birds of passage

Based on characters created by
Ben Aaronovitch & Andrew Cartmel

Robert Mammone

CANDY JAR BOOKS · CARDIFF
2022

Range Editor: Andy Frankham-Allen
Editor: Shaun Russell
Editorial: Keren Williams
Range Consultant: Andrew Cartmel

Printed and bound in the UK by
4edge, 22 Eldon Way, Hockley, Essex, SS5 4AD

Published by
Candy Jar Books
Mackintosh House
136 Newport Road, Cardiff, CF24 1DJ
www.candyjarbooks.co.uk

This book is for Mum – a loving wife, a dedicated and proud mother and Nonna, and an indomitable woman. We all love you, Mum.

'**SPREAD OUT!** Spread out! I want the bastard shot on sight!'

The crackle of fire consuming the farmhouse sounded like the Devil's laughter in Ian Gilmore's ears as he leapt through the window in a flurry of shattered timber. He hit the ground and clumsily rolled to his feet before stumbling down the driveway, trailing streamers of smoke.

Leaping flames from the farmhouse cast twisting shadows, reaching for him in the amber light shimmering in the air. The sharp chatter of submachine guns filled the night, cutting off the screams of those trapped inside.

Dead now. All dead.

Rachel, he thought despairingly.

Staggering along, the satchel thumping against his side, Gilmore checked the Browning. Magazine half full, barrel warm from recent use. The man's face fountained blood as the bullet exited the back of his skull. He closed his eyes for a moment, trying to control his breathing and wrestle the images flashing through his mind into submission.

The shouting around him blurred into a rush of words whose intent was clear. Coming up to a whitewashed outbuilding, Gilmore pressed himself into a doorway while he tried to gather his shattered thoughts. The Chipmunk was in another pasture. The presence of the men hunting him made it as distant as the far side of the moon. Risking a glance, Gilmore saw several figures coalesce around a taller shape standing in the rutted driveway. Staccato orders issued, then the figures spread out.

Gilmore wiped his brow, and the back of his hand came away bloody. He closed his eyes and when he opened them, he saw a light come on in a farmhouse a mile away. Briefly, he imagined the farmer living there waking in the dead of night at the alien sounds. Gunshots. Screams. The mad crackle of fire. He prayed the farmer stayed inside and didn't come out to investigate. Doing the neighbourly thing would only lead to more death. After a few moments, the light went out.

Hesitating, Gilmore heard the distant hoot of a train horn, a long winding note that dwindled into dismal silence. Hope blossomed. In the distance, chugging along, he saw a train emerge from the darkness of a copse of trees. Another horn sounded and he saw, as if in a dream, another train coming from the opposite direction. Between them stood a long, low building buried in shadows about a mile from where Gilmore stood. Was that the local train station? He leaned out from the doorway, hoping to see better, and saw a face staring directly at him. His blood ran cold as he lashed out with the Browning, cracking the figure in the temple and sending him sprawling headlong in the dirt. Someone shouted. The moon appeared from behind a cloud, and Gilmore saw again the train station in the distance. Desperate now, he ran towards it.

Clambering over a wooden fence, Gilmore traversed the open ground at a dead run. Gunfire opened up, and a bullet ruffled his hair, and another ripped open his jacket at the shoulder. Stumbling, he dragged himself upright. Firing wildly behind him, Gilmore fled towards the looming station.

His shoulder burned and he felt blood, hot and urgent, run down his arm. Jamming the Browning into his belt, he clutched his arm with one hand and risked a look over his shoulder. Men climbed the fence. Struggling on, Gilmore made for a short clinker brick incline. Behind, he heard the relentless sounds of pursuit.

A lone lamp stood on the platform, its light fizzing and sputtering. Gilmore pulled the pistol from his belt and shot out the light, plunging the platform and the surrounding area into darkness.

He saw the engine approaching, the cyclopean headlight yawning wider and wider as the clatter of steel on steel swallowed the sounds of pursuit. Gilmore turned at movement behind him. Arms reached for him, and he danced aside, clubbing the pistol into the back of his pursuer's head.

Looking up, Gilmore saw the engine driver staring wide-eyed at him in the night, then the engine passed him. The horn blew, a blast of sound that rattled his hearing. On the other side of the platform, he saw the long line of carriages of the other train appear.

With his pursuers closing, Gilmore scrambled up the incline. The line of carriages rattled past, the clamour of steel wheels on the points deafening. Desperate, he threw himself between the front and back wheels of a carriage. He landed with a grunt on the clinker piled between the tracks, then, gathering himself, rolled between the wheels on the other side, then down the short incline, landing in a puddle of water.

Breath rasping like a buzzsaw, Gilmore pulled himself onto the empty platform. The ticket office window stared darkly at him. He saw his distorted reflection in the glass as he staggered along the length of the platform. At the far end, he leapt onto the ground, grunting at the satchel thudding into his hip.

He landed in a weed-choked section of dirt, in the narrow space created by the two passing trains. The wind picked up, throwing clouds of dirt into the air. The sound was atrocious. Ducking down, Gilmore saw several pairs of legs on the other side of the nearest tracks, thwarted pursuers waiting for the train to pass.

Desperate now, he leapt at a rope dangling from a carriage, numb fingers clutching the frayed end. Pulled off his feet, his body slammed against the carriage. The satchel nearly slipped from his shoulder, and numb fingers just managed to hold onto it. He twisted his wrist, wrapping the end of the rope around it. Dangling precariously, Gilmore pulled himself up, shouting with pain as his wounded shoulder sang. The effort nearly undid him, but he managed to hook a leg through the open door. With an exhausted grunt, he rolled inside and lay gasping on his back. It was only then he saw a pursuer keeping pace with the carriage, weapon trained on him. The eyes of the two men locked. A weapon barked; the bullet's echo was swallowed by a despairing scream...

CHAPTER ONE

Monday – Cambridge. 9am.

IAN GILMORE looked out the window of his single engine Piper as he circled Cambridge, and finally felt the tension that had gripped him since waking that morning ease. The rolling hills, the glint of the pond and the city itself all unfurled before him like a richly knotted carpet. An enclave of tranquillity and learning, Cambridge was a world away from the seething anthill that was London.

The nightmare which had awoken him that morning in a thrashing of limbs and blankets lingered. It was always the Lancaster, always over Berlin, dodging away from the searchlights and flak filling the darkness. The nightmares had been strongest during his first marriage, in the years before he met Rachel again. The memory of the sound of the airframe rippling as wind buffeted the Lancaster while shells from the ground defence burst around it haunted him. His first wife, Edith, had never understood the nightmares, which contributed to their eventual estrangement. Rachel had always understood him better – the shared experience of war meant she could empathise where Edith could only shake her head.

With some reluctance, Gilmore began his preparations for landing. He looked forward to the drive to London about as much as the trip to West Berlin for the trade show, which was another way of saying, not at all.

'When Walsingham says jump, the correct answer is "how high?".' Gilmore didn't like the bitterness in his muttered comment to himself, but there was no denying it. He called down to the radio tower, advising Reynolds he would be landing shortly.

After an uneventful landing, Gilmore taxied the Piper into the hangar. The aeroplane had been a present to himself, second-hand, of course, after the MoD had forced him out of his position. An inheritance from an aunt some years before, and Rachel's encouragement, had made the purchase an easy one.

Clambering down the steps, he patted the fuselage affectionately, then walked to his Jaguar. The flight school was a small operation, but big enough for them to be happy for Gilmore to keep the Piper there, in return for the occasional flight lesson. He waved to Reynolds, who had emerged from the office with a coffee mug in one hand, and a cigarette in the other, then began the drive to London.

Rachel often asked why Gilmore didn't take the train down from Cambridge to London when he was required in the office. He would mouth some platitudes about needing time to think and how Woden covered the cost of petrol. He never told her that the carriage's cramped confines reminded him of a Lancaster but, sometimes, he suspected she knew.

Gilmore turned the radio on to Radio 4.

'...A spokesman for the Ministry of Defence has refused to confirm reports that Soviet fighter planes breached British airspace over the weekend. If true, this would be the thirty-fourth incursion by the Soviets since the beginning of the year. The Minister for Defence, Kofi Bambera, refused to answer questions today upon his arrival at Downing Street for what some have called an emergency Cabinet meeting.

'Tensions between Britain and the Soviet Union have grown in recent months as the Auderly House Accords have come into operation, with the handover of Hong Kong to the Chinese government scheduled to go ahead as agreed. In other news, another night of rioting in the Notting Hill area has called into question—'

Gilmore switched off the radio and sat back, massaging a temple with one hand. Mention of Bambera did little to lighten his mood. The nightmares, the argument with Rachel that morning of his refusal to see a doctor about them... He sighed and shook his head. If not for Dillon's ebullience that morning about the Cerberus launches around the world, Rachel's disappointed silence would've been too much to bear.

As was what waited for him in London.

After navigating the capital's traffic, Gilmore turned off the road and drove down a ramp. The parking garage beneath Woden Armaments was an echoing concrete chamber, studded with pillars that cast long, grasping shadows, even with the fluorescent lights caged overhead. Walking from his car to the lifts had recently begun to feel like walking into a trap. And now, with Bambera...

Gilmore sighed. He grabbed his briefcase and exited the car, making for the bank of lifts. The echoes of his shoes on the concrete fluttered around him like a cloud of bats. The doors opened immediately on him pushing the button, and he stepped in. He closed his eyes, savouring the quiet, when a sudden presence forced him to open them with a snap.

'Hello, Ian. I say, it's an exciting day. Are you going to stay for the launch party tonight?'

James Winterton, one of the sales team, stepped into the lift and stood beside him. The doors slid shut and the lift jolted before starting its ascent. Winterton was young, not even thirty, but he affected an old school manner of speech which he evidently thought made him fit in. It didn't.

'Not really my thing, James. Let the bright young things have their moment in the sun. Anyway, I've got dinner with my wife tonight. She's back from Devesham for a lightning visit. Family time before the trip to West Berlin.'

'You're missing out, old chap. Walsingham has laid it all on, food and drink to celebrate the launch.' Winterton leaned in, as if he were confiding a state secret. 'I hear talk the newest member of the board, Whateley, will be in attendance. You're not going to give up free booze just to keep the old ball and chain happy?'

Gilmore's glance at Winterton could've frozen the heart of a star. Winterton went red, coughed, and stammered an inane response. He almost ran from the lift when the doors opened.

Gilmore made his way to his corner office, overlooking the atrium and the building's public entrance. Staff milled about, setting up for the launch party. He shook his head at the sight of the tables and chairs being assembled in front of a stage sitting at one end. Walsingham knew how to put on a show. Final preparations for the trip to West Berlin filled the day. The trade show was the largest Woden Armaments would attend that year, and Walsingham had signalled his intent to ink as many lucrative deals as possible.

Gilmore thought several times about calling Rachel, and apologising. The argument had been his fault, no question. He still regarded it as a small miracle he and her had reconnected over a decade ago, and a larger miracle that they had survived those harrowing events. But he became distracted with several planning meetings either side of lunch and, before he knew it, the day had come to an end.

Before he left, Gilmore spent several minutes looking once more over the report (an arms deal to Saudi Arabia, which he'd protested and been overruled). The more he read, the more uncomfortable he grew. It had become increasingly obvious that Woden was chasing money from wherever it could get it. Five years ago, even two, the company would've shied away from getting into bed with a regime like Saudi Arabia. Not anymore. Grimacing, Gilmore closed the report and locked it away in his safe.

With hindsight, he wondered if Bambera had known about his protestations over the Saudi deal and chosen that moment to approach him.

Gilmore looked around his office, bare other than a desk, a shelf behind him, and a coffee table and two chairs. When Rachel had visited him several months before, she hadn't spared his feelings.

'So, this is what success looks like in the private sector, is it?'

Thinking on it now, Gilmore decided his wife's withering comment had been the reason he had agreed to take up Bambera's offer.

His blotter empty, Gilmore stood to leave. Even the coldness of the house was better than staying a moment longer in this nest of vipers.

Gathering up his briefcase and jacket, he closed and locked the door behind him. From the atrium drifted the sounds of a party already in full swing. Laughter, the babble of many voices, drifted upwards. Even though Winterton's comment had left him in a fury, Gilmore considered for a moment staying to observe the speeches. The launch was scheduled for the next day, but with so many going to West Berlin, it had been decided to have the party a day early. It was, after all, the crowning achievement in Woden Armaments precipitate rise to pre-eminence in the defence manufacturing sector.

'Ball and chain,' he muttered, thinking what a fool Winterton was. Gilmore had soon enough discovered Woden was full of people like that. Brash. Young. On the make. A new generation who didn't care for the sacrifices of those who had come before them. The world had changed since the Auderly House Accords and, Gilmore decided, not for the better.

Sir Reginald Styles' efforts at the peace conference had met with unexpected success. From a world inching towards all out nuclear war, the British and the Chinese had taken the opportunity to negotiate protocols that had changed the geopolitical situation in fundamental ways. Instead of running headlong into catastrophe, at a stroke, the world now seemed to be entering a new era of comity. Instead of arming for a hot war, the government had banked the reduction in military expenditure the Auderly House Accords promised. Woden Armaments, however, had cleverly manoeuvred itself, through deft political donations, to a position where they could access a larger cut of the smaller defence funding pie. Those self-same cuts in defence spending had pushed Gilmore from his position as air vice-marshal in the RAF, forcing him to seek refuge in the private sector. The move had proved to be an ill-fitting match.

'Ian. Wait up, dear fellow.'

Gilmore turned to see Peter Walsingham coming up the corridor towards him. The CEO and largest shareholder of Woden Armaments cut a bluff, hail-fellow-well-met figure, but beneath the blandly friendly face, Gilmore sensed the fierce, competitive streak that had almost single-handedly dragged Woden from a small-time engineering firm, to the top shelf of British arms suppliers, all within the space of fifteen years.

'Stopping for the party?' Walsingham ushered Gilmore along the corridor, towards the broad sweep of stairs down to the atrium.

'I'd like to,' Gilmore said, happy to lie. 'I'm afraid, though, that family duties call.'

'Yes, I hear your wife has descended from her aery at Devesham to pay you a visit before the launch day itself. This is a great day for the firm. A great day. Everyone said partnering with the government would be bad for business, but I said no, partnering with us will be good for the government.' Walsingham's chuckle grated on Gilmore's nerves. 'Still, resting up for the West Berlin trade show is a good idea. The next step in our expansion. Who knows, you may even be able to ink some deals with the Eastern Europeans.'

The more than subtle hint as to how Gilmore should direct his energies in the next few days rankled. It rankled even more that Bambera had been right about the direction Walsingham had begun to take Woden.

'I'm not entirely sure the military establishment here in the UK would approve us selling equipment to the enemy,' Gilmore said. He tried diluting his words with a smile, but his lips felt stiff.

'Always doom and gloom with you, Ian. Better days are coming, dear fellow. Look, I know you're in a rush to go home to that good lady wife of yours, but I want you to meet our new director, Harry Whateley. Can you spare a few minutes?'

Resisting the urge to check his watch, Gilmore nodded. 'Why not?'

'Excellent.' Walsingham slapped him on the shoulder. 'You'll like Harry. A straight shooter, as our American cousins say. A real man of the people. And he's one of us.'

Mildly intrigued, Gilmore descended the stairs with the CEO to the atrium. A mosaic of a naked figure, hammering a ploughshare into a sword, dominated the rear wall. Underneath was etched a verse, paraphrased, Gilmore discovered when he first joined the firm, from the Bible.

Beat your ploughshares into swords; let the weakling say, 'I am a warrior.'

Gilmore saw a figure standing near the main doors, addressing what appeared to be a group of journalists.

'Never shy of the media,' Walsingham said, nodding towards the animated figure. He continued down.

As Walsingham reached ground level, applause greeted him. He looked like Caesar entering Rome at the head of his army after conquering Gaul, Gilmore observed sourly. The charade went on for almost a minute, before Walsingham turned and beckoned.

'Come along, Ian, this won't take long.' Walsingham led Gilmore towards the figure and the journalists.

The men and women of the Fourth Estate all seemed to hang off his every word. Gilmore noticed another man standing to one side, keeping a careful watch on the man at the centre of attention.

'...and I said to the Prime Minister, "Prime Minister, if you think that's reasonable, then I've got a bridge in Liverpool to sell you." And you know what, he slipped me his phone number and said would I accept cash?'

Laughter erupted, most of it genuine, though two female reporters exchanged glances that were mostly eyerolls.

Gilmore tensed at a sudden presence at his side. 'Ian Gilmore. Air Vice-Marshal, retired. How is the private sector treating you?'

A fellow in a rumpled suit and a hat that sat tilted to one side on a round head smiled grimly at Gilmore.

'Jack Bannerton,' Gilmore said, watching him with narrowed eyes. 'How's the move from Fleet Street to the BBC treating you?'

'Bloody place is crawling with communists,' Bannerton replied, grinning humourlessly. 'It's comrade this and comrade that. Then, in the evening, all the producers are down at their club, ordering scotches from the working-class heroes slaving behind the bar.'

It was Gilmore's turn to grin humourlessly. 'We all make decisions in life we're forced to endure, isn't that right?'

'As you would surely know.' Bannerton glanced at him, then nodded to Whateley. 'What do you think of your newest director?'

'What should I think about him?'

'A man on the make, in business and politics. Shady past, been to places a fellow really shouldn't, if you know what I mean.' Bannerton's mouth turned down. 'I don't much like his politics, and as for his business acumen... Tell me. Why do you think a man with absolutely no business experience is appointed to the board of the premier British arms manufacturer?'

'Off the record?'

'Aren't all the best conversations?'

'Woden wants to expand beyond Britain. Having a populist politician with the common touch who might hold the balance of power after the next election on the board seems prudent, especially when there are pesky things like laws that prevent businesses from selling to the wrong sort of people.'

'I can tell from your tone you're less than impressed with the decision.'

'I'm but a humble consultant,' Gilmore said, not without a trace of bitterness.

'Hmm, I'm sure you are. If you do hear anything interesting about Woden's latest acquisition, I'd appreciate a call.' Bannerton reached into his pocket and pulled out a card, which he thrust into Gilmore's unwilling hand. 'We're old chums, Gilmore. Scratch my back and all that nonsense. Now, watch this.'

Gilmore tucked the card away as Bannerton joined his cameraman. Bannerton raised his hand to catch Whateley's attention.

'Joking aside, Mr Whateley, what do you say to people who argue that a politician can't serve two masters?'

'Which two masters might that be?' Whateley said, his eyes boring into Bannerton.

'Well, the British people, and the Woden shareholders. Aren't you opening yourself to charges of a conflict of interest whenever defence procurement is discussed in the Commons?'

'What a clever little fellow you are,' Whateley said. 'Woden Armaments is a shining example of British industry and ingenuity. It has lifted itself up by its bootstraps to the top rank of defence firms in the world. And all with British skills and know-how. I'm proud, damned proud, to be able to work with them to ensure that Britain continues to be the factory of the world.'

'That's all very well, Mr Whateley,' Bannerton rejoined, speaking over another journalist trying to ask a question of his own. 'But you've not answered my question about a conflict of interest. How can the British people be certain you won't promote Woden Armaments ahead of your competitors?'

'What an outrageous thing to say. Who do you represent?'

'The BBC, though I don't see—'

'Oh, the BBC. It's amazing that an organisation funded by the license fee and leading a charmed existence by virtue of its Charter, can constantly undermine the interests of this country. There can be no conflict of interest when I am representing the best and brightest of Britain! Indeed, I'm sure the British people welcome someone with experience of the real world sitting on those overstuffed seats in the Commons. For too long there has been a class of politicians who have taken it as their God given right to rule over the British people. And see where that has got us. Jobs threatened by people who weren't born here, yet given the keys to the kingdom by an agreement none of our citizens had a say in.'

'You would block the arrival of the Hong Kongers to Britain?' a female reporter said.

'I think the British people will hear much more of what I have to say, what plans I have to improve their lives, when the Prime Minister grows a spine and goes to the Queen to request an election. No, no, that's all I've time for. There's a lovely party arranged behind me to celebrate the fantastic success Woden is about to achieve.'

While the other reporters shouted questions at Whateley's departing back, Bannerton looked at Gilmore and shook his head, as if to prove his earlier point about Whateley.

Walsingham beckoned Gilmore over to him and then motioned to Whateley. The politician's minder stood to one side at a discrete distance. When he saw Walsingham, Whateley's eyes lit up. He lumbered forward, his hand outstretched.

'Peter, my dear fellow,' he said, giving Walsingham's hand a good hard shake. 'Bloody reporters. Follow you around like a bad smell. That fellow from the BBC should be flogged.' A waiter walked past, and Whateley snatched a glass of champagne from the tray. 'I must say, compared to what they serve at Westminster, the nosh and drinks are far, far better in the private sector,' he said, toasting Walsingham before draining the contents of the glass in one go. 'Tonight should be an absolute banger!'

'Oh, we're definitely celebrating, Harry.' Walsingham placed a hand on Gilmore's shoulder. 'May I introduce one of my top consultants? This is Ian Gilmore. Air Vice-Marshal, retired.'

Whateley's gaze switched to Gilmore. He felt the full force

of the magnetism lurking behind the other man's eyes. He hadn't given the announcement of Whateley's appointment to the board of Woden much thought, though he knew it had caused something of a storm in the media and Parliament. He had seen Whateley on the news a few times and heard him on the radio. Those appearances did little justice to the man in the flesh. Over six-foot-tall, bald as a billiard ball and with a battered nose befitting a boxer, Whateley had the physique of a rugby player gone to seed. The skin on his face was rugose, yet the eyes were brilliantly blue, almost otherworldly.

'Air vice-marshal, eh? One of the flyboys. Well done, sir. Well done. Never got the chance to be in the military, but I tell you, if I had, we'd have won a few more than we lost!' His laughing was more like a chortle.

Gilmore had his right hand enveloped in a meaty counterpart that pumped it hard.

'How's the military these days, Gilmore? Badly run down, I bet you agree. Bloody government thinks more about butter than guns, let me tell you. In fact,' Whateley said, leaning in with a leer, 'I'm told Jeremy loves all that butter.' He laughed raucously, and Walsingham joined in.

Gilmore looked Whateley up and down coolly.

'If there's any gaps in our military capacity, I'm sure Woden is picking up the slack. For a fee, of course.' He saw the glance Walsingham shot him and ignored it.

'We'll soon enough need everything Woden can provide,' Whateley said, dropping his voice to a conspiratorial whisper. His eyebrows waggled, but there was nothing humorous about what he said next. 'We might have to turn the guns on our own, if the bloody government lets in all those Hong Kongers. Imagine that. Blacks rioting in the cities while the yellow peril sneaks in and steals the jobs from little Johnny Englander.'

Whateley's minder stepped forward and whispered in his boss' ear, while Gilmore watched, frozen. Walsingham coughed discreetly. Whateley glanced at the man by his side, then looked between Gilmore and Walsingham. For a moment, Gilmore saw something reptilian slide behind those glittering eyes. Then they blinked, and the bonhomie re-emerged.

'Gerald here thinks I've scared you both with idle chatter. Look at you. Like virgins on their wedding night. Relax, relax.

Tonight we celebrate. Who can tell what happens tomorrow, eh?'

'Woden will take care of the future, I can assure you of that,' Walsingham replied. 'These satellites are just the start.'

'Indeed. With those communication satellites, Britain will rule the skies, mark my words. And who knows, I may soon enough rule the nation. Now wouldn't that be a wonderful achievement?'

'Oh, absolutely, Harry,' Walsingham said. 'Don't you think, Ian?'

Gilmore managed a pained smile. Whateley frowned, then his face lit up.

'I'll see you on the flight, Mr Gilmore. We'll paint West Berlin red, eh? Now where's that drink's waiter vanished too?'

Whateley wandered off in search of more alcohol, leaving Walsingham and Gilmore behind.

'Is he part of the delegation I'm leading? When did this happen?'

'Calm down, Ian, calm down,' Walsingham said, smoothly. 'Consider it part of Whateley's induction into Woden. He needs to see how we operate in the field, as it were. He'll only come along to watch, meet a few people, get a feel for the job.'

'Job? His job is sitting on Woden's board, not shadowing me while I'm in West Berlin. And that journalist fellow was right – having him on the board leaves the business open to all sorts of accusations.'

'It was my decision to appoint him, Ian. Not yours, not anyone's. You would do well to remember that you answer to me, not the other way around.'

Icy silence descended over the pair. From the corner of his eye, Gilmore saw Bannerton looking at them with keen interest. Gilmore thought of a dozen things to say and ignored them all. Rachel wouldn't. She would give Walsingham both barrels.

'Well,' Gilmore said, his tone decidedly neutral. 'I must be getting away. Dinner tonight, before I fly out with the team. *My* team.'

'No one said it wasn't, Ian,' Walsingham said, placatingly. He glanced at Whateley regaling a small group of avid listeners. 'Look, he's the future.'

'Future? Whose future?'

'Britain's. Ours. We're the only game in town, Ian. Having Whateley on our side ensures it stays that way. Woden has a lot tied up in him.' Walsingham leaned in. 'Thanks to the Accords, there's a wave of community discontent about to inundate Westminster. Imagine how well placed we would be if he rode that discontent all the way to the top? Downing Street might not be out of his reach.'

'You're banking that a racist becomes Prime Minister, Peter. What sort of thing is that to hope for?'

'He's no more a racist than you or I. He just says what the average man on the street thinks.' Walsingham shook his head. 'Think of your position, Ian. Whateley would need a man with experience in the military to run the MoD, not like that token appointment the PM has made. Think about that, Ian. Think about that.'

CHAPTER TWO

Monday – Cambridge. 6.30pm.

ON THE drive home, Gilmore did think about what Walsingham said. That, and other things. Including Bambera's words to him two months before, when he had summoned him out of the blue to his offices in Whitehall. Those words still resonated. 'Woden is dirty,' Bambera had said. 'Help me bring them down.'

That early excitement at being asked to do something other than shuffle paper around his desk had faded, leaving a feeling of dread. Gilmore wasn't afraid; anyone who had participated in the final bombing raid over Berlin in the dying stages of World War 2 could separate true fear from mere discomfort. But now he was deep in the mire, pushed by his employer to help expand the business into unsavoury territory, and pulled by a minister who might or might not be using him for political advantage.

'Do your duty,' Gilmore muttered to himself, as if the words would be enough to salve that dread.

Light drizzle slanted down in the headlights navigated the streets of Cambridge. Pulling into the driveway behind Rachel's Volvo, he saw the light over the door switch on. The front door opened, and Rachel and Dillon emerged.

'Who's ready for a night out?' Gilmore asked while he came down the path. From somewhere inside the house, he could hear Etta James on the turntable.

'I am,' Dillon chirped, smiling and running up to his father. He hugged Gilmore with one arm, while holding a model rocket in his free hand. Gilmore fondly ruffled his son's hair.

He looked warily at his wife. She had changed into a flowing dress that was at odds with the more practical attire she wore on campus. 'How was your day?'

'Fine,' she said, walking back into the house. Gilmore and Dillon followed. 'I've done some of the housework you seem to have neglected to do, as well as pack for both you and Dillon. And prepare for a finance meeting tomorrow, which is the real reason I came home.' Her smile took the sting from her words. 'Not that I'm happy to be attending it. I thought reaching the upper reaches of academia would be less... bureaucratic.'

'All that and back to Devesham tomorrow,' Gilmore said, ducking into his office to settle the briefcase on the desk. He followed his wife and son into the kitchen.

Rachel had arrived late the night before. She had been too tired for anything more than a short conversation, and had gone to bed.

Rachel nodded. 'How was your day?' She leaned against a countertop.

'Another glorious eight hours spent preparing for the trip to West Berlin. If I could've, I'd still be flying about in the Piper. Instead, I had to listen while bloody Walsingham basically asked me to cut deals with the Eastern Europeans. His insinuations are so blatant I might as well defect.'

'Mind your language, dear,' Rachel said, nodding at Dillon. Their son looked from gazing intently at the model plane and smiled beatifically at them.

'Oh. Sorry, Dillon.' He ruffled his son's hair again.

'So, another delightful day in the salt mines,' Rachel said. She picked up a tea towel and began drying some plates sitting beside the sink.

'Oh, absolutely delightful.'

'Mum's been telling me about the launch,' Dillon said, looking eagerly up at his father.

'Oh yes, and what has she told you?' Gilmore exchanged a wry smile with his wife.

Dillon had talked about nothing else but the Cerberus launches for the last few days, temporarily abandoning his interest in model aeroplanes for modern rocketry. Indeed, he was holding a model of the Saturn V rocket he had assembled over the weekend.

'It's all top secret, or so she says.' Dillon looked accusingly at his mother. 'It can't all be top secret, can it?'

'Well,' Rachel said, screwing up her face in thought, her eyes twinkling. 'What I can say is that three rockets will definitely be launched tomorrow night.'

Dillon frowned. 'There's a show about the launches on the television. I bet you they tell me more than Mum did.'

'Well, you can watch it for a bit and report back to me,' Gilmore said, patting his son on the shoulder. 'But make sure you're ready to go when I call.'

Nodding eagerly, Dillon went into the lounge. After a minute, the tinny sounds from the television drifted through the house.

'How's your headache from this morning?' Rachel asked.

'Not too bad.'

'Exactly how bad is "not too bad"?'

'It's fine, Rachel. Really.'

'Did you have a drink today?'

'Oh, come on,' Gilmore said. 'Don't start with that nonsense.'

'My concern for my husband is not nonsense,' Rachel said, hands on hips.

'I've not touched a drop. At all. It's just a headache. I didn't sleep well.'

'"Didn't sleep well" isn't the half of it. You were thrashing about like Harry Houdini trying to escape a straitjacket. This could all have been dealt with years ago if that woman had taken better care of you,' Rachel said, hotly.

'You mean Edith, don't you, Rachel? You can say her name.'

'Of course I can say her name. Not as freely as you seem to be able.' Rachel set down a dried plate onto the counter with a ringing clatter.

'And what does that mean?' Gilmore suddenly wished he'd had a drink before he drove home.

'When you needed help, that woman left you high and dry. What you saw during the war, that last raid... A woman who would leave a man to suffer like that... Like you do...' Rachel sucked in a deep breath and closed her eyes for a moment. 'After Shoreditch... I like to think I helped put you back together.' She reached out and cupped his face. 'Are you all right, really?'

'Just an ache,' Gilmore said, waving vaguely at the back of his head. He looked at Rachel and gave her a lopsided grin. 'Like

18

Humpty Dumpty, was I?'

'Big and brave and all broken,' Rachel said, suddenly blinking back tears.

'I'm made of sterner stuff. Now. Thanks to you.' Gilmore knew how much she hated being emotional.

'It's not too late to tell Walsingham you can't go to West Berlin.'

He shook his head. Picking up another tea towel Gilmore joined his wife drying the dishes. Though the way work is now, testing the marksmanship of the guards on the Berlin Wall wouldn't be too bad an outcome.'

'Is it that bad?'

Gilmore shrugged. 'Walsingham was less than subtle in his advice about who I cut deals with at the trade fair. He thinks if we push hard enough the Eastern Europeans will agree to buy from us. Nothing happens without Moscow's say. And even if I did somehow ink a contract to sell five hundred bazookas tomorrow to a country behind the Iron Curtain, who does he think they'd be used against? In five years' time our boys might have to face them coming the other way. It's insane. And to cap it all off, he introduced me to a politician.'

'You're always meeting politicians, Ian. Woden must have a dozen or more doing their bidding in Parliament.'

'This one is also our newest director. I assume you've heard the name Harry Whateley?'

'Woden's newest board member is Harry Whateley? Dear God. Harry Hately, my students call him. And worse than that. There's talk that the student body may picket him if he campaigns in Cambridge when the General Election is called.'

'I'm sure you and your anti-war friends will be leading the charge.' He held up his hands to forestall Rachel's response. 'I've always been happy with whatever political position you take, Rachel. Anyway, Whateley seems more like a loudmouthed buffoon. Though Walsingham thinks he's on a glide path into Downing Street.'

'Unless something truly terrible happens during the election, I'd be surprised if he did. Thankfully, Whateley sits on the cross benches with the motliest crew since Blackbeard sailed the Caribbean. He's got as much chance of getting to Downing Street as you or I.'

'I've actually been to Downing Street,' Gilmore said, smiling.

'In case you've forgotten, I was there as well.'

'A lifetime ago. They were grateful, even though I don't think the old duffer understood everything that happened.'

'I'm not sure I understood it all either.' Rachel opened a cupboard and stowed away the dishes. When she turned back, her eyes were distant. She shook her head and looked at her husband. 'And I'm by far the smarter of the two of us. Get along then. Tidy up, and we'll go for dinner. I've booked a restaurant in town on the recommendation of a couple of my students.'

Ten minutes later, Rachel stood in their bedroom, looking critically at what Gilmore had chosen to wear.

'Jeans, my dear,' she had said, her head tilted to one side.

'Jeans?' Gilmore looked at her reflection in the mirror as he completed the Windsor knot. 'You forget, my dear,' he said, turning and pulling her close for a passionate kiss. 'I'm not a young man anymore.'

'You're ruining my lipstick,' Rachel said, swatting him away then breaking into laughter. He took a step back, his hands raised in mock defence, before she grabbed an arm and pulled him back for another embrace.

'Mrs Gilmore,' he said, when they finished.

'Mr Gilmore.' Rachel looked up at his eyes, which twinkled merrily. 'You're hardly an old man. If you are, what does that make me?'

'Matronly?' Gilmore said.

Tie completed, he sat on the edge of the bed and sighed. Even with Rachel home, the pressure from Bambera and Walsingham...

'Not looking forward to the trip?'

'Is it that obvious?'

Rachel shrugged her shoulders. 'I would've thought the delights of Berlin would be enough to keep you amused.'

'You've watched *Cabaret* too many times, my dear. And it's West Berlin. Since we signed the Accords with the Chinese, the Soviets have forced the East Germans to tighten the screws. Increased border checks, delays in food shipments, more demands for hard currency. The locals put on a brave face, but my contacts in the military say the place could crack like a walnut at any time.'

'So, send someone else. It's just a trade fair.'

'It's not just any trade fair, Rachel, and you know it. The West Berlin fair is the largest in Europe. There will be politicians from all over attending. Woden is hoping to coin it in and I'm their point man.'

'You were hired as a consultant, Ian. Not a lobbyist. Walsingham is using you to put a legitimate front on a toxic business.'

'There are larger things at play...' Gilmore shook his head.

Keeping his arrangement with Bambera a secret from Rachel was yet another pressure he felt. He pretended not to notice the way Rachel's eyes narrowed as she watched him.

'Not tonight, please, Rachel. I just want to have a nice meal with my family without having to worry about any of work's nonsense.'

Rachel looked at her husband, a half-smile playing on her lips.

'You can't put it off forever, Ian.'

Put what off forever?

'You're in the middle of it and you don't even notice. You're looking for reasons not to resign, when you desperately want to.'

Gilmore chuckled. 'I'm like a pane of glass to you, aren't I? Would that I could resign, Rachel. Things are at a delicate stage. Soon, though. Hopefully.' He clapped his hands together, as if that would make his troubles disappear. 'All right. We'll talk about it after I get back. For now, I'm dressed, and hungry. Let's go get some grub.'

CHAPTER THREE

Monday – Cambridge. 7.15pm.

IT WAS a quick drive into town. Gilmore parked the Jaguar around the corner from the restaurant and they walked the short distance through streets packed with students ready for a night out.

'This is new,' he said, settling into his chair and looking around the bustling restaurant, which stood on Newmarket Road. Outside, red Chinese lanterns and faux silk banners with Chinese dragons fluttered in a light breeze.

'Recent emigres from Hong Kong, dear,' Rachel said, sitting opposite. Dillon sat next to her, engrossed in a book. 'I heard some of my students talking about it. It comes highly recommended.'

'Especially for those on a budget,' Gilmore said, frowning at the plastic-coated menu. 'Do you get what you pay for?'

'Oh, don't be such a stick in the mud. It's authentic, which is better than the slop they serve at Devesham. The food there is frightful. Anyway, you don't have to eat a mixed grill every time we go out.'

'My dear,' Gilmore said, signalling a waiter. 'It's a little-known secret that the RAF won the war on mixed grills. The messes positively heaved with the stuff.'

'You missed your calling, dear,' Rachel said. 'I understand Eric and Ernie want to expand to a trio.'

The arrival of a waiter saved Gilmore from having to come up with a retort.

'A Scotch, please. Neat.' He did his best to ignore Rachel's warning look.

'Apologies, sir. We don't have a liquor license yet.'

'And yet all these students are dining here. Remarkable how abstemious the younger generation has become.' Gilmore leaned towards the waiter. 'My wife will be ever so pleased at this news.'

'Ignore him, he's in a mood. Which of these herbal teas would you recommend?'

'The Ji Gu Cha helps with fatigue and anxiety. The Qu Shi Cha helps with a lack of appetite.'

'Hmm. The Ji Gu Cha for my husband, please. There's nothing wrong with his appetite.'

The waiter's head bobbed up and down.

'Very good,' Rachel said. 'Dillon, would you put that book down for a moment, please? What would you like to drink?'

Sandy haired and freckle faced, Dillon Gilmore glanced up from his book, a slim hardback with a Sopwith Camel adorning the front cover. He frowned.

'Could I have a Coca-Cola, please?'

'I'm not sure fizzy drinks at this time of the night is the right way to go, son.'

Rachel placed a hand on her husband's arm. 'Maybe this once,' she said. Rachel leaned closer. 'I think he's a bit nervous about the school trip.'

Gilmore glanced at Dillon, who had bowed his head over his book. His fringe hid his features, but Gilmore sensed his wife was right. As usual.

'All right then. A glass of Coca-Cola for the young fella. If you wouldn't mind coming back in a few minutes, we should be ready to order some food.' The waiter nodded then departed in a rush.

Gilmore leaned forward. 'I remember my first trip to France,' he said, winking at Rachel.

Dillon looked up. 'When was that, Dad?'

'Oh, when the dinosaurs still roamed the planet, I'd say.' Gilmore smiled. 'I think it was in 1930. My parents took me for a weekend trip. Got sick on camembert cheese. Make sure you tell the other boys to steer clear of the stuff. Devilishly bad.'

Dillon looked from his dad to his mum, not sure if he was joking. Rachel nodded.

'He's never had a strong stomach for cheese, Dillon. Or

French women, I dare say.'

'Is that true, Dad?' Dillon's eyes twinkled with delight.

'Don't listen to your mum, my boy.' Gilmore patted his wife's arm. 'I can most certainly handle the French ladies...'

Dillon looked nonplussed for a moment then returned his attention to his book.

'Biggles again, is it?' Rachel raised an eyebrow. 'It's been rockets and rocketry recently.' She turned to her husband. 'Isn't he a bit old for that?'

'Oh, I don't think so.' Gilmore picked up the menu again and peered at a page. 'I practically devoured Johns' books when I was a lad.' He looked across the table and smiled. 'A bit of escapism never hurt anyone.'

'Coming from a man who fought in one war and narrowly averted a global catastrophe, that's saying something,' Rachel said, lowering her voice as she spoke.

'We both narrowly averted a global catastrophe, Rachel.' Gilmore looked around before returning his attention to his wife. 'Speaking of catastrophes, how is Mission Control at Devesham?'

Rachel chuckled, a throaty sound that raised the hairs on Gilmore's neck. 'I admire what Allison and Anne achieved, despite all the interference they were getting from both Woden and the government. I've got the technical expertise plus experience running my department at Cambridge. All they needed was someone with a bit more spine to stand up to everyone. Crack enough heads and suddenly everything is humming along.'

'And you were the hard charging general to do it?'

Rachel nodded. 'When those Cerberus rockets achieve orbit, Devesham will be ready to take over.'

'Any noses put out of joint when you were foisted on them?'

'I hardly think "foisted" is the right word, dear,' Rachel said, looking reprovingly at her husband. Gilmore raised his hands to ward off her glare. 'No, I was happy to help them with the project. They'll certainly learn from the experience. I'm not sure what Anne's been up to over the last few years, all very hush-hush, but executive management certainly wasn't involved.'

'When do you think you'll be home, for good?'

'A few days afterwards. We've got some tests to do to confirm their communications capabilities, but once that's done,

I'll be all yours. Both of you.' She looked at Dillon. 'I know you've missed me, haven't you, Dillon?'

Their son nodded without looking up.

'Good. I'm glad to hear it. Home hasn't been the same without you.' As if embarrassed by what he had just said, Gilmore looked around the restaurant, searching for something else to talk about. 'Do they always open these restaurants?' he asked.

'Who is "they" in this instance?'

'Our friends from Hong Kong. Surely all of them aren't restaurateurs.'

'I think you'll find in time they'll contribute something extraordinary to the nation, Ian,' Rachel said. 'We all have to start somewhere. My parents were professors, but when they fled here, their only option was to open a tailor shop.'

'They didn't have a choice.'

'Well, if not having a choice was the difference between the gas chamber or a decent trade supporting their two daughters, I think I know which side of it I come down on.'

Gilmore considered this for a moment. He was about to respond when they heard a commotion at the rear of the restaurant.

'Bloody quit that jabber, will you? Man has a right to hear his own tongue. What the hell is wrong with this country? Harry Whateley will see the lot of you out, you mark my words.'

A hapless waiter wrung his hands as a seated, fat, red-faced man gesticulated wildly at a table near the doors into the kitchen. Heads turned.

'Well, speak up. When is my bloody food coming? Now, or should I come back tomorrow?'

'Dillon, keep your eyes on the book,' Rachel said, her face setting. 'What is that loudmouthed fool complaining about?'

'You'd think if he had those attitudes, he wouldn't dine here. If he doesn't quieten down...'

There was a sudden clatter of shattering crockery. The fat man stood over the waiter, who lay on the floor amid broken plates and spilled food. Several waiters hovered near the table, faces stricken.

'I say,' Gilmore said. He rose from his chair. Rachel placed a warning hand on his arm, but he shook her off. 'I'll be damned if that fat fool ruins my night out with my family.' He pointed. 'You. Yes, you, the fat fellow with the big mouth. I suggest you help these poor waiters clear up your mess and offer to pay for the damages.'

'Who the hell do you think you are?' the fat man said. With his face coloured an alarming purple and sweat pouring down his cheeks, the man had clearly been drinking well before arriving for dinner.

'Someone offering you good advice,' Gilmore said. Suddenly aware all eyes were on him and the fat man, Gilmore stepped forward. 'Come on, be a good chap. Just calm down and—'

The fat man's piggish eyes narrowed. He licked his lips. Without warning, he surged at Gilmore, swinging wildly with both fists. Gilmore swayed back and to the side, like a matador in the ring, and the man staggered past.

'Ian...' Rachel called, rising from her chair.

'I'm fine, dear,' he said. 'I'll have this sorted in a moment.'

Gilmore saw Dillon looking on with rapt attention. Gilmore winked at him, then set himself as the fat man charged again.

'Enough of this.' Gilmore stepped forward, inside the reach of the man's flailing fists, and grabbed a handful of the front of his shirt. He pulled his attacker, who stank of alcohol, close.

'If you want to embarrass yourself further in front of all these people, go right ahead. Otherwise, do yourself a favour and shut your trap.' Gilmore's eyes bored into the other man, who suddenly realised he was caught in a vice-like grip. 'I think our friend has become a little too excited by all this lovely food,' Gilmore said, to general laughter. 'Time to cool off.'

He guided the man with deliberate speed towards the front door. The bell jangled as Gilmore pulled the door open, and then both men were standing in the cool night air.

'You've done me a favour and convinced me my wife is right, not that you'd care. These people call Britain home now, so get used to it. I dare say they've made more of a contribution in six months than you've done in the last ten years.' Gilmore was surprised by the heat in his words. 'Go home before I give you a good thrashing.'

The fat man trembled, whether with rage or fear, Gilmore couldn't tell, neither could he care less.

'They're crawling over this country like maggots. I saw you, with your wife and son. They'll take her in the night and deny him his rightful place in his own country.' Spittle flecked the man's mouth.

It was only when he saw his balled fist in front of his face that Gilmore realised he was moments from striking the man. 'Get away from me, you disgusting creature.'

A greasy smile crept across the fat man's face. Shambling off, he turned a corner and vanished. Gilmore breathed slowly to calm himself. He glanced through the window into the restaurant and saw Dillon staring open-mouthed in awe. Rachel looked less than impressed. Straightening his tie, Gilmore walked back into the restaurant to a sudden outpouring of applause.

'The dashing knight returns,' Rachel said dryly. 'You had quite the audience.' She turned her head to indicate the restaurant.

'He won't come back, will he, Dad?'

'I should say not,' Gilmore muttered. Embarrassed by the applause, he raised his hand in brief acknowledgment. The clapping died away.

'Bloody fool,' Gilmore muttered. 'He might make more friends if he didn't act like an oaf.'

'Are you saying he's wrong about what he said, or how he said it?' Rachel asked.

'Both,' Gilmore said, noting the look in Rachel's eyes but forging ahead. 'I don't have a problem with all this,' – he waved his hand at the restaurant – 'but the government has to take care, otherwise there will be politicians who will argue about the manner in which it's being forced down people's throats.'

'Someone like Whateley might say the very same thing.' The silence that opened between them might have swallowed Titanic.

'Whateley's a pig, like that idiot I saw off,' Gilmore said, keeping his voice low. 'But if the government persists on this course without bringing the community with them, they'll risk destabilising the whole show.'

'The Auderly House Accords were acclaimed the length and breadth of the country,' Rachel pointed out. 'I recall you were especially pleased with them. You said it allowed us to concentrate on our real enemy, the Soviets, instead of always looking over our shoulder in the Far East. This is the price of those agreements – a home for people escaping totalitarianism. Like Britain was for my family. For me.'

'All I'm saying is we can't be expected to take everyone who comes knocking on the door. The public won't like it.'

'I heard him on Radio 4 this morning. He said something like what you just said, about people knocking on the door. And I read an interview with him in *The Telegraph*. He's hardly hiding his light under a bushel.' Rachel placed a hand on Gilmore's. 'He's being heard, Ian. And I'm worried about it. You should be as well.'

Rachel's words reminded Gilmore of the coded language Whateley had used at the launch party. He started to reply when an Asian man in a chef's apron and hat bustled up to their table.

'Many apologies for the disturbance,' the chef said, nodding his head up and down. 'Please, accept this as a token of our appreciation.' Before Rachel and Gilmore could reply, the chef stepped aside, and a parade of waiters swept up and around their table. Within a few seconds, half a dozen steaming dishes had been deposited on their table. Gilmore sat back, a look of incredulity on his face.

'This is very generous of you, but I didn't really do—'

The chef cut him off. 'Please, it is my pleasure. That man,' – his face wrinkled like he'd bitten into a lemon – 'that man has been a bother before. I think he won't come back.' He smiled and gestured at the table. 'Please, enjoy.' Before Gilmore could reply, he returned to the kitchen followed by the flock of waiters.

'Really, this is too much,' Gilmore said, looking at the food piled before them.

'You can always choose not to eat it, Ian,' Rachel said, picking up a pair of chopsticks. 'After all, it's not as if he's forcing it down your throat.'

Gilmore opened his mouth to reply, then decided he had said enough.

Afterwards, Gilmore stopped and waited as Dillon tied up a loose shoelace. Over dinner, he had excitedly talked about the rockets that were launching tomorrow. Rachel hovered near the boy, keeping an eye on him. It was clear she had missed him while she was away in Devesham.

Dinner has smoothed the sharper edges of their earlier

conversation, but Gilmore still detected a frosty note in Rachel's attitude towards him. He shoved his hands into his pockets and sighed. First Edith, and now politics. It wasn't as if this was the first time either subject had caused problems.

Turning to look up the street, Gilmore saw a tatty poster pasted to a nearby lamppost. Something about it caught his attention and he walked to it. When he saw what had been printed on it, his face stiffened in outrage.

'Not pretty, is it?' Rachel said. She had come up to stand beside him.

Gilmore glanced at her, and saw the despair in her eyes. An awful caricature of an Asian man, in the style of Fu Manchu, leered at a cowering white woman, her face a mask of stricken terror. At the bottom, one word, in bold print, shouted to the world.

OUT!

'My parents knew what Hitler promised, even as their gentile friends laughed him off as a braggart and a fool. They fled here, found a home. But the prejudice, even if diluted, followed them. But just like those people running that restaurant, their contributions made this country a better place.' Rachel reached up and touched Gilmore's check. 'You're right. It does take time for people to adjust. But politicians like Whateley don't care about nuance. All they traffic in is slogans and hate.'

Rachel turned her head to look at the passing traffic. A breeze stirred her hair. She glanced at their son.

'I don't want my boy growing up in a world filled with that poison.' Reaching out, she grabbed a curling corner of the poster and ripped it away. Balling the coarse paper in her hands, Rachel threw it into the gutter.

'You and I both know that's where rubbish like that belongs.' She took Dillon's hand. 'Come along then, boys, let's go home.'

Rachel and Dillon walked ahead, while Gilmore trailed behind, deep in thought.

There were many students walking up and down the street, laughing and talking excitedly. The seemed to have hardly a care in the world. Looking at them, Gilmore felt old. He had hoped agreeing to work for Bambera would do something to lift the cloud that had hung over him since joining Woden, but even the thrill of espionage work had quickly dulled.

Rounding a corner, he found his wife and son waiting by the car. Dillon was polishing the Jaguar ornament with the sleeve of his jacket.

'You look glum, dear,' Rachel said.

'Just thinking.'

'I wouldn't worry too much, Ian. Your heart is in the right place.'

'More or less?'

'More, I should think. I mean, you did rough up a racist bully, so you can't be all bad.'

'Now there's an epitaph. "He wasn't all bad".'

Rachel cocked her head and narrowed her eyes. 'Are you feeling all right?'

Gilmore hesitated. He daren't tell her about Bambera, not after deceiving her all this time. But Bambera wasn't the only cause of his mood. 'There are storm clouds gathering on the horizon. At home and abroad. I feel it deep in my bones. I'm not sure what sort of world our generation are going to hand to the lad.'

Dillon glanced up at the mention of him. 'Am I a likely lad, Dad?'

Gilmore chuckled. 'You would be, if you got up to half the mischief those two do.' He looked at his wife. 'What will be, will be, I suppose,' he said. 'Come on, let's go home.'

The Jaguar started with a rumbling purr, then Gilmore pulled out into the street and drove away. A few seconds later, another vehicle, parked several cars behind them, did the same. It followed them at a distance.

Rachel looked up from studying the reflection in the side mirror and glanced at her husband.

'You do know we're being followed, dear?'

'I thought I'd lost him.'

'You did.'

'And?'

'They've found us again,' Rachel said, glancing at the wing mirror again.

'It might relate to those damned letters.'

Vaguely threatening letters, all unsigned, had been turning up for months. Was this a new escalation?

'It's a bit of a jump from writing anonymous letters to following us.' Rachel looked dubious.

'Maybe.'

'Can you lose them?'

'I'll do my best, dear.'

'Of course, you will,' Rachel said. She glanced over her shoulder. Dillon was dozing, his book clasped to his chest. Switching her gaze to the back window, she saw the car keeping pace with them.

'What do you think?' Gilmore's knuckles were white where he gripped the steering wheel.

'You're driving. You decide. Best make it quick.'

The traffic was light, the road slick and gleaming after a recent shower. They had reached the outskirts of the city centre.

'Right then.'

Steering with one hand, Gilmore leaned across his wife and opened the glovebox. Reaching in, he took out a worn leather holster. Dull metal gleamed as the car passed beneath a streetlight.

'You keep the Browning in the car? You're a consultant for a defence firm, dear, not Dirty Harry.'

'As if you didn't know it was there.' He handed the holstered weapon to his wife.

'And what would you like me to do with this?' she asked, glancing down at the Browning. In the back seat, Dillon grumbled in his sleep.

'It's not a hammer, dear,' Gilmore said. He glanced in the rear view mirror, then came to a decision. With a squeal of rubber on macadam, he wrenched the steering wheel to the left and hit the brakes. The Jaguar XJ12 came to rest.

'You know how to use it. Or have those trips to the gun club been in vain?'

'It's not come to this, surely?'

'No. But it doesn't hurt to be prepared.'

Rachel nodded.

'Good. Remember, I'm the fellow with his back to you.' Gilmore suddenly smiled, relieved at having a defined target in front of him.

Without waiting for a response, he shoved open the door and stepped into the night. His blood was up. The cold embraced him, and his breath wreathed his head. The car, which had indeed been following them, came to a halt fifty yards away. Raising his hand against the glare of the headlights, Gilmore glimpsed a figure behind the wheel. The car, a beige coloured Austin Maxi, rumbled quietly to itself.

'A matador without a cape,' Gilmore muttered to himself. He felt his heart pounding, and realised with a start he was enjoying himself. He started forward, his footsteps smacking wetly on the road.

Engine racing, the car lunged straight at Gilmore. He found himself grinning as the car came on. Then, at the last moment, he leapt aside in a windmill of arms and legs. The car rushed by, the wind of its passing whipping Gilmore's hair. Rising to his feet, he tried to make out the number plate. He saw Rachel standing by the open door on her side, legs braced, both arms extended with the Browning in her hands.

Gilmore went to her. The adrenaline began to fade, and his hands shook. Distantly, he heard the city traffic. After the screech of the departing car's tyres, the street was quiet.

Rachel's eyes sparkled in the dim light. Coolly, she handed the gun back to her husband.

'We're going to have a chat about the safe storage of weaponry, Ian.'

He nodded. 'Did you get the number plate?'

Rachel shook her head. 'There was a cloth covering it.'

'Anyone other than the driver inside?'

'No.'

Gilmore nodded. 'Should we stay in a hotel tonight?'

'No. It'll cause too much disruption. You've got your trip, and I've got my funding meeting tomorrow. Then back to Devesham. If we stay in town, it'll put us out.'

'Much as I thought.' Gilmore looked at the empty street. He hefted the gun. 'At least if there's trouble, we'll have this.'

'What is it with the military and their toys?'

'A toy is something that brings happiness,' Gilmore said. He glanced down at the gun and shook his head at old memories.

'Mum?'

Rachel and Gilmore looked at each. Gilmore raised a finger to his lips. Engaging the safety, he slid the Browning into his jacket pocket. Rachel nodded. She turned and walked to the rear of the car and opened the door.

'Dillon. Have you woken up? Those wontons got the better of you, darling?'

'Why's Dad stopped?'

'Thought I might've had a flat, son,' Gilmore said, standing beside his wife. He smiled at Dillon. 'Turns out I was mistaken.'

'And not for the first time,' Rachel said.

Gilmore straightened and stared the way the Austin Maxi had gone. 'On that, your mother is perfectly correct,' he said.

Rachel leaned into him. He still found the smell of her hair intoxicating.

'Let's go home,' she whispered. 'Whoever it was, we'll sort them out.'

The rest of the drive home proved uneventful. With Rachel distracting Dillon with a maths puzzle, Gilmore made sure to arrive from a different route to the one he normally took. If Rachel noticed, and he was sure she did, she said nothing.

After tucking Dillon into bed, Rachel came out of his bedroom to find Gilmore standing in the corridor, watching.

'You're good with him.' Gilmore slipped an arm behind her back and held her close.

'Who would've thought.' Rachel said. 'The ice queen with a head for maths and little else.'

'Who said that?'

'How quickly we forget.'

'Seems like the sort of night for me to ask for forgiveness.' Gilmore smiled. 'He's a good lad,' he said, nodding towards their son.

'He looks up to you.'

'Really? He's keen on maths. More you, than me, I should think.'

'You can't see it, even if it's in front of your eyes. The plane models, Biggles. He'd spend hours in your study looking at your medals and citations if I didn't chase him out. You should take him up in the Piper, when you get back.'

'I will,' Gilmore said, feeling a glow of pride. He kissed the top of Rachel's head. 'Are you going to bed, or will you read over those funding submissions?

Rachel's nose wrinkled. 'Funding submissions, more's the

pity. Damn inconvenient scheduling.'

'Gives us a chance to see you,' Gilmore said. 'Home has been far too quiet for your absence.'

'That's very kind of you, dear,' Rachel said, looking pleased. 'The meeting is in the morning. I waste half my time... I should be doing research, not ticking off requests for money.'

'The price of success, dear.' Gilmore glanced at his watch. 'If you're going to bed, I'll stay up for a bit. See everything is ship-shape.'

'You're worried the driver may have followed us home. Do you think it's linked to those letters?'

Gilmore shrugged his shoulders. 'Maybe. It might just be a coincidence.'

'Should we call the police?'

'It doesn't make sense to do it while we're all away. Whoever it was, they were amateurish at best. Let's not worry the police just yet.'

'All right,' Rachel said, only partially reassured. 'Don't stay up too late.'

Gilmore snapped off a salute as Rachel walked down the corridor.

Gilmore sat with a glass of Scotch in the kitchen's cool darkness, listening to the sounds of the house. The letters that Rachel had mentioned were in a cupboard above the refrigerator. Vile messages, vague threats. Neither of them knew who was sending them.

I should've gone to the police, Gilmore thought.

A breeze moaned around the eaves, and he could hear leaves dancing across the paving stones at the back of the house. Branches scraped at the windows. Memories haunted him, of successes and of failures, the pressure from Bambera.

After he finished the drink, Gilmore stepped outside, pulling his jacket tight against the chill. The Browning's weight pressed against his ribs. He walked around the grounds of their home, from the gate at the front, to the towering hedge at the rear that formed the boundary. He checked the windows and doors on the ground level.

Still not satisfied, he returned to the kitchen and stood in the shadows by the window, staring into the night for a good half hour, the Browning sitting on the counter, its presence like an old, familiar friend.

When Gilmore did go to bed, it was some time before he fell asleep.

CHAPTER FOUR

Tuesday – Cambridge. 7am.

THE PIPS sounding on Radio 4 announced the approach of the news. Gilmore, standing in his bathroom, reached over and turned up the volume. He straightened and gazed critically at his reflection in the mirror. He noted the grey in his hair, and the deeper lines cutting into his face. His moustache was a touch ragged. Gilmore picked up a cup and stirred the lather with a brush.

'This is BBC Radio 4. Here is the news...

'Good morning. Speculation continues to mount that the Prime Minister will visit the Queen to seek an early general election. The Prime Minister, who is under increasing pressure from Harry Whateley's Freedom Party, refused to address questions from journalists last night as he attended a fundraiser...'

'I bet you he didn't want to talk to journalists,' Gilmore said. He continued stirring the lather.

'The successful launch this evening of the three satellites, dubbed Project Cerberus, at Diego Garcia, Banana Island, Nigeria, and at the Woomera Rocket Range in South Australia, will signal a new era in British telecommunications, according to a government spokesman. Woden Armaments CEO, Peter Walsingham, who entered into a controversial public/private arrangement with the British Government, issued a statement saying this would be a great day for British technology...'

'Of course, he would bloody say that,' Gilmore said. 'The taxpayer's paid for half of it.' He realised with a start that a pyjama-clad Dillon was standing in the doorway, watching.

'Hello, Dillon,' Gilmore said. 'Did you sleep well? Where's your mum?'

'In the kitchen.'

'She's making breakfast, I take it?'

Dillon nodded.

'It's not eggs, is it?'

Dillon nodded again. He broke into a fleeting smile.

'Oh dear,' Gilmore said. He straightened his shoulders. 'Well, we'll just have to make the best of it. Why your mother persists in thinking her scrambled eggs are... What's wrong, Dillon?'

'Do you have to go?' his son said, plaintively.

Gilmore paused, then set the brush and cup down. 'We've talked about this, haven't we?' Dillon nodded, but looked miserable all the same. 'It's the scout meeting, isn't it?' Dillon shrugged his shoulders. 'You know I would do anything to come. This trip... I've got no choice.'

Gilmore was aware how weak that sounded. The scout meeting was tonight. Because Rachel was travelling back to Devesham, and Gilmore had final preparations to make for the trip to West Berlin, Dillon would be staying with his Aunt Sarah, who would collect him after school that afternoon. Gilmore had prepared, with some eagerness, a short talk to Dillon's scout troop about his time with the RAF. Damn Walsingham...

'I've spoken with your Scoutmaster, and we've agreed to reschedule my talk to next week.' Gilmore paused, contemplating his son's glum face. 'I tell you what. I've got a spare hour or two in my schedule. The Germans love their planes. I'm sure there will be a hobby shop near my hotel. I'll try to find that Lancaster B III model you've been asking for. How does that sound?'

'Really? That would be great, Dad. What if you can't find it, though?'

Gilmore made a show of rubbing his chin, as if considering something weighty. 'If it's not there, how about something from the other side? The Messerschmitt?'

Dillon immediately perked up. 'The Me 262?'

'Does that sound like a fair compromise?'

Dillon nodded. Gilmore reached out and took his son in a rough embrace.

'I'll make it up to you, all right? Once we're all back home, I'll talk with your mum and see if we can go down to the coast one weekend. What do you think about that?'

'Will you take me out in the boat?'

'When did you become a Navy man?' Gilmore straightened and put on a serious face. 'This is a house of aviators, not sailors.'

'Come on, Dad,' Dillon said. 'Marcus' dad is in the Navy. It's not so bad.'

'Not so bad, eh? Well, if you like the water that much, we'll hire a boat for the day. Let's see if we can do a bit of fishing without sinking the thing, eh? Now, off you go and see how your mother's doing with those eggs. I want fair warning.'

Coughing alerted him to another presence in the bathroom doorway.

'...Aah, Rachel. Breakfast ready, I take it?'

Dillon flashed his dad a guilty look as he beat a hasty retreat.

'It seems I must face this ordeal alone,' Gilmore said.

'You spoil him,' Rachel said.

'As if you don't.' Gilmore lathered cream across his face, and picked up the razor.

'Something has been bothering me,' Rachel said. 'Why did Walsingham ask you to go to the trade fair?'

'I'd like to think it's my acumen and warm, gland handing ability with buyers,' Gilmore said, turning his head slightly as he slid the razor blade past an ear.

'You think there's another reason?'

'Perceptive as ever, Professor Jensen. I'm barely more than a prop these days. Watch as the retired air vice-marshal guides the oil rich sheiks and shady South American caudillos around the best military technology Britain can produce. The way Woden is going about it, they don't care who they sell to, and how much they sell.'

Gilmore paused to rinse the razor underneath the tap. He looked at his wife's reflection in the mirror, her no-nonsense face crinkled with concern.

'What we talked about, last night.'

'We talked about a lot of things last night,' Rachel said.

'I mean resigning from Woden. Give the whole damned mess a proper heave-ho.'

'And what will you do with all that free time? I'd be happy

for you to do so, don't get me wrong. It's just I can't see you keeping bees, Ian.'

'Maybe I'll write my memoirs.' Gilmore looked at his reflection. 'Perhaps I'll look into a diplomatic posting. Or travel.'

'Travel the world and solve its ills? Sounds wonderful.' Rachel put a finger to her lips, masking a smile. 'Though isn't that a younger man's game? You think you're still eighteen and on that beach.' She reached out and placed a warm hand on his shoulder. 'What's that about old soldiers fading away?'

'Bugger that,' Gilmore said. 'And you seem to have forgotten I was an airman. We never fade away.' He rinsed the razor blade again and started on his other cheek.

'You just fly away into the sunset? While you contemplate that delightful thought, breakfast is ready.'

'Eggs, dear, is it?' Gilmore said. He tilted his head and stroked his cheek with the razor blade.

'Of course. My specialty and your favourite, from what I've heard.'

'I'll be finished up in a few minutes.'

The rest of the morning flew by. Before he knew it, they were all standing on the doorstep, saying goodbye.

'Come back safe,' Gilmore said to Rachel.

She held a battered briefcase in one hand. 'It's Devesham, dear. Hardly anything exciting happens there.' She turned to Dillon, who stood tugging at the knot of his school tie. 'You make sure you listen to what Aunt Sarah tells you. And don't stay up late watching television. And enjoy France. I expect at least one postcard, in handwriting I can read.' Her eyes suddenly red, Rachel grabbed her son in a hug and squeezed him tight.

'And you,' she said, looking at her husband after releasing her son. 'I expect you home in one piece as well. No dancing with the *fräuleins*. They'll steal your heart and shatter it if you're not careful.'

'There will be precious little dancing, Rachel,' Gilmore said. He took her hand and squeezed it. 'Till next week, then.'

'Next week.' Again, Rachel blinked back tears. Shaking her head, she walked across the lawn to her Volvo. She waved one final time before driving away.

'Well,' Gilmore said, staring at the empty street. 'Let's get your stuff. I'll drop you off at school and leave your suitcase at Aunt Sarah's.'

'She'll be fine, Dad,' Dillon said, his hand slipping into Gilmore's.

Once he had dropped his son at school and gave him orders to listen to what the teachers said and enjoy his time away, Gilmore stopped at his sister-in-law's house. Sarah Rushton, Rachel's younger sister, offered him coffee after he handed the suitcase over. He demurred, talking about final preparations for his trip away. Truth be told, he was a little frightened of Sarah. He sensed she disapproved of him.

'Rachel sends her regards,' Gilmore said, lingering on the doorstep.

Sarah looked at him, her arms folded. 'You should take her away when she gets back. She's being working far too hard at Devesham. She needs a break.'

'Really?' Gilmore said. 'She's not said anything to me.'

'She wouldn't. But I will. All the trouble they've faced there is down to your employer. Woden.' Sarah almost spat out the word. 'Corner cutting and dodgy practices. Make sure she gets some rest when she gets back. She needs and deserves it.'

'Fair enough,' Gilmore said. 'Keep an eye on Dillon for me, will you. He's not happy I'm off to West Berlin.'

'I don't blame him,' Sarah said. 'Nothing good ever came out of that city.'

Those final thoughts lingered with Gilmore as he pottered around the house. He went over the trade fair briefing papers once more before filing them away. In the mid-afternoon, Rachel called.

'I'm here,' she said, her voice scratchy on the line.

'How was it?' Gilmore asked.

There was a long pause. 'The finance meeting went... as I expected.' Rachel sounded tired.

'How's things shaping up at mission control?'

'Anne and Allison kept a firm hand on things while I was away. We'll be taking over when the three launch vehicles have entered orbit. Look, I must go. Be good, Ian.'

Rachel rang off, leaving Gilmore holding the receiver, the

buzz of static filling the air around him. Something in Rachel's mood rubbed off on him, and he spent the rest of the day rattling around, trying to find things to occupy him. He prepared a perfunctory dinner, then tried to distract himself with the television. He gave up after half an hour. He went to bed and dreamed of Berlin ablaze all over again.

CHAPTER FIVE

Tuesday – Cambridge. 9am.

RACHEL PULLED the Volvo into her spot in front of the Rutherford Building. On the passenger seat sat the leather briefcase her parents had presented to her on her first day as an undergraduate at Cambridge. Inside were a number of funding proposals. One of them, by a long-time colleague, may as well have contained weapons grade plutonium for all the damage it would cause.

'God damn Neville Atkinson,' she muttered to herself. 'Making me go to war over his stupid funding request.'

For a moment, Rachel regretted not being at Devesham, despite all the headaches she had encountered there. Grabbing the briefcase, she opened the door and stepped outside. She closed her eyes for a moment, savouring the quiet for a few seconds more. When she opened them, she drank in her surroundings.

The Cavendish Laboratory had been Rachel's second home before her marriage, before Shoreditch. She preferred its old location at the New Museums Site, with its crumbling Victorian architecture, cramped offices and lecture theatres, and the weight of history stretching all the way back to Newton. Her earliest research had been conducted there. The offices were bigger, the laboratories brighter, but leaving the old site with its history had never sat well with her.

Another thing that didn't sit well with Rachel was the discovery that once she reached the position of tenured professor, her research work began to dwindle, replaced with the minutiae of running an office. A thicket of bureaucracy surrounded her day-to-day life; her diary was filled with meeting after meeting after meeting, covering staffing levels, occupational health and safety, and the horror of endless fundraisers. Rachel had taken to saying to bemused colleagues, as tipsy philanthropists were gently led to their waiting Bentley's or Rolls Royce's after Rachel had turned on the charm to get them to open their chequebooks, 'let the Devil take the hindmost'.

Closing the door with her hip, she walked towards the entrance to the Cavendish Laboratory. A fresh breeze, coming off Payne's Pond, reminded her that winter was not far away. Along the path, she nodded to students going in the opposite direction. She knew they were looking at her sidelong. Professor Rachel Jensen's reputation as a scientist with an acerbic tongue and manner preceded her. There was muttering, within the student body and the other academics, about an incident in her past involving the military. It was, however, her anti-war stance and willingness to speak out against the military that made her something of a heroine among the students.

So caught up in her thoughts was she, that it took the man hurrying behind her two efforts to catch her attention.

'Rachel?'

She slowed and looked over her shoulder. Her habitual frown eased away as a smile lit her face.

'Albert? My dear fellow. How have you been?'

Professor Albert Markson was a portly man, given to velvet jackets and floppy bow ties. Despite the evident eccentricity about the man's dress, his work in the Cavendish Laboratory in Nuclear Medicine had seen him dubbed the Plutonium Prophet by some of the faculty wags. His work, however, in helping to save the lives of countless people thanks to his brilliant insights into treating cancer through nuclear medicine, saw him regarded by many in the field as a saviour.

'While you've been dallying with the white heat of technology, I've been to Paris. Such an absolute delight,' Albert said, breaking into a beaming smile. 'I met the most delightful fellow at the Louvre, wouldn't you know?'

Though in his early fifties, Albert took his fashion cues from the students. While some in the faculty frowned on it, Rachel found the habit, and Albert, delightfully endearing.

'And how is Devesham?' Albert looked at her curiously.

Her secondment to the establishment had caused a minor ruction within the upper echelons of Cambridge academia. The notion that one of their eminent scientists would agree to get her hands dirty with the proles in the real world had many looking askance at Rachel.

'About as you would expect,' she answered, aware she was being deliberately cryptic. 'Stay in the public sector, Albert. You're perfectly suited to it.'

'Oh, I definitely am. Is that husband of yours on his way to West Berlin?'

'He flies out tomorrow.'

'West Berlin is a delightfully decadent town,' Albert said, his voice dropping to a knowing whisper. 'I wonder what he'll get up to in between meetings?'

'Be nice, Albert. Ian is there on business. He'll have barely any free time; with all the meetings he will attend.'

'Speaking of meetings, what odds Neville has a stroke during ours?'

'Given how I think the vote will go, very good odds.'

'What, asking the dons in their gilded eyrie to approve a biological weapons laboratory at Cambridge is a bridge too far?' Albert chuckled.

'Since his wife died, Neville's not been the same...' Rachel paused on seeing a severe looking man in a black suit approach them. It looked to Rachel like he was stalking prey. 'Here's the man of the moment,' she said as an aside.

Lifting her head, Rachel tried on a smile. 'Neville,' she said, nodding to him.

'Rachel!' Neville Atkinson's voice was querulous and angry. 'Do I have it right that you're voting against my proposal when the finance committee meets? May I say you're making a terrible—'

'Professor Atkinson,' Rachel said, more severely this time. 'As you very well know, there is a proper process for discussing your proposal. This windswept concrete path isn't an appropriate venue to—'

Atkinson cut her off by grabbing her arm. 'Why are you so wilfully blind.'

Albert stepped in. 'Take your hand off her, Neville,' he said, his normal avuncular humour gone.

'That's all right, Albert,' Rachel said. Her voice was as cold as old iron. She locked eyes with Atkinson. 'Neville, if you don't release me, I'll snap your arm off at the elbow.' Startled, Atkinson let Rachel go and then took a step back. 'Out of respect for your wife, I'm going to forget what just happened,' Rachel said. 'She was a good woman. The recent decline in your manner and behaviour I can only ascribe to understandable grief over her death. Now, we are all going to act like adults, and engage with each other in the proper manner, in the proper place, with regards to your funding request. Not out here where the entire world can see us arguing.'

Recoiling as if he had been slapped, Atkinson's sallow face tightened, and crimson blossomed on each cheek. Without a word, he turned on his heel and stormed off.

A chill blast of wind from the lake blew through the silence that enveloped Rachel and Albert. Leaves skittered around them, the brittle sound like breaking glass.

'"Snap your arm off at the elbow",' Albert said, sounding shocked and a little awed.

'I've come to learn, Albert, then when your blood is up, you men don't listen to reason,' Rachel said, adjusting her jacket where Atkinson had pulled at it. 'Going for your throats is the only way to get through your thick skulls.' She looked after Atkinson's retreating back and shook her head. 'I'll see you at the committee meeting.'

Inside, the halls echoed with chatting students and staff, making their way to their next lectures. Standing amid the organised chaos, Rachel closed her eyes for a moment, trying to get her bearings after the confrontation with Atkinson. When she opened them again, the space had emptied. She turned and followed the nearest corridor to her office.

'Good morning, Professor. And welcome back.' A young woman with round spectacles looked up at Rachel from behind her desk.

'There's precious little good about it, Penny,' Rachel said, and immediately regretted her tone.

Penny was one of Rachel's PhD students, working part-time

to supplement her scholarship. The young woman paled and looked down at the typewriter sitting before her.

'I'm sorry, my dear,' Rachel said, coming to the desk. 'I had an unfortunate... Never mind. I apologise for my tone. It wasn't directed at you.'

Penny shook her head. 'I'm fine, Professor, really.' She glanced at the desk diary. 'All you have this morning is the finance committee meeting. I've left messages for you on your desk.'

'Thank you. Though I doubt I'll get through many of those messages. I'll take any calls that come through, up until ten minutes before the meeting, all right?'

The committee room was the sort of tired-looking affair Rachel had come to realise was the hallmark of an underfunded university sector. Politicians might talk about the white heat of technology, but when it came to funding it, the purse strings were resolutely knotted tight. Battered chairs surrounded a conference table covered in chipped laminate and coffee rings. Several tired-looking indoor plants sat forlorn in the corners. The miasma of cigarette smoke lingered in the air from the previous meeting, a fug that reminded Rachel of some of the dull thinking the room had hosted.

She was, Rachel decided, rather put out by the whole ordeal to come. Nodding to the other members of the committee on entering the room, which included Albert, she sat in an empty chair. Opening her briefcase, she retrieved the folders from within, spread them across the table in front of her, then looked up.

'Shall we begin?'

Finance committee consisted of several departmental heads reviewing funding proposals for future research, the money drawn from a limited pool of funds provided by the government or by donations. Each session consisted of an interview with the proposer, who would be challenged on the merits of their proposal, and what they hoped to achieve with their research.

'Tell me why we do this again?' Rachel said an hour later, rubbing the back of her neck while they waited for the next applicant.

'For the betterment of mankind?' Albert said, eliciting a

chuckle from around the table.

There was a knock at the door.

'Come,' Rachel called.

Professor Atkinson entered. He may as well have been climbing the steps of a scaffold. He glanced briefly at the people in the room and took a seat at the far end of the table.

'Neville,' Rachel said. Her voice betrayed no emotions. 'The committee is ready to hear about your application.'

Neville Atkinson spent five minutes in a dry recitation of his proposed research. It sounded to Rachel as if he had given up before entering the room.

'According to your proposal,' Albert said, when Atkinson finished and sank back into his chair. 'Cambridge should help fund a biowarfare centre. Do I understand you correctly?'

There was a rustling of papers as the other members of the committee glanced uneasily at each other.

'No,' Atkinson. 'I'm not arguing for anything of the sort. What I hope to achieve with the centre is to better understand the application of biological warfare so we can hope to defend ourselves from it.'

'It seems,' Rachel said, glancing down at her copy of Atkinson's proposal. 'That there is a very fine line separating the creation of biological weapons and merely understanding how they operate. Vanishingly small, I would've said. You walk up to the brink and then look down into what I think is something of a moral abyss. I'm also concerned about the mention in Section D of investigating ethnic susceptibility. You are straying into an area of dubious ethical precedent.'

'Come now, Professor,' Atkinson said. His eyes narrowed. 'We all know that certain ethnic groups are susceptible to particular diseases, more than other groups. Sickle cell disease, after all, is most common amongst the blacks. Why, even—'

'*The blacks?*' Rachel said. Her words dropped into the sudden silence that enveloped the room with all the solidity of an anvil onto concrete.

'Forgive me,' Atkinson said, with a glare that asked for nothing of the sort. 'I stand on solid, scientific grounds. If you want to muddy the waters with talk of ethics, well, that might explain your lack of success in your own research in recent years than anything else—'

'Professor Atkinson.' Rachel paused when she realised she had raised her voice. Atkinson's half smile infuriated her. She pursed her lips, as if she had tasted something unpleasant, and forged on. 'We all acknowledge the research you have done these last two decades as part of the Cavendish Laboratory. So it is with some regret that I inform you the Laboratory will not be approving your proposal.' She waved her hand at the paperwork sitting in front of her. 'Let me be frank. Most of this is half-baked nonsense, and the rest of it borders on outright racism. We are researchers, first and foremost. Not enablers of mass slaughter. Cambridge is in the business of learning. I can't believe I have to say it, but we do not dabble in germ warfare.'

She paused to gather herself.

'Not enablers of mass slaughter? You might want to dig a little deeper as to what is actually happening at Devesham, Rachel...'

'What are you...?' Rachel shook her head. The jealousies of some in the department was all too evident. She frowned and went on. 'Regardless, on a personal note, and on behalf of the committee, we extend our courtesies regarding the recent death of your wife. I think you might be wise to take a period of leave to reflect—'

'Leave?' Atkinson rose suddenly from his chair. 'You've waited a long, long time to do this to me, haven't you, Rachel? Slyness is in the blood, isn't it? I'll do better than go on leave. The faculty shall have my resignation letter by the end of business today. I refuse to continue working with people too blinkered to understand the threat we face. Our entire way of...' Atkinson stopped himself with a visible effort. He glanced at the members of the committee, his gaze lingering longest on Rachel. 'You'll hear from me again; of that you can have no doubt. Enjoy Devesham.' With that, Atkinson gathered his papers and departed.

'Well, that was... I don't quite know what that was,' Albert said.

'That was a man consumed by grief,' Rachel said. She tidied her notes then looked around the table. 'I believe that is all. Thank you for your attendance.'

Albert lingered, to Rachel's annoyance. After Atkinson's outburst, she wasn't in the mood for idle chit chat.

'Don't you have somewhere to be, Albert? A research team to supervise?'

'Are you all right?' he asked, as they left the room.

'Perfectly fine.' Rachel paused, thinking. His eyes narrowed. 'Is something the matter?'

'Do you know what sort of car Neville drives?'

'Car? I don't recall him ever... Why are you asking?'

Rachel shook her head. 'Never mind.' She checked her watch. 'I've got some paperwork to finish, and then I have to get back to Devesham.'

'Ah, yes, the launch, this evening. What do you think Neville was talking about? Devesham isn't some sort of cabal of iniquity, is it?' Albert had a twinkle in his eye.

'It's what it always was, Albert,' Rachel said. She too, was puzzled by Atkinson's reference. Did he know something she didn't? 'HQ for the British Space Industry.'

'If you say so.' Albert glanced at his watch. 'Oh dear. Must dash. I've got a lecture to conduct. Good luck tonight.' With that, Albert hurried away, waving his hand in the air in farewell.

Back in her office, with the door firmly closed, Rachel stood before the windows behind her desk and contemplated the world outside. The image of Neville Atkinson's face, eyes ice cold and brimming with hate, filled her with a sense of foreboding. The language he had used stung with all the memories of childhood taunts.

The phone rang, startling her.

'Yes, Penny? What's his name? William...? He won't give his last name? The cheek. No, tell him I'm busy. Well, if he still wants to see me, he'll need to make an appointment.'

Rachel set the receiver down in its cradle and returned to looking outside. From her office, she could just see the edge of Payne's Pond skirting the southern edge of the West Cambridge facility. A few willows dotted the shore, long branches swaying in the breeze. Sighing, Rachel returned to her desk, spent an hour responding to the messages Penny had collected for her, then decided it was time to leave.

'Good luck with the launch tonight, Professor,' Penny said, looking up from a pile of correspondence on her desk as Rachel closed her office door. 'It seems ever so exciting.'

'You'd be surprised, Penny. Much of it is automated. To think all our advances have really meant the human element has been largely sidelined.'

Rachel paused, thinking. 'That fellow who called before, William, I think you said. What did he want?'

'He just said he needed to see you. Didn't give a reason. He sounded... anxious?'

'How strange,' Rachel said, after a moment's thought. 'It's been ever so long since I've had a gentleman caller.'

While Penny pretended to look scandalised, Rachel laughed. With her mood lightening, she headed off to her car with a spring in her step.

CHAPTER SIX

Wednesday – Island Lagoon Tracking Station, Woomera Rocket Range, Launch Control. 1.30am.

THE MOBILE launcher was locked down on the launch pad. The seven swing arms of the Launch Umbilical Tower were ready for release. The liquid oxygen/hydrogen pumps had been switched off after a last-minute top up when a previously undetected leak in the propellant tanks was discovered. Lights picked out the 360-foot-tall structure. This third XK-7 rocket, one of the three making up the Cerberus project, had been designed in Devesham, built in a facility near Glasgow, and transported via the Suez Canal for delivery by railroad into the barren expanses of South Australia for assembly, was ready to blast into the heavens.

An eerie silence hung over the launch facility. Guards manned their checkpoints, weapons slung or cradled in their arms. Though never presenting a real problem, the anti-nuclear protesters had been bundled away, unable to do more than protest noisily at the main gates five miles distant or penetrate the triple row of fencing surrounding the facility. The baying of German Shepherds attested to a sighting of a dingo, but little else. The Woomera Rocket Range sat inside an exclusion zone the size of Britain. That, and the lingering malignity at Maralinga, was enough to keep all but the authorised away from the facility.

Launch Commander James Salisbury stood beside a chain link fence and stared at the north-western skyline. By rights, he should've been in the control room, overseeing final preparations. But in the months since traversing the globe to take command of a project that had fallen badly behind, it swiftly became his habit to stand outside after the sunset and gaze at the night sky.

Tonight, he felt the awesome spread of the night almost as if it were a weight on his shoulders. Even without the imminent launch, and all that was riding on it, he would've felt that weight. It felt good to simply lose himself in the inky vastness of the universe. The heat, the flies, the dust, separation from his wife and baby boy, the overwhelming sense of loneliness in an arid wasteland – he could live with all of that, as long as he could stand in that spot, alone, and appreciate the majesty of the heavens sprawled overhead.

Looming behind him stood a squat building, a cinderblock affair hastily flung up when the appropriated funds were approved by parliamentary fiat in faraway Westminster. Several hundred yards distant, the skeletal frame of the station's twenty-eight-yard tracking antenna stood picked out in lights. Something of the day's heat lingered in the air, lending it a warmth alien to Salisbury's experience as a boy growing up in Yorkshire. Clad in trousers and short sleeved shirt, he savoured the warmth even as he prepared to return to the control room and the final stages before launch. But before that, one final look at the magnificence of creation.

The facility lights did little to obscure the Milky Way unfurling like a vast carpet across the sky. Orion, the Southern Cross, all were picked out in brilliant points of light, markers on a journey through the cosmos. There, thousands of miles from home, away from the light pollution that blighted urban Britain, Salisbury remained enraptured by the crystal-clear view of a billion billion stars.

He took a drag on his cigarette and glanced at his watch. He rubbed his face. He was exhausted. All the staff on the base were exhausted. Getting this arm of Cerberus up and running had been a last-minute affair. He had argued for more time, but Woden flat out refused. But they did it, poured more concrete in less time than any British civil engineering project since the Second World War. Here, and in Nigeria, and on Diego Garcia, his team had come together and performed the near impossible.

As always, on nights like this, when he preferred to linger

in the heat instead of the air-conditioned comfort of the control room, which played hell with his sinuses, Salisbury's gaze unwillingly shifted, dropping from the awesome sky above, to the sickening glow coming from the Maralinga testing fields. After the clean view of the sky, the ever-present reminder of the nuclear tests in the desert wastes of South Australia was always a clarifying rebuke to man's claim to be planet earth's faithful steward.

'As above, so below,' Salisbury muttered to himself. He dropped the spent cigarette and ground it beneath his heel. He turned, then paused, drinking in the sight of the conical structure looming over the control centre.

The multi-stage launch vehicle stood twenty stories high and native birds wreathed its nose cone.

Salisbury strode along the gravel walk, stones crunching under his boots. He flashed his badge to the guard on duty. He had done it hundreds of times, knew the guard by name, but also knew that without that badge, any attempt to force the door would result in lethal violence.

Salisbury stood in the corridor, preparing himself for the work to come. He felt the pressure of the place, of his role, fall on him like a beam of timber from the Crucifixion. Ahead, a security guard manned a station. Salisbury walked towards it and swiped his card across the reader, stepped through when the metal barrier slid open. He exchanged a nod with the guard, then continued down the corridor.

On his left, the tracking station was a hive of hushed activity. Through glass, he saw men, and a few women, rush about on rubber soles with computer printouts clutched in their hands, making final checks of the calculations. He glanced into the communications equipment room, where the telemetry guidance instructions would be beamed to the payload vehicles as the booster rockets fell away. More guards, more checkpoints, a nod and a wink to the chaps at the recovery operations desk, then Salisbury strode into Mission Control.

He paused to survey his domain, as much to admire it as to put off the inevitable confrontation with one of his team. The control area was split level, dim lighting casting the cavernous room into shadows. A Mercator map dominated the far wall, pinpricks of light highlighting cities, while three lines depicted the pre-planned orbits of the satellites about to be flung into the sky. To the right, three smaller screens displayed locked off images of the separate launch vehicles.

A triple row of terminals sat in the lower area. Figures wearing headsets sat at each, faces bathed in green and amber lights as they intently examined the readouts. Meteorological reports were fed directly from the Bureau in Melbourne, linked by a Telstar Satellite riding overhead in geostationary orbit. More information poured down other screens, alerting their operators to minute changes in fuel loads, shifts in temperature of the exterior skin of the rocket itself, and the metallo-rubber rings that ensured no bursts of super compressed rocket fuel could escape and incinerate the vehicle when the burners ignited.

Walking towards a narrow set of steps, Salisbury acknowledged with a nod the engineers and analysts who turned to greet him. He was pleased by the number of women on his team; after his time at Oxford, he had pushed hard to recruit more women into the aeronautics field.

He stopped next to the steps, fixed a smile on his face, and ascended the platform.

At the top, he turned and looked across the control room. His vantage point gave him a panoramic view of the entire operation. His operation, despite what Charles said. Woden Armaments may've supplied half the money, and Charles may've been Woden's man at the facility, but this was an operation for the benefit of the British Government, for the British people. *For humanity.* Salisbury decided long ago he'd be damned if he'd concede an inch to the man, devil take him.

Salisbury moved to stand behind a central desk. He checked the large clock, mounted beneath the map and which had been counting down for the past week.

It stood at 30m:30s to launch.

'Could someone please remind me why the launch time is at this ridiculous hour?' Salisbury said, as he scrubbed a hand over his face.

The woman beside him handed him a steaming mug of coffee. 'We have to give the BBC sufficient times to package up the details for news broadcast.'

'Oh right,' Salisbury said sarcastically. 'There's an election due.'

'Now, now.' The man on his right tutted. 'I would've thought you public servants were apolitical.'

'Put a cork in it, Charles,' Salisbury snarled. 'Woden's been suckling at the taxpayer's teat for all its worth since the deal was signed.' He ignored Charles' furious glare. 'How's Banana Island and Diego, Alice?' Salisbury swallowed a mouthful of coffee, wincing at its temperature and bitterness. He slipped on a headset and readied himself to begin the final countdown.

'Coming through loud and clear, Commander.' Alice was always more formal than she needed to be, but he appreciated her professionalism.

'What are the weather observations?

'Light clouds over Banana Island, but nothing untoward. The storm has moved south of Diego Garcia, so we won't have to worry about that.'

Salisbury breathed a sigh of relief. Ensuring one rocket launched successfully was one thing, but three, strung out around the globe... He had woken up more than once in a cold sweat in the past week.

Charles coughed. With great reluctance, Salisbury glanced at him.

'Devesham have communicated they will assume command of the satellites once they are successfully launched.'

'Tell me again why I'm giving over control to Devesham, Charles.' Salisbury caught a glimpse of Alice looking sharply at him, but he ignored her.

'Despite what you may think, Woden Armaments have made a substantial investment of their own funds in Project Cerberus. As they say, follow the money, dear fellow,' Charles said. 'After all, we've been supporting the home-grown aeronautics field for years.' He didn't bother to cover his words with a smile.

'Support?' Salisbury shook his head. 'What support have you provided Guy Crayford's family?' Salisbury immediately regretted his words.

The loss of Crayford and his X-K5 craft had hit the British Aeronautics Establishment hard. Some blamed Woden Armaments for pushing that project too quickly.

Salisbury looked down at his terminal, aware that he'd lost

a point in his endless struggle against Charles. He gripped the edges of his desk with both hands, then nodded firmly.

'Alice, send a message to Banana Island and Diego Garcia I'll be assuming single control at fifteen minutes to launch,' Salisbury said, slipping into the clipped tone he adopted when it was time for work.

There was a pause while Alice messaged the other two launch facilities.

'Message sent,' she said. 'And... acknowledged.'

Salisbury keyed a switch on his desk. There was a burst of static in his headset, then he began speaking.

'We're within thirty minutes of launch. Banana Island and Diego Garcia launch sites indicate they are good to go. We will proceed as per our simulations, with a go/no go signal communicated when we enter the five-minute window.' Salisbury paused. He felt a lump in his throat. His wife always told him he was too emotional. 'Whatever happens, I'm damned proud of all of you. What you've done in such a short period of time... Well, no one else could've done it. Project Cerberus is happening because of your efforts.' He smiled to himself. 'All right then, enough backslapping. Let's get these birds in the air.'

The next twenty-five minutes slipped through Salisbury's fingers like water. At the fifteen-minute mark, Salisbury assumed sole control of all three launch sites. He glanced at the screens to the side of the main map. They showed a locked off shot of the rockets on Banana Island, off the coast of Nigeria, and the dependency of Diego Garcia, a tiny island in the middle of the Indian Ocean. He heard a tone in his earpiece, then Alice told him they were approaching the go/no go window.

'Weather conditions remain fine at all three sites,' Salisbury said, taking in the information on his screen.

'Engineering crews confirm all three launch vehicles are in the green zone,' Alice said.

Salisbury glanced at Charles.

'Devesham? They're ready to assume command once we release the satellites?'

'The Gorgons have finally got their act together,' Charles drawled.

It was a little in-joke among the Woden component at

Woomera about the three women in charge at Devesham. Salisbury desperately wanted to punch Charles for what he had just said, and really, everything about the man. That could wait for the tail end of the launch party, he decided, when the drinks had flowed sufficiently for him to take Charles into a storeroom and give him the belting he so richly deserved.

'Go/no go window has been reached,' Salisbury said into his headset microphone. His voice echoed around the control chamber. 'We are set for launch,' he added, after a pause.

The change in atmosphere was palpable. There was no turning back. Save a catastrophic failure on the launchpad, or the rockets themselves breaking apart under the immense G forces they would experience, the satellites would be in orbit within the quarter hour.

The seconds ticked by. Salisbury felt a trickle of sweat running down his neck. He glanced at Alice, who looked stonily at her monitor. Even Charles seemed awed by what was about to happen.

'Switching over to automatic launch controls,' Salisbury said into his microphone.

The lights dimmed for a moment and were then replaced by a low-level series of red lights. The scene before him seemed dipped in blood, and Salisbury scolded himself for his morbidness.

'T-minus thirty seconds,' Alice said, her dispassionate voice echoing around the chamber.

The atmosphere was electric. On the monitors on the far wall, Salisbury could see the images of the three launch vehicles. Birds circled the top of the launch vehicle on Banana Island.

'They'll get the fright of their lives,' Salisbury muttered, ignoring a glance from Charles.

'T-minus twenty seconds.' Alice's voice echoed metallically around the control room.

Salisbury could see information cascading down the screens of the nearest terminal, as sensors went into overload as the ignition sequence began.

'T-Minus ten... Nine... Eight... Seven... Six... Five... Four... Three... Two... One...'

The rest of Alice's words were lost in a rumbling roar that sounded like a million freight trains were passing simultaneously through the control room. Four Star Striker engines ignited with a dragon's roar. The structure shuddered as the Woomera launch vehicle lifted from the launchpad, smoke billowing outward and upward. Then, the rocket began to ascend, slowly at first as it fought against gravity's jealous clutches, then with more speed as the release of energy shattered those chains.

The camera providing the feed panned upwards as the swing arms swivelled back and the umbilical cords fell limp. Salisbury was awestruck, watching the launch vehicle rising into the air, gathering speed against the star sparked velvet of the galaxy. He felt a hand on his shoulder and turned to see Alice smiling broadly at him. He even accepted a congratulatory handshake from Charles.

Sixteen minutes and forty-five seconds into the launch, all three vehicles of the Cerberus Project entered low earth orbit. An hour twenty-two into the mission, with Devesham now in control, the three separate nose cones split open simultaneously, and the satellites emerged. Precisely two minutes after that, Director Allison Williams at Devesham confirmed control uplink. Fifteen minutes and seven seconds after that, an emergency MoD message came through to Salisbury on his screen. He read it as blood drained from his face.

Control of all three satellites has been lost. Repeat – control of all three satellites has been lost.

CHAPTER SEVEN

Tuesday – Devesham Mission Control. 6.30pm.

WHEN RACHEL originally joined Devesham Mission Control, things were, to say the least, not going well. Her former colleague, Allison Williams, was a dedicated, resourceful scientist with a spirit of adventure. Those strengths didn't extend to administering a disparate team of engineers and technicians in a hothouse environment with a corporate backer breathing down their necks. What Allison lacked in people management skills, Rachel made up for in spades. You didn't wrangle a gaggle of eccentric academic dons, while juggling your own research and emptying the wallets of wealthy benefactors, if you didn't know how to browbeat people into line.

By the time Rachel brought the listing ship back to an even keel, with the assistance of Dr Anne Travers (who Rachel had once taught to a much lesser degree than Allison), she felt she had imparted enough of her experience to Allison, that she understood the requirements to run Mission Control and its team. Now, all her efforts were coming to fruition, as Rachel settled back and watched what proved to be a smooth handover from Salisbury's team at Woomera to Devesham itself.

Rachel kept a critical eye on the main control panel as the last of the green lights indicated all the uplinks had successfully connected. Only then did she relax.

'That's it, everyone,' Allison said, turning to the pensively waiting team in Mission Control. 'Devesham is now in sole control of the Cerberus satellites.'

A cheer went up from the assembled team and, soon enough,

champagne began to flow freely in celebration.

'Well done, Allison. We did it,' Anne said. She clapped Allison on the shoulder while sipping from her plastic cup. Anne grimaced and looked dubiously at the contents. 'This isn't the top shelf stuff I was promised.'

Allison laughed, the sound dying in her throat when her gaze drifted to a piece of equipment sitting in the shadows at the rear of the room.

It was an oddity amidst the workstations, computer mainframes and celebrating technicians. The equipment looked like a stylised throne, with high sides and a low cowl mostly hiding the figure seated within. This was, as Anne said a few months back, the dirty little secret at the heart of their operation. The comment provoked an argument with Allison, who took great pains to point out that Anne was as responsible as she was for the figure linked into the machinery. A figure the team unofficially dubbed the Child, even though the girl inside the machine was in her early twenties.

Anne felt her smile curdle. She knew that Allison had met the Child before, an experience she refused to discuss. Whatever suffering the Child had experienced, it somehow made her a prime candidate for the paradigm shift Woden promised the government it could achieve; the synthesis of man and machine. It would give them the edge over the powerful Soviet mainframes. Where the Soviets pummelled numbers into submission with the massive networks built up since Turing's creation emerged stumbling into the world during the war, Woden would go down a different path, harnessing man and machine to make the intuitive leaps needed to project power into orbit around the globe.

Of course, as Anne knew very well, there was a very good reason the Child stayed mostly hidden. The technicians feared her. It was as simple as that. Only a few wisps of hair clung to her skull. Thick veins formed an ugly delta beneath the scalp, twisted and knotted and bunched. She sat hunched forward, spindly arms crossed over her lap, spittle hanging from slack lips. The surgery caused considerable disquiet among the Devesham team. With some difficulty, the concern had been tamped down, mainly because only Allison and Anne dealt directly with the Child. On her arrival, it was common knowledge that Rachel had reservations about the surgery performed on the Child. Only Allison and Anne knew what she really felt.

Anne was sure at one point she'd heard Rachel talking to the Child, calling her *Judith*.

Anne watched the Child. Only the eyes, fixed open in a waking REM dream, moved, twitching from side to side, working through the reams of data pumped into her brain via the two cables screwed into plugs embedded in the rear of its skull. Anne didn't need to see the cables, but she knew they were there.

After all, she had assisted with the operations that sunk the plugs deep into the Child's brain.

'Well, this dreck will just have to do,' Anne said, trying to lighten the mood.

Distracted, Allison nodded towards a figure standing at ground level. He looked up at the celebrating technicians, a scowl warping his features.

'Hemmings doesn't seem happy,' Anne said, raising her cup and toasting him. His scowl deepened. Rachel joined them.

Unconsciously, the younger women made room for their mentor. Old habits died hard.

'Mr Hemmings is never happy,' Rachel said.

'He needs a good woman,' Anne said, chuckling.

'I wouldn't wish him on any woman, good or bad.' Rachel looked at them both. 'Any updates on the telephone issue?'

'Nothing,' Allison replied. 'Which is why Hemmings is probably filthy. With our telephone lines down, he won't be able to phone Woden and claim credit for our work.'

'We're all in the same boat,' Anne said. 'I'd love to ring my husband.'

'What about the village?' Rachel asked.

'Blackout extends to the village,' Allison said. 'The lines went down just before you arrived.'

'Just in time for the launches.'

'With the sort of complexities we've had to work with,' Allison said, 'I'm surprised everything, and I mean everything, held together as well as it did.' She glanced again at the Child sitting slumped in its chair. 'What's she thinking, I wonder?'

'I shudder to think,' Rachel said. 'If I'd been in charge from the start...'

Allison raised her hand, interrupting Rachel. 'You weren't, Rachel. I was. It was my decision.'

Rachel scowled. 'It should never have come to that. What Judith needed was help. Not this... exploitation.'

It was the first time Rachel had spoken the name so openly. Anne watched the two old friends spar over a shared history she still didn't understand. Anne would have to contact the Brigadier soon; Alistair would be able to find out what happened at Shoreditch eleven years ago. She knew the Doctor had been involved; she'd known that for years. But the specifics still eluded her.

Allison scowled. 'And yet you're still here, Rachel. Why is that?' Respect for a mentor went only so far.

'There's a higher purpose here I can just... and I emphasise *just*... agree with that legitimises what was done. These satellites will revolutionise communications around the globe. And yet...'

'I know she was in ill-health,' Anne said, fishing for information. 'But for her parents, for her, to agree to your proposal...'

'She was never the same after Shoreditch,' Allison said, shaking her head.

'How's that?'

'She didn't fit in,' Rachel cut in, glancing a warning at Allison. 'Not after what was done to her as a little girl. Her nightmares were singular. What happened to her unlocked something in her brain, gave her... powers that ordinary people don't have, or not to the level documented with her. I think we've all experienced events in our lives that are outside what one would consider the everyday. The trauma made her amenable to...' Rachel shook her head. 'Her parents couldn't control her. She took to drink and drugs, just to cope.'

'And that's why this was the only way,' Allison said, cutting in. 'She was basically a vegetable when her parents contacted me. I'd stayed in touch, after Shoreditch. They were desperate to keep her alive. Knowing what was originally done to her, I was able to copy the process. It helped her, Anne. What we did. Connecting her into our communications systems in a manner that melded the mind with machine intelligence. She's alive today because of what I did. For her parents, that's enough.'

Allison sighed. 'This is hardly the way we should be celebrating.'

At that moment, Hemmings started up the steps towards them.

'Another reason to be depressed. Eyes front,' Anne muttered. 'Here comes trouble.'

'How's my girl doing,' Hemmings said, nodding to the Child.

'She's not *your girl*,' Rachel said, her nostrils flaring.

'Come now, Professor. Can't take a joke? Just asking after the health of the main component in our operation here. I could sack all these technicians scurrying around like so many ants, but without her, those satellites may as well be drifting junk.'

'She's doing fine,' Allison said. 'All indications are she's operating within normal tolerances.'

'Good. Good. She's a valuable piece of kit, Director Williams.' For Hemmings, Allison's title was a way to needle her. 'Wouldn't want anything happening to her.' Ignoring the looks of outrage, Hemmings glanced around at the celebrating staff. 'How long do my Gorgons intend to keep this little party going?'

'I might remind you, Mr Hemmings,' Rachel said, warningly, 'that if you keep referring to my colleagues and I in that manner, we'll have no choice but to report you.'

'To whom, I wonder?' Hemmings said. He had a broad, blocky face, the sort that a sculpture might think unfinished. Thin lips over a square chin and watchful eyes too closely set made for a memorable, if ugly, face.

'The government, of course,' Rachel said, attempting to rein in her temper.

'But my salary comes from Woden. Woden doesn't care one way or the other what you think of what I say. Again, when are you returning to work?'

'They'll celebrate as long as I say,' Allison said, tilting her chin defiantly. 'Just because you're Woden's man here doesn't mean you can tell me how to run my team. They've worked their guts out over the last six months. I think a chance to let their hair down is well-deserved. If you're so concerned about their productivity, getting the phone lines reconnected will help morale no end. I'd very much like to contact my fiancé.'

'Yes,' Anne chimed in. 'My husband is expecting a call from me as well.'

'And mine,' Rachel said, crossing her arms.

Hemmings irritably waved away their words. 'For all this talk of Women's Lib, you all seem terribly reliant on your menfolk. Harden up, ladies.' His smirk spoke volumes. 'Apparently, there's some strike action happening in the south, and the local repairmen have decided to go out in sympathy.' Hemmings ran a hand through his thinning hair. 'I'm reliably informed it should only be for a day or two.'

'Really?' Allison said, her voice heavy with incredulity. 'We may as well send a letter by carrier pigeon. It'll be damned quicker.'

'Be that as it may, you have bigger fish to fry. Or have you forgotten the test that was scheduled before the launch?'

'All work and no play, is it?' Anne said, her eyebrows arching.

'Quite.' Hemmings looked around the room with disdain. 'Your people have worked hard, I concede. But make no mistake, they'll be required to work even harder. Make sure this place is neat and tidy, and your team ready to proceed. I'll return with the co-ordinates shortly. I'm sure our most valuable member will absolutely gobble them up with relish.' Without waiting for a response, Hemmings turned on his heel and departed.

'He's quite the martinet,' Allison said.

'He who pays the piper calls the tune.' Rachel looked at his departing back like she wanted to shoot him.

Anne smiled, appreciating Rachel's feelings all too well. If someone like Hemmings threw his weight around back at the Fifth...

'So Woden has deeper pockets than the British government?' she asked.

'Woden has more reason for this to succeed,' Rachel said. 'This is their stepping stone into global communications. They've just demonstrated to the government and the British people that Britain has a home-grown space programme that can compete with the best in the world. They might be standing on Bernard's shoulders, but now they've... *we've* succeeded so spectacularly, the next step is control of global communications.'

'So, now we crack the whip?' Allison asked.

Rachel nodded. 'It's your show, Allison. I'll leave the honours to you.'

'Heavy is the head that wears the crown?' Setting aside her cup, Allison clapped her hands loudly several times. 'All right, all right. Everyone, settle down for a minute.'

A dozen expectant faces turned.

'What we've just accomplished has catapulted Britain to the forefront of global communications. But this is just the beginning.' She waved away a scattering of applause. 'You all deserve the accolades that will surely follow. But the work never ceases. Our paymasters are eager to try their new toys out. We will shortly commence Phase One testing. Enjoy yourselves. But not too much.'

Despite the murmurs, the team, including Allison, Rachel and Anne, pitched in and soon enough, all signs of the party in the control room had been cleared away.

Anne lingered beside the figure under the cowl, checking the medical data on the display set into the unit itself. Her gaze drifted to the pair of black cables snaking from the rear of the Child's skull, then hurriedly looked away.

'All clear?'

Anne jumped.

'Easy does it,' Rachel said. 'How's our... friend doing?'

'Judith, you called her.' Anne frowned. 'What happened to her?'

'You know I can't say, Anne.'

'I signed the Official Secrets Act, years ago now.'

Rachel nodded slowly. 'Yes, and you know well enough that does not cover every single secret.'

Anne glanced up at the half visible face. The black veins snaking beneath the waxen skin made her nauseous.

'In the end, it was their choice,' Rachel said. 'They did it to save their daughter. Not one I could've made.'

'You saw your boy when you were home?'

Rachel nodded, a fleeting smile crossing her lips.

'You're lucky. Bill and I have tried for a... Well, no joy yet. He's in the military, just like Ian was.' Anne wasn't sure why she said that, perhaps to remind Rachel that she did understand the need for secrets?

'Really? He and Ian would get on like a house on fire. Which branch?'

Anne smiled. 'Scots Guards Special Support Group. At least, that's the official name on paper.'

Rachel nodded. 'Oh yes, the Home-Army Fifth Operational Corps,' she said, lowering her voice. 'My husband was instrumental in its formation.' Rachel smiled. 'Well, I guess you and I have lived similar lives.'

'Perhaps. Similar enough, at least.'

Hemmings walked in, clutching a sheaf of papers. When he reached the top of the steps, he stopped short of Allison. Rachel and Anne joined them.

'Well, are you ready? I have the co-ordinates here.' Handing the printouts to Allison, he watched impatiently as she paged through them, her lips pursed. When she finished, she looked at Hemmings.

'These co-ordinates are... where, exactly?'

'An atoll in the Indian Ocean,' Hemmings said. 'Uninhabited, barely a few yards across.' He paused and licked his lips. Rachel shuddered involuntarily. 'You will be testing the satellite's precision guidance systems and its ability to link to remote regions. Three months ago we set up a radio tower on that atoll.'

'If the atoll is uninhabited, who will be there to confirm the test transmission is received?' Anne asked.

'The British navy has been kind enough to supply a boat for this very purpose. They'll make sure you've hit the target.'

'Target?' Rachel said.

'A mere turn of phrase,' Hemmings said. He stared meaningfully at the printout in Allison's hands. 'Can you do it, within the timeframe I've requested?'

'These are very particular, be we can do it,' Allison said. 'How about we call you when we're ready?'

Hemmings nodded. Not lingering, he descended the steps and left the control room.

'I trust him about as far as I could throw him,' Anne said, watching him leave.

Rachel shrugged her shoulders. 'Without Woden's money, you'd be a decade away from achieving what we've started.'

'I still don't trust him.' Anne's eyes went distant for a moment, then she clicked her fingers. 'Have we activated the cameras aboard the Diego Garcia launched satellite?'

Allison nodded. 'Last time I checked, they were operational, but not transmitting.'

'Well, we'll soon fix that. Now, where's Phillip...'

Anne buttonholed a bespectacled technician who looked vaguely frightened by her sudden appearance at his side. Shaking her head, Allison returned to the main terminal at her desk, where she began feeding the co-ordinates into the navigation circuits. Rachel stepped back, keeping a weather eye on proceedings. In the time since coming on board to straighten things out, Rachel had gradually receded into the background. She itched to be home.

Over the next thirty minutes, the control room became a hive of activity as technicians, under Allison's command, set themselves up for the test. People rushed about or stood in clumps consulting screens and checking calculations. Hemmings returned after a while and stood to one side, observing proceedings with a calculating glare. Keyboards clattered, information was fed into the terminals, and printers chattered in response. Over it all, Judith remained silent and still. Anne hovered near the Child, observing her vitals. A tone sounded.

Allison looked at Anne, who nodded. She crooked a finger at Hemmings, who swiftly ascended the stairs to the upper level.

'Do you care to say a few words?' Allison said. 'This is the moment we've been working towards for months.'

'Not really,' Hemmings said, coming to a halt beside Allison's desk. He stood with his hands clasped behind his back. With his swept back hair and black jacket, Allison thought he looked like an SS officer from a very bad World War Two movie.

'Well then,' Allison said, turning to look up at the main display. It showed a corner of the Indian Ocean, several hundred miles west of the Burmese and Bangladeshi border. A red circle enclosed a black dot. The atoll. 'Let's begin, shall we?'

Midshipman Walter Green strode across the foredeck of HMAS *Hellion*. Overhead, the Milky Way spread out in a glowing banner that twisted and turned, countless stars strewn across the velvet blackness with a child's glee. He saw a globe of light crawling across the sky. A plane? An errant satellite? He shook his head and smiled.

Even at that time of night, it was warm, the northerly maintaining the day's temperatures. The destroyer's bow carved a path through the slight swell, the water phosphorescent against the black sea. After the punishing heat of the day, Green welcomed the relative cool. There was no sunlight glinting off the ocean like glass daggers into your eyes, nor were the steel plates forming the deck and hull painfully hot. And yet, Green loved every moment of life aboard.

Right now, he was heading towards the mess for a bite to eat. The galley was open twenty-four hours a day, catering for the changing shifts. The morning crew had just taken over, and Green had decided he could do with some toast and marmalade before turning in. The mess would be almost empty, which he welcomed. In a letter written to his mother before departing Goa a few weeks ago, he had told her it was the early mornings, when *Hellion* was at its quietest, that he truly appreciated.

He glanced up at the bridge – large panels of darkly tinted glass ran around the structure, forming a rectangular patch of black from which to observe the ocean. He had been on the bridge several times, delivering messages to the officers. The atmosphere was always hushed, like the officers were at Mass. He had thrilled to stand at the beating heart of *Hellion*. Though his visits tallied to only a handful of minutes, it inspired in him a thirst for improvement. One day, he hoped to be the one receiving messages.

One day, he thought.

A sudden flash of light overhead caught his attention. He glanced up, curious. Was it a meteor? Nothing. He had seen lightning appear out of a clear blue sky, a marvel that made the other, older sailors, laugh as he recounted it. But the conditions weren't the same. He stopped in the shadow of the bridge and stared up at the stars.

At that moment, he went blind.

Five seconds later, Midshipman Walter Green was dead, a stinking, burning, bubbling smear of grease on *Hellion's* deck.

Within twenty seconds, despairing screams and vast plumes of smoke filled the air. The destroyer's superstructure came apart, like a candle in an inferno. By the time the gas-powered turbines exploded, what remained of *Hellion* as it slipped beneath the waves was hardly a ship at all.

CHAPTER EIGHT

Tuesday – Devesham Control Room. 7.30pm.

'**WELL, THAT'S** a success, if ever I saw one,' Allison said, looking proudly at the display.

Anne came over and watched the information flow across the screen. 'What's that?' she asked, pointing at a number.

'Thermal detector.' Allison pursed her lips. 'That doesn't look right.'

'It bloody well doesn't. Three thousand degrees Celsius?' Curious, Rachel joined them.

'It must be a blip,' she said, leaning in for a closer look. 'See, the detector has settled down. Twenty-four degrees. A glitch in one of the sensors.' Rachel glanced at Allison, who looked uncertain. At that moment, Hemmings turned and looked at them.

'A success, ladies?' His smile made Allison's skin crawl.

'It appears so.' She peered at a data readout. 'All indications are the satellite manoeuvred into position with a hundred percent precision, and the test transmission we sent was received on the atoll. We haven't heard from the ship yet, but all indications from our end are the satellite worked to design. Oh, and there was an issue with a temperature sensor.'

'Details, details,' Hemmings said, rubbing his hands together.

Allison wasn't sure which disquieted her the most – Hemmings in a fury, or Hemmings looking as pleased as punch.

'I'd like a report on my desk in the morning. Mr Walsingham will be very happy.' Hemmings smirked. 'We're going to do great things together. I can feel it.' With that, he left them.

'How about pleasing us and getting those phones working again,' Anne called out.

Hemmings raised a hand in acknowledgement but didn't turn around. The door closed with a note of finality.

'Is it me or does this place feel more and more like a cell, and less and less like a control centre?' Allison asked.

Anne nodded absently. She tapped the display screen. 'I'm not happy with that thermal detector,' she said. 'Can we check the programming on it?'

'I can get Carl to conduct a diagnostic check.' Allison glanced at her. 'Why?'

'Just a hunch,' Anne said. 'I also want to look at the satellite camera video feed.' She glanced at Rachel. 'We have total control over the link?'

'All three video feeds on all three satellites are routed through this centre,' Rachel confirmed. 'It was one of the first things I made sure was in place. We can't be fully in control of the satellites if we can't see what they see.'

Allison nodded. 'It will take a while for the recording to download. Our mainframe capacity is stretched as it is.' Her brow furrowed. 'You look worried.'

'I am. All of us should be.' Anne rubbed her chin. 'There's something not right here.'

Allison shrugged. 'Woden have always wanted things done their own way. This is the big bad world of public-private partnerships.'

'It's not that.'

'Well, tell us.'

'Hemmings is being even more dictatorial than normal. The phone lines go down just before the launch. I bet you if we asked, he'd bar us from entering the village itself.'

'There's not much more we can do right now,' Rachel said. 'But you're right to be suspicious. Ian doesn't say much, but he's not happy with Woden's attitude on many things.' She looked at her watch. 'That said, even though it's early, I'm just about dead on my feet. Unless you need me, I'm going to get some kip. Will you two be all right to manage this shift?'

'I think the students have learned all they can from the master,' Anne said, stifling a smile.

'I think someone has been watching far too much *Kung Fu* on television,' Rachel said, sniffing. 'My son loves it, I must say.' She smiled. 'I'll see you in a few hours.'

Allison and Anne watched Rachel leave the control room.

'Have you noticed she's moved into the background more and more?' Anne asked.

'I have. It makes sense. The place is humming along, now. We have her to thank for that.'

'I like to think we would've got there in the end.' Anne glanced at the Child, silently communing to itself. 'She seems to be coping.'

'Vital signs are all good,' Allison said. The Child never slept, though she was never fully awake, either. 'She did very well,' Allison added.

Running the communication systems through the machine/human interface had sped up the testing process ten-fold. It may've made them both queasy, but the blending of brain and computer worked.

'What is she thinking, I wonder?'

'Nothing, I hope,' Anne said. 'I think if she had even a scintilla of self-awareness, she would go mad.'

Several hours later, someone shook Rachel awake. A vague figure loomed over her, blurred and grey in the dim light.

'I said wake up.'

It was Allison.

Rachel blinked several times. 'What is it?' she asked, suddenly alert. She dimly remembered collapsing onto a camp bed in the dormitory, which now seemed eons ago.

'Something's wrong.'

'Is it the satellites?'

'Worse,' Allison said. She glanced at the door. 'Come with me. Act like everything is fine.'

'Isn't it?' Confused, her senses tingling, Rachel rose from the bed. Tugging her sweater into place, she followed Allison out of the dormitory and down to the main control room.

A black uniformed man stood by the entrance. Rachel hadn't seen him before. She saw Allison tense as they approached.

'ID,' the man barked. His narrow set eyes bored into Allison.

'I'm the Director,' she responded.

'Don't care. ID. Now.'

Allison pulled her ID card from a pocket and held it before the guard's face. He scrutinised it for what Rachel thought was far too long to be anything other than a calculated insult.

'Yours too,' he said, nodding curtly at Rachel. He gave her ID a perfunctory glance, then he pulled a walkie talkie handset from its clip and clicked the button.

'Two to enter,' he said, then glanced at Allison. 'The blonde one is a bit mouthy; keep an eye on her.'

Before Allison could react, Rachel grabbed her by the elbow and steered her through the door, which opened from the inside. Another uniformed man glared at them as they entered. The door slammed shut.

Inside the control room, there was no sign of the earlier atmosphere of triumph. Rachel could see the looks of unease from the members of the team as she and Allison walked up the steps. Anne looked up as they arrived.

'When did these guards show up?' Rachel wanted to know.

'An hour after you went to bed,' Anne said. 'I've tried raising Hemmings but he's not available. Or so that fellow,' she said, nodding to the guard beside the door, 'keeps on saying to me.' Anne tapped the keyboard, and the screen, with its lurid green text on a black background, came to life. 'There's something else, though.' She pointed to the screen. Several graphs were visible.

Rachel leaned closer, absorbing the data. She looked at Anne and Allison, her eyes wide with shock.

'This can't be right,' she said.

Anne shook her head. 'We've run the numbers a dozen times. They're accurate.'

'This is saying the communication arrays increased the temperature at sea level to 3,400 degrees centigrade for nearly a minute. That's not... That's not possible.'

'I've gone over it again and again,' Anne said. 'Plus, Carl ran a diagnostic check for me on the thermal detector systems. Everything confirms the information from the satellite over the Indian Ocean.'

'But my research, the same research used on these satellites, couldn't achieve an outcome like that. These are communications satellites. It's physically impossible for the transmissions to generate that sort of heat.' Rachel felt a sudden fear grip her. 'Do we have any satellite images of that test area?'

Anne nodded. She moved to another terminal and punched in a code, and the screen lit up. Instead of green on black, the monitor showed images in colour. A blue expanse appeared.

'I had to access archived images during the day. These are the same co-ordinates.' Anne pressed a button, and the image leapt forward. Again, and again, and then again.

'All I can see is water.' Rachel looked at Anne and Allison. 'Where's the atoll? Why would Hemming want us to target water?'

'That's the thing,' Anne said, leaning over the keyboard. 'I've accessed the thermal imaging video feed from the satellite. This is what it recorded.' She tapped several keys, and the day-old image disappeared, replaced by an image clearly taken at night, overlaid with the distinctive halo of infra-red.

Rachel watched a shape appear at the edge of the screen and slowly crawl across the water.

'Is that some sort of craft?'

Anne nodded as she chewed on a thumbnail.

They watched the ship edge towards the logged co-ordinates of the test and, with each fractional movement, Rachel felt her stomach tighten. It entered the test zone, and the co-ordinates turned red to signal target locked, then the screen went white. When it returned to normal, the distinctive sharp edges of the ship had been replaced with a glowing blob that soon disappeared.

'What's that?' Rachel said, tracing a finger across a smudge that drifted away from what remained of the ship.

'Smoke,' Anne replied.

Rachel shook her head. 'What about the test? We received confirmation the signal from the satellite was received.'

'I haven't been able to work out how they've done it, but I sourced the response signal from Malaysia.'

'It was a fake?'

'Yes,' Anne said, her voice dropping. She glanced at Allison, who nodded. 'And there's something else.'

'Something... what?'

'It's Gupta,' Anne said, nodding to an Anglo-Indian technician sitting blank faced at a nearby terminal.

'What about him?'

'Shortly after the guards arrived, he tried to leave the facility. To go into Devesham. Said he wanted to get out, that he was tired of being cooped up in here.'

'Tired?'

Anne nodded. 'The guards turned him around. Said that no one could leave Devesham Control without Hemmings' say so.'

'That's... insane.'

Rachel reached across and lifted the receiver. Punching in an external number, she held the receiver to her ear, waited a moment, then dropped it back in its cradle.

'Phone lines are still down,' she said. 'We're trapped here, aren't we?'

Anne nodded. The women looked at each other, then at the screen. The smoke had disappeared.

'What the hell is going on?' Rachel said.

CHAPTER NINE

Wednesday - Cambridge. 8.30am.

THE MORNING after the launch, Gilmore was getting ready when the telephone rang. After hearing the radio reports announcing the successful launches, he had tried telephoning Rachel, but there seemed to be a problem with the line. He hoped that Rachel might call before he left the house. He walked from the bedroom to his study and answered the telephone.

'Hello, Rach—'

A familiar voice, not his wife's, interrupted. He listened intently, a look of anger slowly spreading across his face.

'Now you listen to me,' he said, when the voice stopped. 'We agreed that I would help when I could. Now you're expecting me to drop everything before I fly out and come and meet you? I understand... No, you don't understand. I'm hanging on by the skin of my teeth—'

The voice interrupted Gilmore.

'What? You've sent someone? This is intolerable. I said when I agreed—'

A sudden sharp rapping came from the front door. Gilmore closed his eyes. His hand tightened on the receiver. The plastic groaned.

'We're going to have to discuss our arrangement. Otherwise, you can consider me out.'

There was a click, and the call disconnected, leaving Gilmore to listen to buzzing static. Carefully, belying his rising anger, he settled the receiver in its cradle.

Ignoring the insistent rapping on the door, Gilmore took his time collecting the suitcase from his bedroom before making his way to the front door.

Opening it, Gilmore was confronted by a tall, lean figure in a dark suit and tie. His black hair was swept back from a high forehead. Parked in front of the gate was a dark grey car.

'Air Vice-Marshal Gilmore?'

'Mr Gilmore is fine. You're Stanhope? You're my MoD driver?'

'I am,' Stanhope said, smiling cheerily.

'We've had some problem with strangers, recently. I know who you say you are. But I'd like to see some identification, please.'

'Oh, forgive me,' Stanhope said, flashing another smile. He pulled a small wallet from his breast pocket and flipped it open. Stanhope smirked as Gilmore inspected it. 'What do you think?'

'Looks legitimate enough. You're lucky. The mood I'm in, any hint of chicanery and I might've had to shoot you in my front yard.'

Stanhope's smile grew strained.

'We're on the clock, Mr Gilmore,' he said. 'Our mutual friend is impatient, given the night's events.'

'What's happened overnight?'

'Above my pay grade, I'm afraid. Really, I'm just an errand boy.' Stanhope gave him another smile. 'Best you hear it from the horse's mouth.'

Biting down on a retort, Gilmore nodded. 'Have it your own way then.'

The drive down the A10 to London proved uneventful. The flat agricultural land around Cambridge gave way to the fens, which then grew into undulating hills as they drove further south. There was a brief snarl as they made their way into and through Royston. The traffic quickly dispersed and Stanhope picked up speed.

After an hour, the car slipped into London. Traffic was, for the time of day, surprisingly light. The drive had, for the most part, been done in silence, which only added to Gilmore's irritation.

'Any idea why the minister wants to see me?'

'It is important, Mr Gilmore, but aside from that, I've not been made aware of the particulars. As I said—'

'Yes, you're an errand boy. Point taken.'

Frustrated, Gilmore glanced at a copy of *The Times* sitting with him in the back seat. Above the fold, there was talk of another summit with the Chinese. Below the fold, an article about protests at the anticipated influx of immigrants from Hong Kong prominently featured Harry Whateley's name. Frowning, Gilmore set the paper down.

Stanhope turned into the Victoria Embankment. The Thames appeared on Gilmore's left. He looked across the sluggish water at the people walking along. His thoughts drifted to the trade fair in West Berlin, and his irritation deepened.

'I assume you work for the minister?'

Stanhope glanced into the rear view mirror. He gave a noncommittal shrug. Gilmore was beginning to think the man wasn't just a driver. The traffic became stop-start for a few minutes. Gilmore checked his watch more than once and drummed his fingers on the seat in agitation. He took a deep breath to calm himself. It worked, for a little while.

The pips sounded on the radio, and Gilmore shifted his attention from the view outside the car.

'Rioting overnight in the Notting Hill area is now under control, according to District Superintendent Burke. A protest over race relations late yesterday afternoon grew violent when men wearing balaclavas approached those marching. An altercation quickly became a brawl, sending onlookers running for cover. Superintendent Burke said the riot squad moved in shortly after 7pm, quickly dispersing all sides. Property damage is estimated to run into thousands of pounds.'

'Problems inside and outside the country,' Stanhope said. 'I understand your wife is something of an anti-war advocate. A world away from the halls of academia?'

Gilmore narrowed his eyes. Stanhope was definitely more than just a driver. Rachel's political leanings had drifted further and further to the left in the waning years of the '60s, before she embraced the anti-war movement in the wake of the American debacle in Vietnam. He imagined that had attracted the attention of the security services, though not enough to veto her work at Devesham.

'She has firm convictions in that area,' Gilmore said, stiffly.

'Seeing as how she fought in the war, it's a strange change of mind, don't you think?'

'War changes everyone who participates in it. You'd know if you served,' Gilmore said. 'Did you?'

He saw Stanhope's eyes narrow in the rear view mirror. 'Too young,' he said, shortly.

'Ah. I see. Well, count yourself lucky, then.'

Images of burning bombers falling from the skies over Berlin painted themselves inside his skull for a moment. The two men fell silent, and the radio news concluded noting the Prime Minister was expected to shortly visit the Palace.

Through the trees, Gilmore glimpsed the vast white bulk of the MoD Main Building that hove into view like a wallowing ship at sea. A sudden rush of memories flooded him as Stanhope drove into Horse Guards Avenue.

Gilmore hadn't been back to the building in the year and half a since he had been forced out of the RAF.

Stanhope turned off Horse Guards Avenue and came to a stop before a white barrier. A uniformed figure stepped from the guardhouse, with a clipboard in one hand. He wore a service revolver strapped to his hip. Another guard stayed inside, watching a bank of flickering monitors.

Stanhope's window slid down and he handed a card to the guard.

'There's no need to worry about the chap in the back,' Stanhope said.

The guard looked hard at Stanhope, then again at the identity card. 'What chap in the back, sir?' the guard deadpanned.

'There's a good fellow.' Stanhope took back his card.

The guard turned and waved to his companion inside the guardhouse.

The white barrier lifted, and Stanhope drove through the entrance. There was a brief shadow as they passed between two narrow buildings, before they emerged into the light and a large courtyard. A sign pointed to the right, and Stanhope followed it. They drove onto a ramp, which spiralled down into the underground carpark. Within a minute or two, Stanhope had parked. Both men alighted from the car.

'Almost there,' Stanhope said.

He led Gilmore towards a set of lift doors. Pressing a button, Stanhope stepped back beside Gilmore.

'I'm afraid we're meeting the minister in the cellar. For your privacy, I should imagine. Anyway, I'm sure you've seen the inside of the minister's office before. This will be much more interesting. Henry the Eighth stored his wine down here, did you know?'

The ride in the lift was thankfully short. Stanhope's smug demeanour irritated Gilmore so much he breathed a sigh of relief when they stepped out. Lights had been strung up along one whitewashed wall. The floor was rough concrete and sloped away from them. Somewhere, water dripped.

'Exactly how paranoid is Bambera?' Gilmore asked, looking around.

'Very,' Stanhope said. 'Come along.'

He walked off, forcing Gilmore to hurry after him. They followed the ramp down, before it cut to the left. With each step, Gilmore felt the weight of the earth and the building overhead settle on him.

After a few minutes, they emerged in a long gallery. The walls were of cut stone, with oaken beams interspersed throughout. At the far end, in shadows, stood a figure. As Stanhope and Gilmore approached, the figure stepped out of the darkness.

He had the physique of a wrestler. Wide at the shoulders and narrow at the hips, despite the grey peppering his short-cropped hair, the minister looked capable of tearing telephone books in half.

'Mr Gilmore.' Kofi Bambera's voice was like the low rumble of an approaching train.

'Minister,' Gilmore said. His nostrils flared. 'I really must protest about the cavalier way I've been treated—'

Bambera raised his hand and Gilmore faltered to a stop. 'If there was another way, I would certainly have found it by now. Instead...' Bambera gestured to their surroundings.

'Instead, you summon me into this warren of corridors. Isn't it enough I've provided you useful intelligence on Woden? What else could you want of me?'

Bambera stared at Gilmore for a long moment. He regretted his peevishness. Bambera clearly didn't tolerate fools, as Gilmore never had. Bambera's response, when it came, surprised him.

'What can you tell me about Project Cerberus?'

'Project Cerberus? Only what I read in the papers. And what little my wife has told me about her work at Devesham. I heard on the radio the launches overnight were a success.'

Bambera nodded. 'Shortly afterwards, however, we received confirmation that we had lost control of all three, including the one in position over the Indian Ocean.'

'You... what? You lost control? How is that possible?'

'That's what we're asking ourselves.' Bambera's brown eyes narrowed. 'There's another thing.'

'What?'

'An hour later, shortly after midnight GMT, contact with HMAS *Hellion* was lost.'

'Where—?'

'The Indian Ocean.' Bambera's voice had taken on a staccato cadence, as if lingering over the words caused too much pain. 'Two hundred and forty-three men lost. Not to mention a twenty-two-million-pound state of the art vessel.'

'The burden of command,' Gilmore said, not unkindly. He didn't like Bambera, but as someone who too had lost men under his watch, he knew the agony Bambera clearly felt. 'When you approached me to spy on Woden, I was more than willing to help. Woden has lost its way. So why am I here today?'

'You're here, Mr Gilmore, because the satellites the government and Woden have been working on aren't communications satellites.'

A prickling sensation stole up Gilmore's spine. 'I'm getting the sense that the loss of the satellites and your ship are linked.'

'Very much so,' Bambera said. 'Tell me, what does your wife work on up in Cambridge?'

'My wife... What does my wife have to do with this?' Mention of Rachel only reminded him of his deceit.

'Just answer the question.'

'Just answer... Am I compelled to be here, Minister? I've attended out of consideration of my patriotic duty.' Gilmore paused, gathering his temper. 'Is my wife suspected of doing something illegal?'

Bambera looked at Gilmore for a long moment, then sighed and shook his head.

'We are in the midst of a crisis—'

'The satellites.'

'Yes, the satellites,' Bambera said, nostrils flaring at the interruption. 'Two hundred million pounds of research and investment, not to mention the prestige...'

'The domestic communication satellites the government has spent six months trumpeting to the world,' Gilmore said. 'The ones you just told me weren't communications satellites.'

Bambera's smile in return was not friendly. 'No, they are not communication satellites.'

'Then what are they?'

Bambera looked at Gilmore through hooded eyes. 'Bear with me a little while longer, Mr Gilmore. Since the Auderly House Accords, the rapprochement between Britain and China has allowed us to concentrate on our true enemies.'

'The Soviets?' Despite his confusion, Gilmore's curiosity grew.

'It was ever thus, from even before the Bolsheviks toppled the Tsar.' Bambera rubbed his jaw. 'This entire conversation is covered by a D-notice I issued early this morning when reports of the loss of control over the satellites came through.'

'I'd be stunned if it wasn't.'

'You've proven your worth with information about Woden. I've looked at your record, Gilmore. I have no idea what the Shoreditch Incident was, but since neither has anyone else in the Ministry, it's indicative that you can keep quiet about important matters.'

Gilmore simply stared at Bambera, who smiled ruefully.

'And of course, you know who Harry Whateley is.'

'I've met him. Very likely a bounder and a cad. My wife says her students call him Harry Hately, and given his views, I'm not surprised.'

'If only he were a bounder and a cad,' Bambera said. He glanced at Stanhope, who had been conspicuously silent during the whole exchange.

Gilmore frowned. 'With all respect, Minister, what has any of this to do with your missing satellites and *Hellion*?'

'Everything. Whateley is coming at issues of defence and immigration from the right, hoping to outflank the Opposition and suck up their votes. Our internal polling indicates his Freedom Party will win twenty seats at the next election. At the very least, he'll have a bloc of votes to throw behind anyone who will offer him the Prime Ministership.'

'Whateley? Prime Minister? That's... insane.'

'No, that's politics. What's insane is what happens afterwards. Whateley cloaks himself in slogans about patriotism, but scratch the surface and he's an out-and-out racist. He's funded by some shadowy corporate interests we can't touch. He won't stop at closing the border to the Hong Kongers. There will be camps set up the length and breadth of this country, and the first to be marched in will be my people.'

Gilmore looked at Bambera carefully, considering his dark skin and the awful history that told.

'Did you know I have a daughter, Mr Gilmore?'

'I did not.'

'Winifred. And when I think of what kind of world Whateley would make for her generation...'

Gilmore could understand that. Dillon would never have the experiences Bambera's daughter would, but nonetheless Gilmore still sometimes found himself worried about the world Dillon would be handed.

'But the country is prosperous,' Gilmore said, trying to latch onto the positives. 'Unemployment is low, inflation is under control. Why would anyone vote for him?'

'Britain is changing, for the better, if anyone was bothered to ask me.' Bambera squinted. 'They've got more to lose. They've spent so much time on top, they don't want to share the bounty.'

'*They*, Minister?'

Bambera smiled. 'Let me tell you a story my father told me. He was assigned with another private to clean the latrines. This other private, Anderson, complained to the sergeant. "Anderson, you may be both cleaning the dunnies," the sergeant said, and turned around and pointed to my father, "but at least you aren't him." It's people like Anderson who are seduced by Whateley's ideas. They may be white and cleaning latrines, but at least they aren't like my father, or me.'

Gilmore chewed his lip. 'I'd have never encouraged it with my men, but I trust your father belted both?'

Bambera's smile was genuine. 'Thirty days in the brig, but every one of them worth it, he said.'

Gilmore nodded. 'All right then. I've taken the bait. How are the missing satellites and Whateley connected?'

'With the Chinese content to digest Hong Kong, while we embrace their best and brightest, the Soviets have been testing our capabilities. An assassination in an ally's capital here, a coup there. I'm sure you've seen the reports about the incursions into our airspace via the North Sea. The Soviets don't like the idea of Britain having an... Ally is too strong a word. Friend, perhaps? Yes, a friend of China's size. The Soviets hate looking over their shoulder at their southern border. So, they're striking out elsewhere to distract us. The satellites... They're our insurance policy against Soviet aggression if they feel they are being squeezed too tightly.'

'They're weapons platforms, I take it?'

'Exactly. Solar powered laser arrays capable of targeted destruction on the scale of a nuclear warhead, but reusable and without fallout. Couple that with effectively infinite range and being almost impossible to knock out of the sky and Britain has... *had*... a strategic edge. Cabinet signed off on the project immediately after the Accords were agreed. We knew that someone like Whateley would curry favour with the electorate by saying we'd gone soft. So, it was decided the satellites would serve two purposes – hold the Soviets at bay and kerb someone like Whateley's attempts to cut into our vote.'

'But that would only work against the Soviets if the world knew about them.'

'We were planning on making an announcement and sweetening it with a cut to our nuclear weapons stockpile.'

'You don't think Woden has anything to do with the loss of control of the satellites?'

Bambera nodded. 'It's a possibility. They claim they're doing everything they can to re-establish contact with the satellites.' He paused. 'Have you tried calling your wife at the Devesham facility?'

Gilmore nodded. 'Couldn't get through. Problem with the telephone lines?'

'Maybe that's true. Regardless, I've decided to play along, to give them enough rope to hang themselves.'

Gilmore looked dubious.

'It's not perfect, I admit. But the facts are the facts. Woden's behaviour recently has been... suspect at best. Their desire to sell beyond the Iron Curtain is a red flag. That doesn't happen without the Soviet's agreeing to it. That's why I asked you to spy on them.'

Gilmore noticed Stanhope's eyes widen, before they subsided. Bambera noticed, and chuckled.

'Need to know, Mr Stanhope. Up until now, you didn't.'

'I see,' Gilmore said. 'So, it's expose Woden, and we bring it and Whateley down at the same time. You may not call it politics, but it stinks of it all the same. Not only that, but you're playing with fire. If Woden is working with the Soviets, don't you risk more lives?'

'It's a risk I'm willing to take.'

Shaking his head, Gilmore could only laugh. 'All right then. Isn't the government concerned the Soviets will develop satellites with similar capabilities? Aren't you simply creating a new balance of terror? Nuclear weapons. Satellites armed with lasers. It's all the same, surely?'

'Our analysts believed the Soviets were at least a decade behind us in terms of the technology. We believed we had time on our side.'

'Were?' Gilmore grew uneasy.

Bambera nodded. 'We've recently received intelligence that the technology has been passed to the Soviets. Technology your wife developed.'

There was a moment of stunned silence as Gilmore attempted to absorb this new piece of information.

'Rachel would never... My wife would never sell out Britain. Are you accusing her of being a spy?'

'Your wife's antecedents have worried us for some time,' Stanhope said, speaking for the first time. 'Her father was a member of the Polish Communist Party, wasn't he?'

'Who exactly are you, Mr Stanhope?' Gilmore said, seeking a target for his rising anger. He glanced at Bambera. 'Not someone from Defence, that's for sure. He reeks of MI6.'

'Sticks and stones, Mr Gilmore,' Stanhope said. 'We have... copious notes about your father-in-law's activities, here, in Britain.'

'And what, just because her father was a Communist, somehow, she's one... in secret? I've been married to her for almost a decade, man. She's no more a Communist than I am.'

Raising a hand to cut off Stanhope's response, Bambera

stepped in.

'Please calm down, Mr Gilmore. Your wife has done admirable work for many years. But we are in a war, a cold war, with the Soviets. Nothing, absolutely nothing, can be ruled out. See it from my position. Our mortal enemies have somehow gained possession of technology your wife developed. Given her parents fled Eastern Europe, it would be negligent if we didn't suspect her.'

'Suspect her? Holy God, man. Her father may've been a Communist, but they came here, not Moscow. She fought for her country, *this country*.' Gilmore shook his head, furious. 'This is utterly outrageous. What proof do you have?'

Bambera nodded to Stanhope

'You'll need to show him the photograph. He's loyal to his wife.'

'I wouldn't expect anything different.' Stanhope pulled a scuffed folder from his inner jacket pocket and held it out to Gilmore. 'Go on. It won't bite.'

Gilmore looked venomously at Stanhope, before accepting the folder. Opening it, he saw a grainy, black and white photograph of a circuit board.

'I have no earthly idea what this is, or what it has to do with my wife.'

'That, Mr Gilmore,' said Stanhope, 'is the forerunner to a piece of circuitry which sits at the centre of the machine intelligence aboard all three Cerberus satellites. It was developed by a team of scientists at Cambridge. A team your wife led.'

'Where did you get this image?'

'MI6 has assets in East Berlin who funnel information to us on a regular basis. Three days ago, our team in West Berlin was contacted by one of our assets on the other side of the Wall who said he was sheltering a Russian defector. The defector claims to be a technician on their own rocket programme, and that he wants asylum.'

Gilmore glanced again at the photograph.

'We needed proof that our Soviet friend was on the level, as our American cousins say,' Stanhope said. 'So, we asked him to provide evidence to demonstrate we weren't allowing a double agent into our midst. The intelligence community in Moscow is made up of men whose bread and butter are building scheme after scheme after scheme. He provided this as a demonstration of his bona fides.'

'There's no way on God's green earth she would sell her work to the Soviets. If any of what you say is true, why was she allowed to work at Devesham?'

Bambera exchanged a look with Stanhope.

'Right,' Gilmore said. 'You wanted to see if she would hoist herself on her own petard. How's that going, by the way?'

'Your wife is annoyingly loyal, Mr Gilmore,' Bambera said, with a ghost of a smile on his lips.

Gilmore could've laughed at the absurdity of it all. 'I can't believe it's my wife. The idea is simply absurd.'

Again, Stanhope and Bambera exchanged a glance. Stanhope cleared his throat.

'We have other options. If it wasn't your wife, Mr Gilmore, then we believe the firm you work for, Woden Armaments, sold it to the Soviets. Those are the only two possibilities.'

Thunderstruck, Gilmore could only switch his gaze between Bambera and Stanhope. He felt as if he was trapped in a nightmare.

'So, this is the real reason you recruited me? To test my loyalty, just in case something big came over the horizon?'

'It doesn't get any bigger than this, Mr Gilmore,' Bambera said. 'The Soviets are clearly on a dual track – stealing our technology to catch up with us, or failing that, they're trying to hijack our satellites at the same time. Possibly in connivance with Woden.'

'This is... This is insanity. First you accuse my wife of espionage, now you point the finger at me?'

'You're either the largest victim of circumstance I've ever seen, or the most highly placed Soviet mole in the British establishment since the 1930s,' Stanhope said.

Gilmore felt as if the ground had vanished from beneath his feet. Everything he had ever worked for, his country, his family...

'None of this will stand up in court,' he said, aware he was blustering.

'In here, Mr Gilmore, the rule of law doesn't apply.' Bambera's eyes narrowed. 'You must understand our position. We have evidence the Soviets have access to top secret British technology. Technology developed by your wife, and technology adapted by Woden Armaments, your employer, for satellites armed with laser arrays.'

'So, that's it then, is it? You called me here just so you could lay all this evidence in front of me, before bundling me off to Wormwood Scrubs?'

'You're not wrong about him being stiff-necked,' Bambera said, glancing at Stanhope.

'You can relax, Mr Gilmore,' Bambera said, after a moment. 'This is not going anywhere near the courts. We've bigger fish to fry.' He nodded to Stanhope, who retrieved the folder from Gilmore and slipped it back into his jacket pocket.

'We don't believe you've engaged in espionage,' Stanhope said.

'Only for the British Government,' Gilmore shot back.

'We don't believe you've engaged in espionage,' Stanhope repeated. 'But your wife...'

'I've told you; Rachel isn't capable of that sort of thing.'

'All the more incentive for you to prove it, then.'

Gilmore didn't like the way the conversation was going. 'Prove it? I've been feeding you direct information about Woden's activities in the marketplace. Contracts, future development plans, minutes of meetings with buyers. What else do you want from me?'

'More, Mr Gilmore,' Bambera said. 'Your years of exemplary service in the RAF, including the incident in 1963 and beyond that you refuse to talk about, plus your recent help, demonstrate your loyalty. You are, however, tainted by association with Woden.'

'Yes,' Gilmore said, bitterly. 'I note that I'm the one in the frame here, and not Walsingham.'

'The CEO of Woden will be dealt with when the time is right,' Stanhope said. 'You remain useful, Mr Gilmore. Your attendance at this conference in West Berlin is fortuitous.'

'How?'

'Our Soviet defector is holed up in a safe house in East Berlin,' Stanhope said. 'We've assembled an extraction team, which will form part of the BRIXMIS team conducting their usual inspections on the East Berlin side.'

'I see,' Gilmore said. 'And what role do you require me to play in this nightmare?'

'Simple,' Stanhope said. 'You're going to help our Soviet friend defect.'

Looking between Bambera and Stanhope, Gilmore could only laugh. 'This is madness. I'm not even in the RAF anymore. The East Germans are thugs, but even thugs are smart enough to work out from the paperwork that I'd be nothing more than a civilian prancing around in military uniform.'

'Civilian?' Bambera said. 'Who said you were a civilian?' Producing an envelope from an inner pocket of his jacket, he handed it to Gilmore.

Eyes narrowed, Gilmore opened the envelope and removed a single, folded sheet of typewritten paper. He recognised the seal at the bottom of the page, and he felt his pulse quicken.

'Under the Defence of the Realm Act, 1914,' Bambera said, with a sly smile on his face, 'I'm empowered, in certain emergency circumstances, to recall any officer grade member of the military who has left the service. This is, you will agree, an emergency. I don't need a spy anymore. Unfortunately, an air vice-marshal would draw a little too much attention, plus field duty is below such a paygrade. So, for the duration of this mission I think a temporary reduction in rank will be necessary.'

CHAPTER TEN

Wednesday – Heathrow Airport. 12pm.

'**WILL YA** look at this.'

Gilmore's cab driver swore to himself in a thick Irish accent as cars and trucks jockeyed for position after emerging from the tunnel. Cigarette hanging from his mouth, the driver waved furiously at the other drivers as he somehow managed to steer with his knees and change gears with his free hand.

Amid a chorus of blaring horns, the cab pulled up at the kerb. Gilmore leaned forward and paid. Grabbing his suitcase, he stepped onto the footpath and watched the cab shoot off into the stream of traffic.

Shouting from the entrance attracted his attention. About twenty people, watched warily by almost as many constables, were noisily protesting. A couple of television cameramen jostled for position as they recorded images for the nightly news, while a pair of reporters prepared notes for their stand up to camera.

'Racism damns us all,' a young woman in a paisley top and stained jeans shouted. For a moment, Gilmore's eyes locked with hers, then she snarled at him. 'Capitalism is racism, down with Whateley.'

Quite how that formulation worked was beyond Gilmore, who forced his way through the press to the doors beyond. Free of the raucous crowd at last, he shook his head, then entered Terminal 1.

Inside, there were more crowds, better behaved, and in Gilmore's view, better dressed. With the chatter of a dozen languages filling the air, Gilmore found the check-in desk. Handing over his suitcase, he looked up at the clock on the wall opposite. There was nearly an hour until departure. Frowning, he looked around. Coming towards him at the head of a group of Woden executives was Harry Whateley. His minder drifted along behind them. The looks on the faces of the men around him reminded Gilmore of dogs eager to please their master, yet fearful of being kicked.

'As I live and breathe,' Whateley declared as the group came to a halt in front of Gilmore. 'If it isn't our pet air vice-marshal, retired. How are you, Ian?'

'Fine,' Gilmore said. 'How was the launch party?'

'I don't think the shareholders would appreciate how much of their money we spent celebrating, but it was all worth it, I say.' Some of the men closest to him chuckled. Ostensibly, this was the team Gilmore was meant to lead in West Berlin, but Whateley had clearly co-opted them.

'You've managed to miss your welcoming committee outside,' Gilmore said, indicating the protestors at the main doors.

Whateley's face darkened.

'Slander and worse,' he said, almost spitting out the words. 'Never worked a day in their lives, and who knows what filth they're injecting into themselves. They dog me wherever I go, and it's sure to get worse when the PM grows a spine and calls the election.' The crowd in the terminal swirled around them. Some recognised Whateley and pointed. He perked up a little at the attention. 'Still, it'll all be worth it to see their faces when the Freedom Party wins a clutch of seats. There will be a reckoning after that.'

'I'm sure,' Gilmore said noncommittally.

'Well,' Whateley said, looking at the group clustered around him. 'We're heading to a bar until they call us to the flight. Will you join us? After all, you're the leader of this pack.'

'I'll catch you up,' Gilmore said, fumbling for an excuse. 'I... ah, need to get some items from duty free.'

'Refresh the liquor cabinet at home. I understand perfectly.' Whateley already looked bored. 'Well, when you're ready, you'll find us easily enough.' Without waiting for a reply, Whateley left, his entourage in hot pursuit.

'I need a bloody stiff drink after that,' Gilmore muttered, ignoring the look from a woman walking past him. He headed in the opposite direction, making for another bar further down the concourse.

He took a seat at an empty table next to a set of floor-to-ceiling windows overlooking the northern runway. A waiter came over.

'Whisky, neat.'

The waiter nodded and walked to the bar. Gilmore turned to admire the aeroplanes lined up at the terminal, waiting to be filled. A figure loomed next to him. Gilmore turned, surprised that the waiter had returned so quickly.

'You're not the waiter,' he blurted out.

'I should bloody well hope not,' said a young, black woman. She slipped into the seat opposite him. She wore jeans and a dark leather jacket with exaggerated lapels over a loose linen shirt. Her dangling gold earrings winked in the light.

'Are you lost, perhaps?'

'Certainly, not.' There was a faint Jamaican lilt to her voice.

'Then who are you?'

'Hannah Gordon,' she said, extending her hand.

Somewhat nonplussed, Gilmore shook it. 'I must say you look very different on TV,' he said, suspecting that this Hannah was probably tired of being compared to the famous blonde actress. He narrowed his eyes. 'Did Stanhope send you?'

'Bingo,' Hannah said, smiling brightly.

'You're with MI6?'

'Don't shout it from the rooftops, Mr Gilmore.'

Gilmore was struck by how young she looked. 'Where is Stanhope?'

'He'll be on another flight. A paperwork problem. We'll meet him at London Block.'

'London... Oh, you mean the UK military HQ in West Berlin?'

'That's the one,' Hannah said.

'So, you're my nursemaid while I'm in West Berlin?'

The waiter appeared with Gilmore's drink. He set it down, and Hannah reached across the table and took it.

'Thanks,' she said, tilting the glass towards Gilmore before drinking the contents in one swallow.

Gilmore and the waiter exchanged a glance. 'Better get

another one, this time for me.'

The waiter returned to the bar.

'Whisky, neat.' Hannah's eyes watered, but they twinkled in amusement. 'And not cheap either. Nursemaid is slightly patronising, Mr Gilmore. Though Mr Stanhope is the patronising kind, I must admit. I'm your... minder. That's it. A minder.' Hannah sat back, looking very pleased with herself.

'Look,' Gilmore said, leaning forward. 'I've been left with little choice about this mission. I certainly don't appreciate having someone assigned to me for the duration of my stay in West Berlin.'

'I dare say we both don't have much choice in the matter.' Hannah looked around. 'Aren't you travelling with a team from your company?'

'They're at a different bar,' Gilmore said, a little sourly. 'Our new director, Whateley, has absconded with them.'

'Harry Whateley?' Hannah's mouth twisted in disgust.

'Yes.'

'I'm glad I'm not minding him. The man's a pig. Still, this gives us the chance to get to know each other. We're going to be spending a bit of time together over the next couple of days.'

At that moment, the waiter arrived and handed Gilmore his drink. Settling back with glass in hand, Gilmore watched Hannah over the rim as he took a swallow. Despite her freewheeling attitude, Gilmore found himself warming to her.

'How long have you been in MI6, Hannah? Or should I call you Miss Gordon?'

'Hannah's fine, Mr Gilmore. And its Ms Gordon. It's the '70s, after all.'

'Quite,' Gilmore said, repressing a smile. 'How long?'

'Six months.'

'A lot of responsibility for one so young.'

'The world is a dangerous place, no matter how old you are.'

Gilmore toasted her answer. 'True. I wasn't much older than you when I enlisted.'

'And here you are,' Hannah said. 'A born survivor.'

Gilmore didn't reply. His thoughts wandered backwards in time. Ignoring Hannah's curious look, he glanced out the window at the row of aeroplanes lining the terminal. 'Been to West Berlin before?'

'First time. I hear the sauerkraut is delightful.'

'You like sauerkraut?'

'I like the idea of sauerkraut, possibly more than what it tastes like.' Hannah grinned.

'Why do I need minding?'

Hannah's eyes narrowed. 'Because Berlin is a playground for the intelligence services of Europe. If it isn't the CIA running operations without telling its supposed allies, it'll be the Stasi crawling over the place like lice. And we know for a certainty the GRU has elements there as well.'

'Hand in glove.'

'The iron hand in the iron glove,' Hannah said.

'Am I in danger? Is that why you've been assigned to me?'

'We're all in danger.' Hannah leaned forward. 'The Soviet defector is the Stasi's and GRU's top priority, according to our intercepts. The Stasi want to capture him so they can be petted on the head like good little dogs by the GRU.'

'And the GRU?'

They want him dead as much as we want him alive.'

'How are we getting him out?'

Hannah shook her head. 'Not here. You'll be briefed tonight.'

'You do know what the BRIXMIS protocols are?'

'I do.'

'So, you understand how risky this is?'

'I do understand, Mr Gilmore. Do you?'

'More than you could know.'

The tannoy system hummed and an impersonal female voice spoke.

'Flight WB1944 to West Berlin now boarding. Please proceed to Gate 16. Repeating, Flight WB1944 to West Berlin is now boarding.'

'That's us.' Gilmore finished off his drink, and waved to the waiter, who came over. Gilmore handed over a note and waved away the offer to get his change.

'All right then, Ms Gordon. Let's see if we can take West Berlin by storm.'

By what Gilmore assumed wasn't chance, he and Hannah had adjoining seats. After a two-hour flight, their aeroplane began its descent. Gilmore, who had the window seat, glanced through the glass at Tempelhof Airport.

'That used to be the biggest building in Europe.'

'What happened to it?' Hannah asked.

'The Second World War,' Gilmore said, drily.

The warning light to fasten their seat belts and extinguish all cigarettes lit up. Engines revving, the aeroplane completed its turn and began descending towards the runway. Gilmore glanced at Hannah and saw how wide her eyes had become.

'Don't worry,' he said, smiling. 'This is the easy bit.'

'What's the hard bit?' Hannah said, swallowing.

'Mostly, it's staying up in the air.'

The cavernous interior of the main terminal echoed with the clangour of thousands of people arriving and departing. After exiting the air bridge, Hannah and Gilmore made their way to the carousel, around which clustered dozens of travellers waiting for their luggage to be disgorged from within the airport's innards.

'I'll see you tonight,' Hannah said, as she plucked a small suitcase from the carousel.

'What will you be doing in the interim?' Gilmore said, curious.

'There's going to be a protest outside the trade fair,' Hannah said, scanning the crowd. 'I think I see some of your people.' She nodded to the other side.

Gilmore looked, and recognised his colleagues, with Whateley the ever-present centre of attention.

'Are you going to be monitoring the protest?' Gilmore asked.

'Monitor?' Hannah shook her head. When she spoke, her accent abruptly changed to an authentically Jamaican one. 'The Jamaican Brothers and Sisters Leftist Brigade protests against all forms of capitalism, including the military industrial complex that makes slaves of us all,' she said, her drawl evoking a wry chuckle from Gilmore. She leaned in. 'It's also perfect for observing who attends the trade fair.' She looked over at Gilmore's colleagues. 'Have fun with the lads. Don't do anything you'd be embarrassed to tell Mrs Gilmore.' She took a step, then turned around. 'Stanhope has arranged for a little surprise in your room.'

With a wink and a smile, Hannah walked off, vanishing into the crowds. Shaking his head, Gilmore spotted his suitcase. He pressed forward and took it off the carousel. Someone placed a hand on his shoulder, and he turned around.

'My dear fellow,' Whateley said, his eyes struggling to focus and his breath rank with alcohol. 'Were you speaking with that delightful young black woman? They'll be the end of you, did you know that. Special powers. What would your wife say?'

Gilmore decided the minute he arrived back in London, he would hand in his resignation. To think he had to answer to someone like this.

'Say? It's not what she'd say that should have you worried, Whateley. It's what she'd do that should give you nightmares, let me tell you.'

CHAPTER ELEVEN

Wednesday – West Berlin, Approaching British Section. 3.50pm.

'**HEY, BOSS.** Have you been to Berlin before?'

One of Gilmore's Woden colleagues, Freddy Thompkins, sat up in his seat. Gilmore had disliked Thompkins from the moment he laid eyes on him – a wide boy, to use the current parlance, whose boastful commentary at last year's Christmas party about his exploits with women had earned him a place in Gilmore's black book. That, and his juvenile refusal to call Gilmore by his name.

The shuttle bus had left the airport behind ten minutes before, and now trundled along a busy road, heading towards the hotel that also served as the trade fair's venue. The other members of the team, a good dozen, eagerly looked through the windows at the passing buildings. Whateley, who had put away enough alcohol back at Heathrow and during the flight to refloat *Titanic*, snored quietly in his seat. His minder sat in the chair opposite him.

'Only the once,' Gilmore said.

There was something about the snide tone in Thompkins' voice that riled him.

'What was it like back then? The *fräuleins* must've been frisky, eh?'

'I couldn't tell,' Gilmore said. 'I was thirty thousand feet in the air dropping incendiary bombs on their heads.'

Thompkins' smirk turned greasy, and the good humour in the bus dissipated. Gilmore sensed the eyes of the driver on him in the rear-view mirror. Annoyed with himself, he looked out the window until they reached their destination.

Outside, Gilmore was glad of the fresh air. He grabbed his suitcase from the driver, who handed it to him with a glare, then joined the rest of the group as they walked towards the hotel's entrance. To his relief, Thompkins kept his distance. Standing to one side, a noisy and cheerful group of protesters waved flags and banners, and chanted words Gilmore couldn't make out. A couple of bored looking policemen kept an eye on the group.

'Bloody lefty idiots,' Whateley said as they mounted the steps towards the revolving doors. He looked very much worse for wear.

'Only kids, really,' Gilmore said, catching a glimpse of Hannah leading the chanting. She saluted him with a broad smile.

'If they were my kids, they'd be over my knee, and no mistake,' Whateley said.

Inside the lobby, the atmosphere was cool and calm, unlike the protest outside. Marble floors and walls muted the sounds of conversation. Dozens of people moved about or sat talking. There was a general sense of community here, and Gilmore quickly realised most of the people talking were there for the trade fair.

He saw Saudis in traditional garb, deep in conversation with suited Japanese. An African, wearing an army uniform arrayed with an astonishing selection of metals and epaulets, talked to a barrel-chested Scandinavian. There was even a fellow in a cowboy hat who, by his drawl, likely came from the deepest part of Texas, expounding loudly about his intentions that day.

After the group checked in, they scattered to their rooms to freshen up before assembling in the bar. Given the opening of the trade fair wasn't until later in the evening, and that there was no way he could stop the team from relaxing with drinks, Gilmore acquiesced. As for himself, Gilmore went to his own suite. He dropped the suitcase on the bed, then sat in his chair and closed his eyes, hoping for the tension to ease. It didn't.

Perhaps it was being in this city. Gilmore's thoughts drifted back a good thirty years. Explosions ripping across the skies sounded in his head. The cold inside the Lancaster bit deep, despite the lambskin jacket buttoned up to his throat. Pressure waves from the anti-aircraft weaponry rocked the plane, making the airframe groan and shudder with a noise that still haunted his sleep. The sound of tracer bullets stitching across the fuselage, the metallic pinging that forced his heart in his throat.

The sudden surge of the Lancaster leaping higher into the air as the bomb bay doors clanked open, releasing their payload. The whistle of frigid wind, the scream of bombers all around them bursting into flame and plunging towards the devastated city, and a horrified glimpse into Hell as Berlin burned...

Shaking his head, Gilmore clambered to his feet, suddenly clammy. He looked around. The room was dotted with heavy furniture, and the curtains were thick, letting in little light. Desperate for a glimpse of the sky, he pulled aside the curtains, and late afternoon sunlight washed into the room. Wiping his forehead, Gilmore unlatched his suitcase and picked out some shirts Rachel had packed for him.

Rachel, he thought. Whatever Bambera wanted of him, Gilmore was only here to clear his wife's name.

Going over to the wardrobe, he pulled open the door and froze.

Hanging inside, tucked neatly into a clear plastic shroud, was a familiar blue grey uniform. A cap, with a burnished symbol at the peak, sat beside a pair of highly polished shoes. Next to them was a latched, metal box. So, this was Stanhope's surprise.

'Hello, old friend,' Gilmore said.

He unfolded the shirts and hung them on the hangers provided, then took out his uniform and laid it on the bed. He stared at it for a long moment, wrestling with the memories it evoked, before turning to look at the metal box. He picked it up, flicked the latch and opened the lid.

Lying nestled inside a tray sat a service issue sidearm. The Browning Hi-Power's dull grey metal seemed to drink the light. A magazine sat above and below the Browning. Gilmore moved to lift the weapon from the box, then paused. Again, memories assailed him.

Shoreditch, this time. A pistol in hand, pouring fire with his men into the hulking shape of the Dalek in the shadows of the junkyard. The feeling of impotence washed over him again, then the rage at losing men to an evil no weapon could scratch.

Slamming the lid shut, Gilmore slid the box into the back

of the wardrobe. He returned the uniform to its hanger.

After emptying his suitcase, he completed a circuit of the room. He checked the time. Still a few hours before the official opening of the trade fair. Cocktails, canapés and inane chatter. The real deals occurred in hotel suites, well away from prying eyes. For those more adventurous, the dingy bars across the Western Zone provided a suitable venue to cut a shady deal.

Feeling claustrophobic, aware the BRISMIX mission was bearing down on him like a Spitfire on a Messerschmitt, Gilmore decided he needed some fresh air. The prospects of leaning against a bar with the Woden cronies filled him with horror. But where?

Of course!

'The Lancaster B III it is,' Gilmore said out loud. The idea of stepping outside cheered him up.

Grabbing his jacket, he left the room and headed for the lifts.

CHAPTER TWELVE

Wednesday – Devesham Mission Control. 2pm.

'**THOSE SATELLITES** aren't designed to facilitate communications,' Rachel said quietly. 'They're laser arrays. They've perverted my research.'

The atmosphere in Mission Control had deteriorated with each passing hour. The number of guards had increased, and with it, the disquiet amongst the team. Allison had demanded to see Hemmings, but the lead guard, who disdained to provide his name, had simply told her to return to her desk.

'Let's look at the facts,' Rachel said.

She, Allison and Anne were gathered around the central platform overlooking the room. On the main screen, they could see the path each of the Cerberus satellites as they circled the globe.

'Facts?' Allison said. 'The main fact is we're hostages. By the very people we're meant to be working with.'

'But why?' Anne said. She shook her head. 'It doesn't make sense.'

'The facts,' Rachel insisted. She began counting them off. 'One. The satellites were never designed to facilitate worldwide communications. Two. The temperature sensor on board the Indian Ocean satellite proves that. Three. The destruction of that ship proves they're clearly designed as weapons of war. Four. If Woden isn't allowing outside communications, they mustn't be working with the UK Government. Five. At some point, they'll make their move.'

'Move? Why does that sound ominous?' Anne asked.

'If they're not working for the UK Government, who... the Soviets?' Allison's eyes widened. 'Are they working for the Soviets?'

'Working for them? No. Working with them? It's likely.' Rachel drummed her fingertips on the desk, thinking hard. 'Ian mentioned to me how Woden is angling for contracts behind the Iron Curtain, an effort to broaden their market access. Who controls the Warsaw Pact countries?'

'The USSR, of course.' Anne glanced at the two women. 'So, they've sold us out to make money?'

'Treason comes in all sorts of flavours,' Rachel said. 'Woden has grown very quickly, very fast. They may be stretched for cash. Developing the Cerberus rockets with advanced UK technology and using it as a bargaining chip for greater access to Eastern Europe may've been their intent all along.'

'How could they think to get away with it?' It was Allison's turn to look confused.

'Remember all that pilfering that was happening before I arrived? I've checked the registers. It's easy to miss because it was happening over such a long-time frame. The sort of equipment that went missing is sufficient to build a replica, albeit smaller, of this control room.'

'My God,' Allison said. She closed her eyes and shook her head. When they opened, they glistened with tears.

'You can't blame yourself,' Rachel said. 'It's clear there's been a concerted plan over a long period of time to get to this point.'

'What about us? The team?' Anne asked.

'That's where they think they can get away with it, I imagine. The dead tell no tales, isn't that what they say?'

'Kill us all?' Anne shook her head again. 'There would be some sort of evidence, surely?'

'We're isolated. The phone lines are down. All the guards were supplied by Woden, from the very beginning. Hemmings and his goons have all the time in the world to turn this place and everything in it to ash.'

'Unless we do something,' Allison said. 'But what?'

'Engineer our escape.'

'Against armed guards? Come on, Rachel, we're defenceless here.'

Rachel glanced at Allison, then at Anne. 'I've heard a lot

about you, Anne, about the sort of things you've been up too in recent years. And Allison and I have experienced a lot of similar things since 1963. Things... not of this world. And we survived. And prospered. Are you saying a group of armed men who don't look terribly bright are enough to stop three of the smartest women in Britain?'

'Only Britain?' Anne said, wryly. 'How then?'

Rachel drummed her fingers again on the desk. She paused, then snapped them as an idea flared. A slow smile spread across her lips. 'We use our brains. And if I'm right in what your husband does...'

'You probably are.'

'...Then we have to contact him.'

'How?'

'Cleverly.'

It was, as Rachel said, clever. And very, very subtle. While the security guards glowered at the team, who went about their work monitoring the satellites, Rachel, Anne and Allison began engineering their escape.

'What do you have in mind, Rachel?' Allison said. She knew well enough that when Rachel had the bit between her teeth, you either got out of the way or were trampled.

'As I understand it, the Scots Guards Special Support Group is affiliated with UNIT, and Ian once told me that UNIT maintain a network of listening posts within the UK. Not that they're meant to, of course, and not that they intentionally listen in on domestic communications.'

'Alistair certainly wouldn't allow that. Definitely not,' Anne said, deadpan.

'I'm glad to hear it. Regardless, we transmit a message, via Morse code, on a frequency that blankets the country.'

'From here?' Anne looked dubious.

Allison, however, suddenly looked excited. 'How?'

Rachel opened her mouth to answer, but it was Allison who jumped in. She pointed to the ceiling, but it was a much higher place that she really meant.

'The satellites?'

'How do we do it?' Anne wondered. 'And how do we do it without Hemmings finding out?'

In the end, it was simpler than any of them had anticipated. With Hemmings locked away, no doubt planning something nefarious, it became easy for Anne, Allison and Rachel to carry out their plans. Under the guise of a series of tests, they gave out instructions to their team.

'What they'll be doing is arranging for a series of electronic pulses to be transmitted across the UK by the nearest Cerberus satellite,' Anne said. 'The laser arrays will act as transmitters, not of focused light, but instead what are effectively bursts of static.'

'But as a coded message?' Allison asked. 'And you think these listening posts will... what, pass on the message?'

'Oh definitely,' Anne said, smiling.

CHAPTER THIRTEEN

Wednesday – West Berlin. 3.25pm.

DESCENDING THE steps to street level, Gilmore paused to look at the protestors. Their numbers had swollen, padded out with several men and women who looked like they'd bunked off their afternoon lessons at university. Hannah was in the front line, haranguing anyone who walked by, in English and German. Gilmore was impressed by the performance. Everyone was fair game – flustered *hausfraus* in the city for a day trip, bemused buttoned-downed businessmen on their way to a meeting, even a gaggle of school children who listened to her raptly before their teacher shooed them along. Hannah and the group reserved their strongest denunciations for the international entourages who arrived, often by BMW or Mercedes, and were ushered up the stairs into the hotel by blank-faced men who moved like sharks and who spoke into their wrists.

Eventually, Gilmore grew tired of the spectacle and went in search of a model shop. The UK sector of West Berlin looked clean and well run. Trolleys rumbled down the centre of the main streets, crisscrossing the sector and providing a cheap means of transport. There were clear signs of new buildings having gone up in the last twenty years, repairing the devastation the bombing raids of the '40s had wreaked across the city. A few older buildings remained, somehow escaping the final storm by land and air. If he looked carefully, Gilmore could still see the scorch marks in the upper brickwork of those buildings, signs of how close they had come to succumbing to the firestorms. Drifting along the footpath with a tide of people, Gilmore's thoughts returned to his sole bombing raid.

Oddly, the pressure that had been building in him in his suite began to lift. He enjoyed the sun on his face and the architecture and the happy, smiling people around him. In an odd way, the guilt over his involvement in that final raid began to ease – he had helped rain death upon Berlin but, here, as everywhere, life simply went on.

He saw a police officer standing at the nearest corner. Deciding he couldn't spend all day walking the streets in search of a model shop without a clue where one was located, Gilmore went up to the officer. With a mixture of English, broken German and some hand waving, the officer directed Gilmore to a shop two blocks over. Thanking him, Gilmore began to walk purposefully along the street.

It was then that he became aware that he was being followed. At first, it seemed a coincidence. A face in the crowd, crossing the street when he did, keeping pace along the footpath. Skin tingling, Gilmore paused to look in a shop window, nodding to an assistant rearranging the display. From the corner of his eye, he saw the figure slow to examine a notice pasted to a pole.

More intrigued than alarmed, Gilmore continued.

Halting at an intersection, he glanced across the street, spotting the figure's reflection in a shop window. The image was too indistinct to make out the face, but his hunter wore an overcoat, and a hat jammed low over his eyes. Then Gilmore saw Hannah pacing along further down the opposite side of the street, and his blood ran cold.

Instinct took over.

Gilmore crossed the intersection, eyes fixed ahead. He sensed the twin presences behind him. A sudden mania to look back gripped him. He imagined himself as Orpheus, leading his wife to freedom from death's cold grip, only for it all to be undone by a human need to make eye contact. He took a deep breath and pressed onward.

The sign to the model shop came into view over the heads of the other pedestrians. Gilmore slowed, instinctively checked his flanks, then he ducked inside.

A bell jangled. Standing behind a desk was an older man, with thinning hair and a drooping moustache. Peering over half-moon glasses, he smiled and nodded at Gilmore.

Reciprocating, Gilmore plunged into the shop.

Shelving filled the small premises, packed with model kits of all shapes, sizes and origins. With clichéd German efficiency, the shelves were ordered by historical period, starting from Ancient Greece and moving up to the recently concluded Vietnam conflict. Miniature soldiers cast in lead appeared to be a specialty, ranks upon serried ranks of men and arms down the centuries all on display inside glass cases. There were painted examples dotted around the shelves and, despite his earlier alarm, Gilmore took some pleasure in examining them in detail.

The paintwork was exquisite – whoever did them had a sharp eye and steady hand for the job, as well as apparently endless patience.

'Do you like them?'

Gilmore turned and saw the shopkeeper watching him.

'They're very good,' Gilmore said, nodding to Napoleonic era Prussian Hussars arrayed in a case.

'My grandson painted those,' the older man said in a thick accent, smiling at a memory.

'He's got a good eye. I'm looking for something a bit more modern.' Here, Gilmore hesitated. He suddenly realised with a thrill of embarrassment he was about to ask the man if he had a model of an aeroplane that had been instrumental in almost levelling the city.

'You are English, *ja*?' the old man said, smiling. 'You want something from the Second World War?'

Gilmore nodded, feeling a flush creep up his cheeks. 'A Lancaster B III. For my son.'

'*Ja, ja*, we have those. Come, follow me.' The old man moved deeper into the store.

The bell over the door jangled. Gilmore hesitated, suddenly uncertain. A heater ticked somewhere behind the front desk, and the sounds of the street were a distant murmur. He saw the shopkeeper pause and turn to look at him, beckoning with one hand. Frowning, Gilmore followed.

The rear of the shop heaved with more model kits. Tanks, battleships, jeeps. Model helicopters of all sizes and descriptions. Submarines, battle cruisers and frigates. The shopkeeper looked around, then moved to the nearest shelf.

'You have your choice of manufacturers, of course, *ja*?' he said, nodding to several shelves.

Gilmore glanced over his shoulder but couldn't see whoever had entered the shop. Smiling weakly at the shopkeeper, he turned his attention to the model kits.

'Does your son prefer the maker? Of course, being a good German, I would say that Revell is the best, but that is just me.' The shopkeeper rested a hand on his chest and smiled. 'However, Airfix would be the maker of choice for a patriotic Englander, *ja*?' He pointed to a shelf. The shopkeeper reached for a plastic covered box and pulled it down. 'The Lancaster B III,' he said, looking at the image of the bomber emblazoned on the lid. 'Four wing mounted Rolls-Royce Merlin piston engines. A truly remarkable aircraft. The Revell model is more intricate than the Airfix, so your choice must depend on your son's skill level.'

Gilmore nodded, pretending to think. Instead, his thoughts turned to whoever had entered the shop, thinking they probably stood just on the other side of the shelf, making meticulous notes recording everything he said into a small black book.

'I think my son will enjoy the challenge of the Revell,' he said, suddenly aware the shopkeeper was staring at him. 'I'll take it. Would you mind wrapping it for me?'

The shopkeeper beamed. 'Of course, of course. I will be a few minutes. Please, please, you are welcome to look around the shop. Take your time.'

Gilmore nodded. The shopkeeper left. The doorbell jangled again.

Hannah stood at the end of the aisle, a finger to her lips. She wore her protest clothes, and a bag hung from her shoulder. With her other hand, she motioned towards the other side of the shelf. Then she beckoned Gilmore towards her.

She kept her finger pressed to her lips, until he bent his head towards hers.

'You've got a friend,' she said, her voice the barest whisper. 'You should leave.'

To her surprise, Gilmore looked at her and shook his head. Ignoring her glare, he turned and walked quietly to the rear of the shop, where the owner had just finished wrapping the kit.

'There, all done,' the old man said, sitting a brown paper covered box on the counter. He stared at Gilmore with hard eyes, capturing his attention. Those eyes then flicked towards the front of the store, then back to Gilmore. An understanding, almost psychic, passed between the two men. Gilmore nodded once, then pulled a twenty deutsche mark note from his wallet and handed it to the shopkeeper, who rang up the sale and presented Gilmore with his receipt and change.

'Tell me,' Gilmore said, lowering his voice. 'Is there a rear exit?'

'Rear... ah, yes.' The shopkeeper nodded. He lifted the counter flap and beckoned Gilmore forward. 'If you would, please.'

Gilmore followed the shopkeeper into the rear of the shop, which contained a small kitchenette with a gas stove and a small sink. The shopkeeper unlocked the door and opened it

'West Berlin is a place where secrets are respected,' he whispered, raising his eyebrows and nodding towards the front of the shop.

'I'm glad to hear it,' Gilmore said. He lifted the package and nodded. 'For my son, and for me, I thank you.'

Clapping Gilmore on the shoulder, the shopkeeper ushered him through the door.

Picking his way up the surprisingly clean alley, Gilmore paused for a moment beside a drainpipe, watching the street. People walked by, in pairs or singly, going about their normal lives. For a moment, he felt the crushing distance between where he stood, and his family. Holding the parcel to his chest, he imagined how delighted Dillon would be when he opened it. Sighing, Gilmore shook his head. He started forward, then felt a hand clamp onto his shoulder.

'Get your—'

Hannah stepped back under the shadow of Gilmore's raised fist. 'Well, there's no doubting you're jumpy today, Mr Gilmore.' She looked over her shoulder.

'How did you get into the alley?' Gilmore asked.

'I'm very persuasive. Plus, I think your shopkeeper mate is no friend of the Stasi. He buttonholed the man following you. Drove him out of the shop yelling bloody murder about shoplifting. It does sound more menacing in German I have to say. Your Stasi shadow has had his cover blown, at least for today.'

'Stasi? Have we been compromised?'

'No,' Hannah said. 'It's because you're English. And you work for a major defence contractor. Stanhope reckons West Berlin is lousy with Stasi right now. You're risking the mission if the Stasi bundle you into a car and take you for a drive over the border.'

'Isn't that a bit far-fetched?'

Hannah looked at Gilmore. For a long moment, Gilmore felt like an insect being considered by an entomologist, just before they dropped a chloroform-soaked ball of cotton into the jar.

'This isn't a game, Mr Gilmore. West Berlin is a dream of democracy surrounded by a nightmare of tyranny. My instructor told me that, though it sounds better if you sound posh. I signed up to the Service to make a difference, not play nursemaid to a soldier who's forgotten how to fight.'

'Now just a minute,' Gilmore said, hackles rising. 'You can't speak to me as if I'm a—'

At that moment, Hannah's eyes widened. 'Is that...' she breathed, staring hard at a car that had just come to a stop across the street.

Startled, Gilmore followed her gaze, and saw two men inside the vehicle. The driver was obscured by the car's central pillar, but there was no mistaking the figure sitting in the rear.

'Whateley? I thought he was in the bar back at the hotel. What the hell is he doing?'

'I don't know,' Hannah said. 'But I want to find out.'

'Wait,' Gilmore said, grabbing her arm.

Hannah tried to shrug him off, but he held on. 'If you don't let go of my arm, I will punch you.'

'You can do that after you agree not to be so damned impetuous,' Gilmore said, his gaze on the car.

'Impetuous?' Hannah's mouth worked, but she backed down. 'All right. I'll be a good little girl. Now let go of my arm.'

Gilmore complied. 'A racist like Whateley will spot you a mile off. Hang back and we'll see where he's going.'

Angry or not, Hannah could see the sense in what Gilmore said. They watched for any movement.

After a minute, the driver stepped out of the car. Gilmore recognised Whateley's ever-present minder. The minder opened the rear door and Whateley stepped out. He wore an overcoat, and jammed an astrakhan low on his head. While his companion looked up and down the street, Whateley walked across the footpath to a nondescript door. He knocked. After a few seconds, the door opened and Whateley entered.

'Now that is interesting,' Hannah said, glancing at Gilmore.

'What's he up to, I wonder?'

'We should find out.'

'He could be at a meeting with a...' Gilmore coughed and went red.

'I think you're trying to say, "lady friend", Mr Gilmore, when you really mean *prostitute*.'

Gilmore started, then chuckled. 'You're not quite as naïve as I thought.'

'I hope so. Spying isn't a game for kids, that's for sure.' Hannah stared at the building. Whateley's driver had returned behind the wheel. 'A prominent member of Parliament, also one of Woden's directors, on a trip to West Berlin, walks into a nondescript building. If he's chatting up the local prostitutes, it leaves him wide open to blackmail.'

'And if it is something more innocent?'

Hannah chuckled. 'If you believe *innocent* and *Harry Whateley* go hand in hand, I've a bridge straddling the Thames I'm more than happy to sell you.'

'All right,' Gilmore conceded. 'We need to be careful. The driver has seen me before.'

'When?'

'A couple times. Woden threw a party for the Cerberus Project launches, and Whateley was there. Heathrow as well. That fellow hovers like a hawk. If we're going to do this... How?'

'Carefully,' Hannah said, without any trace of irony. She looked him up and down. 'I don't suppose you want to buy a coat and hat, by any chance?'

CHAPTER FOURTEEN

Wednesday – West Berlin. 4.15pm.

AS THE afternoon shadows lengthened, Gilmore walked down the street, dressed in a long overcoat and a homburg hat. A black silk ribbon ran around the crown, with a red cockade pinned to it.

Hannah's German was astonishingly good, and the staff had attended to Gilmore with a rapidity he found astounding, given his experiences shopping for clothes at home.

'You're quite the pimp,' Hannah said. 'I'm not quite sure I should be seen with you in public.'

'In other words, it's perfect?'

'Amazing, isn't it?' Hannah's cheeky grin was infectious.

'I'm not sure my wife would appreciate knowing that,' he said, drily. They stopped at the end of the street, diagonally opposite Whateley's car. The driver remained in position; a newspaper propped on the steering wheel. Of Whateley, there was no sign.

'The idea is to draw attention to what you're wearing, not your face. In case Whateley notices you.'

'As a disguise it's as thin as tissue paper.'

'The best thing we could do at short notice,' Hannah said. 'So, you're happy with the plan?'

'Such as it is. Why don't we just report this to Stanhope? An MP visiting prostitutes, anywhere, would be a massive red flag for MI6.'

'Stanhope right now has other things to worry about,' Hannah said, looking impatient. She opened her bag and showed

Gilmore the contents. What looked like a small tape recorder was nestled inside. 'We'll tell him when we've got actual intel.'

'And of course, you'll look good if you do catch Whateley in a compromising position.' Gilmore shook his head. 'Nevertheless, we should find out what he's up to.'

'That's the spirit.' Hannah grinned broadly. 'Keep your eyes and ears open and stay out of trouble. And for the love of God, don't take that hat off. Whateley will make you in two seconds flat.'

Before Gilmore could reply, Hannah stepped into the street, waiting for a trolley to rumble past before disappearing down a narrow alley.

Gilmore jammed his hat lower then crossed, passing the rear of Whateley's car and walking up to the building's entrance. He could feel the eyes of Whateley's driver boring into his back and resisted the urge to glance over his shoulder. He rapped on the door and a shutter slammed open.

'*Ja?*'

Gilmore froze. He felt Dillon's gift pressing against his chest and, on instinct, lifted it and waved it in front of the suspicious eyes glaring at him. The shutter closed with a bang, and he heard bolts being thrown.

The door yawned open, revealing a shaven headed man with a black skivvy and pants. '*Nach oben,*' the man said, in a surprisingly high-pitched voice.

While Gilmore had no idea what he was saying, the guard jerked his thumb over his shoulder at a set of rickety-looking stairs behind him. Taking his cue, Gilmore ascended the stairs to a landing. Behind him, the door slammed shut.

Gilmore looked around. A longer corridor ran ahead of him, light spilling from a dozen half open doors. Music and laughter drifted towards him. Moving cautiously down the corridor, he glanced into the first room he came to. Several men sat around a table topped by green felt, gazing intently at playing cards. A woman, in a bustier and short skirt, appeared from deeper within the room, carrying a glass in each hand. For a moment, her eyes locked with Gilmore's. They were cold, hard as chips of ice. They transformed when she paused to place a drink in front of one of the card players. She suffered a slap on the backside, then disappeared into the rear of the room. Gilmore went on.

It quickly became apparent he was in some sort of illegal gaming house, and not, to his considerable relief, a brothel. In the next room, several men clustered around a table, and the dull sound of tumbling dice underscored their raucous, alcohol-soaked laughter. It reminded Gilmore of *Cabaret*, and he suddenly felt very homesick.

'How the hell did I end up here?' he muttered.

As he reached the third room, the door swung open, and a pair of very drunk men stumbled out, laughing and slapping each other on the back. At the sight of Gilmore, they sobered up long enough to sidle past. When they did, they immediately dissolved into gales of laughter, all the way down the stairs.

Turning back from watching them, Gilmore saw another woman, again in a bustier and short skirt, staring frankly at him. She looked him up and down and nodded.

'English?'

'Why... ahh, yes,' Gilmore stammered.

'Good. We have a space available at the card table. Please come *herein*.'

Aware he was risking exposure, Gilmore nodded and entered the room with several tables. Men sat at each of them, playing cards. One table stood by an open window, with two men deep in conversation. Gilmore's heart skipped a beat when he saw one of the men was Whateley. The other figure was a heavy-set man, grey faced, eyes hidden behind folds of flesh. Gilmore promptly sat at the nearest table, his back to Whateley and his companion.

Opposite Gilmore at the table was an Asian man, probably Japanese, staring sourly at a hand of cards. On his right sat another fellow, smelling of garlic and cloves, smoking a thin cigarillo. He was morosely counting through a small stack of chips. On the Japanese's left sat a bluff looking fellow, red brick tanned, looking worse for drink.

The woman returned with a tray containing more chips. Hurriedly taking out his wallet, Gilmore handed over a fifty Deutsche mark bill. The woman frowned and he hastily added another fifty. A smile transformed her face and she handed him a stack of chips, before sauntering away.

'Play much cards, fella?' The tanned man's voice boomed

with a broad Australian accent.

'A little,' Gilmore said softly, aware that his card playing skills amounted to a few sessions in the mess hall sometime in early 1945.

'A little? That's good enough for me. Deal him in, Abe.'

The Japanese man glanced at the Australian with a look of barely concealed contempt, which seemed to delight the Australian no end. Five cards flew across the table, landing in front of Gilmore with the precision of munitions in a bombing raid.

'Five card stud,' the Australian said, as if that had any meaning to Gilmore.

In the centre of the table were five more cards – several face cards, and a couple of number cards. While Gilmore pretended to sort through his cards, he strained to listen to the conversation behind him.

'Come on, come on,' the Australian said. 'Play or fold.'

Gilmore looked up at the Australian, whose easy attitude had transformed into impatience. Looking at his cards, then at those on the table, Gilmore picked up a couple of chips and tossed them into the centre of the table.

'Just how good a hand do you have?' the Australian rumbled, squinting at Gilmore.

Gilmore gave him the same look of disdain he would give a recruit who dared appear on the parade ground with unpolished boots. The Australian smiled.

'All right, all right, pal. Take it easy. It's all fun and games until money gets between a pair of fellas like us.' The Australian looked at his cards, swore colourfully under his breath, and folded.

The man with the cigarillo took a drag, blew a spiralling plume of smoke into the air, then matched Gilmore's bet and added another chip to the table. The Japanese looked like he was ready to commit seppuku. He muttered angrily in his native tongue then threw down his cards in disgust.

'I bet you he said the same bloody thing when he bombed Darwin,' the Australian said, his booming laughter filling the room.

The conversation behind Gilmore went quiet, then, after the Australian called the waitress for a drink, resumed.

Gilmore caught a few words from Whateley and his partner while the smoker looked intently at his cards.

'The timing isn't right,' Gilmore heard Whateley say. There was a pause, then the other man responded. 'The timing is not up to you anymore.'

The accent made Gilmore sit bolt upright. The slurred, thick words were tinged with an unmistakable Russian accent. He began to stand, when the Australian reached across and grabbed his arm.

'Where do you think you're going, mate? We've got a card game on here.'

The conversation behind them paused. Gilmore sat down. He hunched his shoulders, pretended to care what cards were in his hand, then looked up at the cigarillo smoker. The ghost of a smile played on the man's lips as he returned Gilmore's gaze. He threw several chips into the middle of the table and smirked. Frustrated, Gilmore pushed his entire stack of chips forward. The Australian whistled.

'Here I was thinking you were a weak-kneed Pom, but you've got guts, I'll give you that.'

There was a flicker of doubt in the smoker's eyes. He glanced at his cards, then at the pile of chips, then threw his hand away in disgust, muttering in French.

'He got you there, Frenchie,' the Australian said, chortling away. He reached across and plucked Gilmore's cards from his fingers. He looked at them and his face went white. He laid the cards face up. 'Nothing. The cheeky bugger had nothing.'

Gilmore had had enough. He rose again, ready to shake off the Australian's attempts should he wish to stop him. He made it halfway to the door, aware that Whateley was only a few yards away, when the Australian called him.

'Hey mate, you've left your chips.'

'Keep them,' Gilmore said.

The conversation at the rear of the room stilled. He heard a chair slide backwards. He grabbed the door handle and opened it. A hand clamped on his shoulder.

'Here, you sound familiar.'

The sound of shattering glass echoed sharply around the room. Wild oaths in Russian exploded, and the hand gripping Gilmore's shoulder suddenly loosened. Risking a glance, Gilmore saw the Russian showered in glittering fragments of glass. Whateley had turned away from him, looking at the scene at the table. The Russian stood half-in and half-out of the window, struggling with a lithe figure. For a moment, he looked like he might be able to pull them inside. Then Gilmore swept up an empty chair and hurled it at the Russian's back.

Whateley, with his own back to Gilmore, lumbered towards the dazed Russian, who sprawled across the table. The figure on the outside stairs had fled. Gilmore did likewise.

Standing in the doorway, as players and waitresses spilled into the corridor, he nodded to the Australian who was staring open-mouthed at him.

'Keep the change,' Gilmore said, nodding at the chips on the table.

Adrenaline coursed through him. Then, with Dillon's gift under one arm, he bolted for the stairs.

'*Polizei! Polizei!*' he shouted, thinking quickly. 'The police are raiding the place!'

Mention of police in an illegal gambling den created the desired effect. The corridor heaved with people attempting to escape the imaginary police raid. Gilmore took advantage of his head start to clatter down the stairs, past the shaven headed goon who was heading up. Hoping to add to the confusion, Gilmore grabbed him by the skivvy to get his attention.

'They're killing each other up there! Hurry!

The doorman shrugged him off, leaving Gilmore to grapple with the bolts at the entrance. As the commotion overhead grew louder, and screams and shouts filled the air, he flung back the door and plunged outside.

Pulling the door shut, he looked up and down the street, ignoring the stares of passers-by. Hannah emerged from an alley, frantically beckoning him. He ran to her.

'We have to get out of here,' she said. Sweat sheened her face, and Gilmore thought she was about to vomit.

'What did you see?' he said, grabbing her arm, which was covered in glittering shards of glass.

'I crouched on the exterior stairs bolted to the back of the building. I heard it all,' Hannah said, her eyes wide and wild. In one hand she clasped the tape recorder. 'I've got it all. He's in bed with the Soviets. Bloody Whateley is a traitor!' She shook her head, as if unable to believe it.

'Are you sure?'

'You were up there. You must have heard what they were saying.'

Gilmore started to shake his head, then stopped. 'The timing is not up to you anymore.'

'I heard that too. And there was more. That's torn it. Whateley's taking his marching orders from Moscow!'

Numb at the prospect, Gilmore nodded. 'We'd best get back to the hotel,' he said, as a pair of police vehicles pulled to a stop, their tyres shrieking and sirens wailing.

People poured from the building, scattering in all directions as four police officers emerged, batons in hand.

CHAPTER FIFTEEN

Wednesday – West Berlin, British Section. 6.15pm.

THE HOTEL lobby teemed with guests. Gilmore and Hannah, who had arrived after a circuitous walk back, were busy arguing over what to do next.

'I have to tell Stanhope,' Hannah said.

'What we have to do is sit down and think this through,' Gilmore urged. He felt terribly exposed in the lobby. There were too many people, and too many vantage points to be observed.

'What's there to think through? Whateley is a traitor. I have it on tape, for God's sake. And I recognised the man he was talking to.'

'Who?'

'It's an attaché at the Soviet Embassy in East Berlin. His name is Sergei Sachenkov. Late of the GRU. He's military intelligence.' Hannah looked shocked at saying the words.

'All right,' Gilmore said, his voice taken on a parade ground sternness. 'Up to my room, now.'

'You can't be too paranoid, isn't that what they say?' Gilmore opened his wardrobe and took out the metal box.

'You don't know the half of it,' Hannah said.

Gilmore noted that her Jamaican accent was more apparent when she was stressed. He opened the box and removed the Browning and a clip. He slapped the clip into the pistol's butt, checked the safety, then rested it on the bed. He shook his head.

'I signed on to help the government keep tabs on Woden. Now I'm hip deep in the treason of a Member of Parliament.'

'An MP with a real chance of controlling the balance of power,' Hannah pointed out. 'That's why we need to tell Stanhope immediately.'

'It will be like a nuclear bomb going off in London. It's bad enough the Soviets suborned our own intelligence apparatus before the war. But if they have their hooks into someone like Whateley... What will Stanhope do?'

'Message HQ. God, that will set the cat amongst the pigeons. Harry Whateley meeting with a member of the GRU.'

'Woden brought Whateley onto its board, with Walsingham pushing for it. It's looking more and more like Woden is somehow working with or for Soviets.'

'The defector's information will show whether that's true or not,' Hannah said.

'With me smack bang in the middle,' Gilmore said. 'All right, we tell Stanhope. Then what?'

'We wait for our betters to make a decision.'

'Hazard a guess at what that might be.'

Hannah frowned. 'Nothing, for now. It's too close to the election. If Whateley disappears...'

'MI6 wouldn't disappear him, would they?' Gilmore looked shocked.

'Your naivety is touching. If he disappears, it sets off a scandal.'

'And if the allegations leaked to the press to discredit him are treated as the security services picking a side in the heat of an election, the firestorm will polarise the country for a generation and strip the intelligence services of their legitimacy,' Gilmore concluded.

'Like I said, we wait for our betters to make a decision. In the interim, we have to prepare to bring the defector into the UK sector.'

Gilmore shook his head. 'We still have that to do. What a mess. All right. Call Stanhope. Get him up here.'

While Hannah had reception connect her through to Stanhope, Gilmore went over to the window again and looked outside. The day was shading into evening and, with the shadows, a subtle change came over the city and over Gilmore's view of it. No longer did West Berlin seem a haven amid a sea of tyranny. The protestors had vanished, leaving rubbish in their wake. Instead of wide streets thronging with people, all Gilmore now saw were isolated individuals scuttling about like insects, their faces masking their true natures. He almost jumped when Hannah touched his arm.

'Stanhope arrived half an hour ago. He'll be up in a few minutes.'

'Why'd your parents come to England?' Gilmore asked. He needed a distraction from the afternoon's events.

'Opportunity. For my father, it was either breaking his back in the cane fields, or fall into a life of crime, like his brother did. As soon as he married Mum, they came over.'

'You were born in England?'

Hannah nodded. 'Born and bred an Englishwoman,' she said. Gilmore detected a hint of pride in her voice.

'What was it like, growing up?'

Hannah turned her head a little, her eyes distant. 'For the most part, it was fine. Kids, when they're young, they don't really understand the sorts of things that rile up their parents. Of course, when it wasn't fine, well... let's just say there were more people like Whateley when I was younger than today.'

'Maybe they've just learned to hide their prejudice better.'

Hannah opened her mouth to reply, then closed it. She nodded. They heard a quiet knock at the door.

'Who is it?' Gilmore said as he picked up the Browning. He moved to stand beside the door.

'It's not bloody housekeeping, I can assure you.' Stanhope's familiar growl sounded impatient.

Glancing at Hannah, Gilmore held his pistol by his leg, then unlocked the door, stepping away as it opened.

'Well, this is a welcoming party if ever I saw one,' Stanhope said, nodding at Gilmore's Browning.

'Shut the door,' Gilmore said.

Glancing between Hannah and Gilmore, Stanhope frowned. 'What the hell have you two been up to?'

Hannah looked at Gilmore, who nodded. She quickly sketched the afternoon's events. Gilmore admired the dispassionate way she outlined their discovery of Whateley's betrayal. Stanhope took it all in without reaction. When Hannah finished, he was silent for a few moments.

'You're sure that it was Whateley and Sachenkov?'

'As sure as I am that you and I are having this discussion, sir,' Hannah said. 'Plus,' she said, opening her bag and pulling out the recorder. 'I have their conversation on tape.'

'Play it.'

Hannah rewound the tape and pressed Play. Sounds of laughter, the clink of glasses, and raised voices emerged tinnily from the speaker.

'We have to wait.'

'The timing is not up to you anymore, Vatley.'

Silence. Then... *'So that's it. For all my work—'*

'Comrade Vatley, your allegiance to the Motherland is not unappreciated. But events are moving at their own pace. When the election is called, you will do as I have instruct—'

Then, a shattering of glass. Hannah pressed Stop.

'Well then,' Stanhope said, running a hand through his hair and glaring at the recorder. 'That's put a spanner in the works.'

'A whole box full,' Gilmore said, watching Stanhope carefully. 'What now?'

'We stick to the mission. In fact, if you hadn't called, I was going to send someone anyway. We're bringing it all forward.'

'When?' Gilmore said, feeling his heartbeat rise.

'Tonight. In the next hour.'

'Why?' Hannah said.

'We've received intel that the East Germans have called in the GRU. A team arrived this morning, according to our sources in East Berlin. It's not enough those filthy Stasi bastards are sniffing about, they've asked the breakers to come in and tear the place apart. We have to get the defector across the Wall and into the British sector.'

'When's the go signal?' Hannah asked.

'Fifteen minutes. We'll assemble in the hotel parking garage and drive to London Block. We'll wait for nightfall, then head across the Wall.'

'Fifteen minutes? We've not been read in on the details...'

'There'll be time when we get to London Block,' Stanhope said, cutting her off.

'Hang on,' Gilmore said, exchanging a glance with Hannah. 'We can't run a BRIXMIS inspection in the dead of night. We may as well walk around with loud hailers announcing our intention to spirit the defector across the Wall.'

'Allied treaty nations have the right to conduct a BRIXMIS inspection at any time. We've never notified the East Germans ahead of time of an inspection.' Stanhope shrugged. 'They do it to us, so...' He looked at the tape player. 'I'll take that tape.'

'Protocol says the agent of record maintains the chain of custody,' Hannah said. 'I'll take good care of it.'

Stanhope's gaze lingered on the tape recorder. He had a hungry look but nodded.

'You've always been a stickler for protocol, Gordon. Very well.' Stanhope checked his watch. 'I must call London about this Whateley mess. I'll meet you both downstairs.' With that, Stanhope left the room.

'Don't let that tape out of your sight,' Gilmore said.

'I won't.' After a moment's hesitation, Hannah went on. 'Why?'

'Insurance. Woden has got connections deep within the government and the bureaucracy, particularly the security services. As does Whateley, for all his posturing. Lose track of that tape and who knows where it will end up. Keep it until we get back to London.'

'All right,' Hannah said. She thought for a moment. 'What do you think about going across the border earlier than planned?'

'He's risking lives going in mob handed like this,' Gilmore said.

'He knows what he's doing.'

'Does he? It sounds an awful lot like he's jumping at shadows. What's his background?'

'Old Etonian. A few years in business, travelled abroad, then decided to work for Queen and Country. Arrogant as hell, but capable. Very capable.'

'Doesn't matter how capable someone is if they make a mistake. Not only will people die if he cocks this up, but if we can't get this defector across the Wall with his evidence, my wife's name will be damaged beyond repair.'

'We'd best make it go flawlessly, then,' Hannah said. She went to the door. 'I'll see you downstairs.'

When Hannah left, Gilmore set himself into motion. He took his uniform from the wardrobe and laid it on the bed. Removing his wallet, he considered tossing it into his suitcase, then thought better of it and slipped it into his uniform jacket pocket.

Swiftly, he changed out of his clothes and into the uniform. The crispness of the shirt and trousers immediately took him back to his days in the service. The jacket fitted like a glove. It was only when he placed the cap on his head and looked in the mirror did the memories of Shoreditch come flooding back.

Screams, grinding words of hate, flashes of light that bleached all life from the world...

Group Captain Ian Gilmore fixed the holster to his belt, then slipped the Browning into it, along with the spare magazine. He nodded at his reflection, then left his room.

The ride down the lift was short. It arrived with a bump and the doors opened into darkness. Gilmore mulled the emptiness for a moment, then stepped into the parking garage. Silhouettes confronted him, as did the fizzing of fluorescent lights in the distance. He saw movement in the distance around a bulky object, and his hand dropped to the butt of his Browning.

A light flashed and Gilmore saw frozen in that instant several figures standing in front of a Mercedes. A shorter figure detached itself from the group and came to meet him. It was Hannah, wearing an RAF uniform. On her upper sleeve was emblazoned a patch with the British flag and the BRIXMIS title beneath. With a smile on her face, Hannah saluted. Gilmore snapped one in return.

'Group Captain Gilmore? If you would come this way.'

While Hannah led him to the car, Gilmore reflected on how easy it felt to slip back into the old rank. Stanhope was waiting for them.

'Group Captain. Glad you could make it.' Stanhope wore a British Army sergeant's uniform.

'What's the plan?' Gilmore said, as he and Stanhope sat in the back of the Mercedes. Hannah slid behind the steering wheel and started the engine. Above its revving, Stanhope looked across at Gilmore.

'We're going to meet the rest of the BRIXMIS team at the Olympic Stadium,' Stanhope said.

Gilmore nodded. 'London Block. How do we know the defector hasn't been caught?'

'As of two hours ago, we're certain he's at the rendezvous point.'

'Many's the slip betwixt cup and lip.'

'You'll just have to trust to the brilliance of my plan, Mr Gilmore,' Stanhope said.

Gilmore caught Hannah looking at him in the rear vision mirror as they exited into the early West Berlin evening. He raised his eyebrows and then subsided into silence.

They raced through quiet streets. Most of the pedestrian traffic had vanished, giving over this part of the city to cars and delivery trucks. Hannah passed a trolley car, and Gilmore saw the pale face of a woman staring down at him until Hannah sped away. After a few minutes, he saw the bulk of a stadium loom against the star speckled sky.

Stanhope checked his watch, the luminescent dial illuminating his face. 'Ten minutes, Gordon. You made good time.'

Hannah circled the stadium until she turned down a side road. In short order, they stopped before a white horizontal barrier. A uniformed figure, armed with a submachine gun, stepped from a booth, clipboard in hand. For a disorienting moment, Gilmore was back at the Ministry of Defence entrance. Hannah rolled the window down, showed her identity card while exchanging a few words with the guard, before the barrier rose and the Mercedes rolled down the ramp to a lower level.

'All I seem to be seeing lately is parking garages,' Gilmore said as he clambered out of the car.

'All haunted by the best spooks, old boy.' Stanhope strode ahead towards a barred door with a security camera set over it.

'Old boy?' Hannah stage whispered to Gilmore and giggled.

'That's enough of that,' he said, stifling a smile.

At the door, Stanhope held a plastic security pass in front of a camera set in the wall. The lens whirred as it focused on the card. A series of beeps issued from a mechanism within the door, followed by a hollow clank as the locks disengaged. The door swung open on well-oiled hinges, and an armed guard, standing just inside, stood with the barrel of his submachine gun trained on them.

'These military types have no trust, do they, Gilmore?' Stanhope said, as he swept through the door and down a short concrete corridor.

Gilmore ignored him, nodding to the guard as he and Hannah entered the bowels of the stadium.

'BRIXMIS was set up as a liaison force, to enable the Allied Powers occupying West Berlin an opportunity to investigate East German facilities on the other side of the border.' Stanhope's voice echoed in the corridor as he waited at another door. 'It does mean USSR personnel can also cross onto this side for similar missions.'

'Doesn't that mean they can gather intelligence about us, in return, sir?' Hannah said.

Stanhope didn't answer immediately; he waited for the door to open first. When it did, he turned to address them.

'Everything comes with a price. The group captain would agree, I'm sure.'

Gilmore looked around at the command centre. A dozen uniformed figures from all branches of the UK military manned workstations, going over charts or reports. At one end sat a large glass panel, a map of the divided Berlin picked out in intricate detail; roads, train tracks, major facilities and buildings, with the Wall splitting the city from top to bottom. A sergeant came over from his workstation and snapped off a brisk salute.

'Group Captain Gilmore? Staff Sergeant Hawkins.'

Gilmore returned the salute. 'Impressive set up you have here, Sergeant.'

'We think so, sir. If you'll all come this way, we're about to have the briefing session for the next tour.'

Hawkins took them from the centre to a conference room. Nine other figures, men and women, were seated around a table. All had reports open in front of them. A man stood at the far end of the room, in front of a chart hanging from the ceiling. Everyone in the room stood. Gilmore realised he was the ranking officer. He waved them back into their seats.

'I don't stand on formality, especially when time is short. Please continue, Lieutenant.'

'Thank you, sir. I'm Lieutenant Harrison and this is our team for tonight's outing. We were waiting for your arrival before beginning formalities. Well then. This is an inter-service trip, but of a different sort to what BRIXMIS usually engages in.'

Harrison turned to the map and pointed to an area in East

Berlin. 'Three days ago, MI6 received information that a Soviet engineer had defected. Getting him onto our side of the Wall is easier said than done. Which is where we come in.'

'How exactly do you mean to extricate our defector and bring him back to West Berlin?' Gilmore asked.

At that, Harrison smiled. 'Well, sir, the heart of it lies in the numbers.'

CHAPTER SIXTEEN

Wednesday – Approaching Checkpoint Crossing to East Berlin.
11.55pm.

MOVING AS a convoy towards a checkpoint, came three Opel Admiral B cars, all with tinted windows. Once again, Gilmore sat in the rear with Stanhope, while Hannah drove. They were the second car in the small group. Another member of the BRIXMIS team, Private Reggie Drummond, sat in the front passenger seat. He was, to Gilmore's consternation, quite the conversationalist. He was also the lynchpin of their plan.

'Been in West Berlin for three years coming up to Christmas,' Drummond said brightly. He wore a drab olive pullover, with his regimental beret tucked into a shoulder strap. An L64 assault rifle sat across his knees. Indeed, everyone was armed, per BRIXMIS regulations. 'Just in case World War Three kicks off,' Stanhope said as they left the meeting.

'Oh, yes,' Gilmore said. The lad's chatter did get on his nerves, but his enthusiasm was an antidote to Stanhope's insufferable smugness. 'How are you finding it?'

'Oh, it's been a real experience, sir, if you don't mind me saying. Me mum was against it, joining the Army. She thought it'd be wars here and there, but it turns out, there's hardly any danger to it at all.'

'Oh, of course,' Gilmore said, hiding his smile behind his hand.

'Checkpoint,' Hannah said, and the mood in the car tightened.

The lead car stopped at the rear of a line of cars. Men with

Alsatians walked up and down, staring through windows while the vehicle occupants watched stonily from within. Searchlights chased each around the checkpoint. Guards with clipboards made notes as they asked questions of the drivers.

Craning his neck, Gilmore could just see beyond the car at the head of the line a cobblestoned section of road, empty of anything other than a pair of guards walking across it. The checkpoint interrupted the run of the Berlin Wall, the combination of fencing and razor wire terminating for a scant few yards before resuming.

'See the guard towers?' Drummond said, turning in his seat to look at Gilmore and Stanhope. 'We've got snipers on our side, and they've got snipers on theirs.'

'And never the twain shall meet, hopefully,' Gilmore muttered. He glanced at Stanhope. 'How long will we have to wait?'

'Not long. See... Here he comes.'

A guard exited a booth and marched towards them. The driver in the lead Opel wound down their window. A short conversation ensued, then the guard waved. The lead car broke out of the line. Hannah followed suit, as did the last car in their little convoy.

Overtaking the waiting vehicles, they drove through the no man's land between the barriers, tyres sounding a beat across the cobblestones. They stopped at the barrier manned by an East German guard, and as a chorus of honking horns from waiting cars rose into the night, the guard lifted the barrier and waved them through.

'Special privileges, ain't it,' Drummond said, turning again in his seat to look at Gilmore. 'None of the locals, either side of the Wall, like it, but that's the price of losing the war.'

Following the lead vehicle at a safe distance, Hannah drove down a short tunnel and suddenly, they were in East Berlin.

'Quite a shock, when you see the contrast,' Stanhope said, staring out his window.

The convoy briefly passed through a wasteland of weed and rubble. Gilmore saw a pair of watchtowers overlooking the narrow road the convoy raced along, powerful searchlights atop each. Guards paced around the observation decks, rifles hanging from their shoulders, their vigilance unwavering. Then, the watchtowers passed from view, the convoy exiting into a dingy street bracketed by tall, abandoned buildings.

Stanhope hadn't been wrong, Gilmore reflected. East Berlin was a dark and foreboding place. Whereas West Berlin still had people out and about on the streets, East Berlin had all the warmth and grace of an armed prison camp.

'Not where I'd want to retire,' Gilmore said, which elicited a chuckle from Drummond.

'It's like the clocks all stopped ticking back in '45.' The private shook his head. His mournful tone hung like a cloud over them.

'Where's the first stop?' Gilmore said.

'Radio tower,' Stanhope said. 'It's on the list handed out at the meeting. We're not looking for anything. Just keeping up appearances.'

'Do the authorities here like midnight visits?'

'They hate it,' Stanhope said. 'Which is a good enough reason to do it.'

The streets widened a little, though the sense of claustrophobia and abandonment lingered. Where West Berlin was marked with decades of reconstruction, East Berlin was the reverse. It looked like a mouth full of missing or decayed teeth. Empty buildings, some blackened shells, others with their roofs fallen in or their walls collapsed, still stood. Here and there, brick strewn craters could be seen, the remnants of a direct hit from a bombing raid.

Occasionally, Gilmore saw a man or woman moving down the otherwise empty footpaths. At the approach of the vehicles, they would freeze in the headlights, only moving when the convoy moved on. Other times, they would scuttle deeper into the shadows, their faces averted from sight.

'What a damn depressing place,' Gilmore said.

'Good enough to visit, but definitely wouldn't want to stay,' Stanhope said. He leaned forward in his seat. 'Look lively, Gordon, the stop is just ahead.'

The brake lights of the car ahead flared crimson, and the vehicle slowed to a halt beside a brick building that had seen better days. Hannah tucked in behind it, then killed the engine. The lights from the rear car briefly filled their cabin, before they too were switched off.

'What now?' Gilmore said.

'We wait. Shouldn't be more than a few minutes.'

A few minutes later a uniformed figure emerged from the building. Light spilled into the street. The figure beckoned. Car doors opened and the members of the BRIXMIS team stepped into the night.

'Right, then.' Stanhope looked at Gilmore. 'You're up, Group Captain. Lead the way.'

With the details of the briefing to mind, Gilmore marched straight up to the officer waiting for them. The two men looked at each other, and as one, snapped off salutes.

The officer, a captain, was cordial enough, though reserved. His English was good, if heavily accented.

'Another night visit,' he said, as the team entered the building. 'We will have to return the favour soon.'

'I'm sure you will,' Gilmore said.

The shabby interior of the building spoke volumes about its importance but, as Stanhope said, they had to keep up appearances. While several East German soldiers led other members of the BRIXMIS team around the facility, Gilmore, Hannah and Stanhope waited.

'I have not seen you before,' the East German officer said. He lit a cigarette, a foul-smelling thing that Gilmore was sure had come from the black market.

'New boy,' Gilmore said, wandering over to a workstation. He glanced at the paperwork on the desk, but what little German Gilmore understood was easily defeated in written form. A man in uniform sat at the desk, headphones on, listening intently while glaring at the receiver sitting in front of him. Gilmore looked at the officer. 'What are you listening for?'

The officer's smile crept across his face and Gilmore decided he didn't like the man one bit. 'Why, transmissions from our Allied friends across the Wall. Your men and women do like to... how do you say it, *chit chat*?'

Gilmore's smile didn't reach his eyes. He glanced at Hannah; her face was stony. The station may very well have been monitoring Allied communications. After all, the Allies monitored radio traffic in East Berlin and East Germany as a whole. But it was clear to Gilmore, and likely Hannah, the station's main purpose was monitoring the people of East Berlin. The number of receivers equipped with recording gear was testimony to that.

After a few minutes, Drummond returned with the rest of the team. 'All clear, Group Captain.'

'No reds under the beds?' Gilmore said, eliciting a chuckle from some in the team.

Stanhope stood by the door, watching the room like a hawk.

The East German officer cleared his throat.

'Well, I think we've seen enough,' Gilmore said. 'Back in the cars, everyone.' The team members filed out. Gilmore lingered. 'Do you enjoy this?' he said to the officer, ignoring Hannah's warning look.

'Enjoy? Why of course. The uniform has its privileges.'

'You know what I mean,' Gilmore said. 'You've got a shortwave antenna on the top of this building. There's no way you're monitoring our communications. You're spying on your own people.'

The officer waved his hand holding the cigarette, trailing smoke like a comet. He shrugged. 'People's treasonous thoughts are their own. But if they make the mistake of opening their mouths...' His voice trailed off, but his intent was clear.

'Right,' Gilmore said. His eyes blazed.

'You're going to have to keep your scruples in check,' Stanhope said, as the convoy moved away.

'Is this what BRIXMIS does? Pokes and prods without being of any use whatsoever?'

'BRIXMIS serves its purpose, Gilmore,' Stanhope said. 'We've gained valuable intel over the years of its operations.'

'Just as the East Germans and their Russian masters have gained intel on our side of the Wall,' Gilmore said, hotly. 'How is any of this achieving anything?'

'The world isn't black and white. I thought you understood that.'

'Don't tell me what I...' Gilmore grimaced. He clamped his mouth shut and stared out the window.

CHAPTER SEVENTEEN

Thursday – East Berlin. 12:50am.

THE STREETS were empty. A thin mist lingered. East Berlin slumbered fitfully. Approaching the next stop, the tension in the car grew. The briefing had made the plan seem so simple, easy, really. Now that they were in the heart of darkness, or the 'belly of the beast' as Stanhope had said to laughter around the conference room, the plan's logic seemed threadbare.

'Is this going to work?' Gilmore muttered, as the cars drew up to a building.

'It will, because it has to,' Stanhope said. 'For you and your wife.' He reached forward and patted Drummond on the shoulder. 'Ready for the quick change, Private?'

'Ready as I'll ever be,' Drummond replied. The thin sheen of sweat on his face told another story.

'That's the spirit. You might have to cool your heels for a day or two, maybe even a week, but they'll hand you back. There are people in London ready to start making calls if they don't.' Stanhope glanced at Gilmore.

'And you, Group Captain. Are you ready?'

Gilmore nodded.

'Good,' Stanhope said. 'We'll keep them busy, while you three get going.'

Gilmore stepped out of the car, walking up to a wide-eyed guard who had exited the building at the sound of the approaching vehicles. While Stanhope waved a piece of paper about, and the guard signalled frantically at someone inside the building,

Gilmore, Hannah and Drummond furtively went down an alley to a ruined building standing about a hundred yards away from where they had parked.

'What do they make back there?' Gilmore asked, checking anxiously over his shoulder.

'Radio sets,' Drummond whispered. 'For the East German military. Not sure why it's done in a blinking wasteland like this. No sense to it.'

'Quiet,' Hannah whispered. She pulled a torch out of her pocket, and, with one hand masking the lens, clicked it on. A dim glow emerged, tinged red from the blood in her hand. A doorway appeared.

'This is a safe house?' Gilmore said incredulously as Hannah led them inside.

It was cold and quiet. The ceiling had fallen in, probably decades ago, lumps of plaster melting into the floor. Pigeons cooed to themselves in their sleep.

'Don't expect the Ritz in East Berlin,' Hannah whispered. 'It's the best we could do at short notice. Once we got the transmission from our people, we had to move him somewhere quick.' Abruptly, Hannah raised her hand.

Gilmore couldn't see her clearly, but he saw her head turn at a distant sound. It came from below.

'He's down in the basement. The stairs should be just ahead.'

Hannah's assertion proved true. A hole in the wall led to a set of rickety wooden stairs that looked barely capable of supporting a child, let alone three adults. Hannah went first, the faint light swallowed by darkness. Then they heard a low whistle, and the light reappeared at the bottom of the stairs, revealing Hannah's face.

'Come on down, he should be—'

An arm appeared from behind her. A hand clamped over her mouth, cutting her off, while the arm dragged her back into the darkness. She dropped the torch. It rolled around on the floor in lazy circles, sending shadows sprawling across the walls.

Gilmore launched himself down the stairs, the wooden risers groaning beneath his weight. By the time he reached the bottom he feared the whole lot was about to come down on his head.

Scooping the torch up in one hand, he swiftly drew the Browning with the other. Legs braced, he aimed both torch and pistol.

The beam of light pinned Hannah and a figure looming over her against the rear wall. Hannah's eyes bulged as she struggled against her assailant.

'Let her go,' Gilmore growled, aware he had to keep his voice down.

He noticed a satchel lying at the feet of the man holding her. Was this the defector? Behind him, he heard Drummond coming down the stairs.

'Goddamn it,' Gilmore said, raising his voice a little. 'Let her go or I'll put a bullet in your brain.'

He was surprised to hear a throaty chuckle in response. The hand clamped over Hannah's mouth fell away, then the arm pinning her to him. She staggered off, drawing in great, whooping breaths. The man held his hands up in mock surrender.

'A mistake. Just a mistake,' he said, in heavily accented English. 'We are all friends, yes? English friends?'

'Put the gun away,' Hannah said through a gasp.

'This idiot tried to strangle you,' Gilmore said.

'This idiot is our defector. Please put the gun away before you accidentally blow his head off.'

'There won't be anything accidental about it,' Gilmore muttered, before he nodded curtly and holstered the Browning. He walked up to the defector. 'Yuri? Yuri Gorkovich?'

The man nodded. He bent and scooped up the satchel and held it to his chest.

'I thought you would never come. We go now?'

'Not yet,' Gilmore said. He waved off Hannah's protest. 'Show me what's in the bag.'

'No,' the Russian said, stubbornly shaking his head. It reminded Gilmore of a child refusing to give up a favourite toy.

'If you are who you say you are, and you have what you say you have, then show me what's in the bag. Or we can leave you to the tender mercies of the Stasi and their GRU friends.'

Gorkovich switched his gaze from Hannah to Gilmore. What little defiance flickered in his eyes, went out. He nodded. Unzipping the satchel, he pulled out a sheaf of papers and handed them to Gilmore.

With the torch tucked against his chest, Gilmore rapidly flicked through the pages. Some of them were in Russian, the rest English. With a sinking heart, he saw the Woden Armaments insignia at the bottom of the pages typed up in English. There were technical plans, schematics, drawings of circuit boards. At one point, he stopped with a jolt and saw his wife's name mentioned at the bottom of a page marked 'Laser Technology and its application in communications'.

'So, it's true,' he said, slowly shaking his head in disgust. He handed the paperwork back to the Russian engineer, who hurriedly stuffed them into the satchel.

'You can confirm they're documents from Woden?' Hannah said.

Gilmore nodded curtly. 'That damned dog Whateley... and Walsingham. Nothing like this could happen without him knowing about it. His plans to expand into Eastern Europe.' Gilmore shook his head again. 'Selling those documents to the Soviets must've been the price he had to pay to get a foot in the door.'

Hannah turned to Drummond, who had been watching all this play out in silence. 'Well, Private, this is it. The group captain and I will give you both some privacy.'

Hannah turned to Gorkovich and, to Gilmore's surprise, reeled off instructions in fluid Russian. Gorkovich's eyes widened in amused delight. He nodded eagerly, and as Gilmore and Hannah moved towards the stairs, Drummond and Gorkovich undressed.

'Will it work?' Gilmore said, as the two other men stripped down to their underpants. It was cold in the basement, and Gilmore didn't envy what the men were doing, no matter how brief their exposure.

'It has to,' Hannah said, echoing Stanhope. 'Otherwise we're courting the biggest diplomatic incident since Powers was shot down over the Soviet Union in 1960.'

'Just what I needed to hear,' Gilmore said.

Hannah looked at him. 'Those documents. Are they...?'

Gilmore nodded. 'Your technical people will want to check if they're doctored, but my gut tells me they're legitimate.' The tension in his shoulders made them ache. 'There's going to be hell to pay when we get home.'

'This and Whateley,' Hannah said, as the two other men stepped into the light.

Drummond now wore the shabby clothes the Russian had changed out of, and the Russian wore Drummond's uniform. It looked tight at the waist, but it would pass muster.

'Keep your head down,' Gilmore said, after he shook Drummond's hand.

Behind them, Hannah and Gorkovich ascended the stairs.

'Sure thing, sir,' Drummond said. He blinked rapidly in the light.

'Follow the instructions and you'll be fine,' Gilmore said. 'Tomorrow, a coded message will be sent to the local authorities. They'll pick you up and you will confirm who you are. The cover story is you did this on a dare. Free beer at the mess for a month and all that. They'll interrogate you for a day or two, then we'll arrange to get you back across the border.'

'I surely hope so,' Drummond said. Then, he straightened and saluted.

Affected by the man's devotion to duty, Gilmore snapped off a salute in return. The two men nodded to each other, then Gilmore turned, leaving Drummond in the dark.

Carefully, Gilmore climbed the stairs, joining Hannah and Gorkovich.

'All right,' he said, switching off the torch. 'Here comes the hard part.'

CHAPTER EIGHTEEN

Thursday – Devesham. 12am.

Hemmings and several guards entered the control room. He carried a sheaf of paper with him. Accompanied by the guards, he marched up the steps and stopped where Gupta Mengu, one of the senior technicians, was seated.

'You, boy,' Hemmings barked. 'I want you to enter these numbers into the system.'

Gupta looked up to where Allison stood with Anne and Rachel.

'Don't look at them. I'm the one giving orders here. Do as you're told. I've got two sets of co-ordinates that need entering. If you know what's good for you, you'll do as you're told.'

'What's going on here, Mr Hemmings?' Allison began descending to Gupta's workstation.

'If you know what's good for *you*, Director Williams, you'll stay where you are. This little fella is going to do what he's told, aren't you?'

'If Director Williams is unhappy...'

Hemmings cuffed Gupta behind his ear. The technician sprawled forward, the clatter of his keyboard as his head hit it like a death rattle. A sudden silence filled the room.

'What in God's name do you think you're doing?' Allison stopped on the steps opposite Hemmings.

'I'm exercising the power Woden has given me,' Hemmings said, in a deceptively mild tone. He leaned over Gupta, who blinked dazedly up at him. 'Enter the data, or you'll get what for.'

Gupta shook his head. 'I'll not do anything without Director Williams' approval.' With an effort, he sat straight, clinging to his dignity.

'Why do you people think you've got any right to... Jervis. Get over here.'

A guard clattered up the steps. Allison noted with alarm that he was armed.

'It's time to make it clear to these egg-headed ne'er-do-wells who actually is in charge. If he doesn't start entering this information in the next ten seconds, shoot him.'

There were muffled cries of alarm from the other technicians.

'You've gone insane,' Allison said. 'Gupta, under no circumstances will you do anything of the sort. He's bluffing.'

'I never bluff, Director Williams.' Hemmings began counting down.

'Allison,' Rachel called out. 'I think you should—'

A slash of Allison's hand silenced Rachel. She glanced at Anne.

'You might want to reconsider,' Hemmings said cheerfully, interrupting his countdown. 'Five, four, three...'

Gupta's eyes were wide, almost pleading. He closed them when Hemmings reached zero.

'No?' Shaking his head, Hemmings shrugged his shoulders. 'Oh well. Jervis...?'

With deliberate care, Jervis removed his pistol from his holster and aimed it at Gupta. He paused and looked at Hemmings.

'I gave an order. Do it.'

A shot rang out. Allison screamed. Gupta slumped backwards in his chair, his right eye a ruin. More screams filled the room.

'Get this thing out of here,' Hemmings said, as if Gupta was a discarded piece of broken furniture. 'Now. You,' he said, pointing at a stricken woman standing nearby. 'I trust you're smarter than your friend and your boss?'

Allison, mute, only shook her head. Within a few minutes, the twin sets of data was fed into the workstation. With a grunt, Hemmings left with his guards, leaving the shellshocked room to absorb what had just happened.

*

'Why did he have to do it?' Allison said, teary eyed. 'Gupta did nothing to them.'

'They made an example of him,' Rachel said. Her face too was pale, but her eyes were steely.

'It's been two hours,' Allison said, wiping at her eyes. 'Did they even get the message?'

'We transmitted on as wide a frequency as possible,' Anne replied. 'I'm sure there are some puzzled truck drivers and ham radio users out there. You need to relax, Allison.'

'Don't tell me what I nee—' Allison stopped herself with a visible effort. The side of her face twitched, and her hand rose to touch her cheek. 'I've put years of my life into this project,' she said, almost talking to herself. 'Built it from the ground up, despite all the interference from Woden. Almost sacrificed the life of that... thing.' She glanced at the Child, silent and calculating in its throne, then looked hurriedly away. 'They murdered Gupta,' she said, her voice a whisper. 'And it's all been for nothing.'

'Not nothing,' Rachel said quietly.

Below them, the control room was quiet. Only a few technicians remained at their stations, monitoring the sensors aboard the satellites. Since the shooting, Hemmings had kept clear. The guards remained, giving the place an atmosphere that something drastic was about to happen. And soon.

'If nothing else, we've exposed a conspiracy to betray the nation. If Anne's husband gets here in time, he can roll up this lot of tin soldiers like a tatty rug—'

Shouting came from the bottom of the control room. Guards stood straighter as the door slid open and Hemmings entered, with several more guards flanking him. He shouted orders, and the guards dispersed up the steps, dragging the remaining technicians from their workstations. Hemmings followed at a trot until he reached the observation platform.

'What the hell are you playing at?' Rachel said, rising from her seat. 'Don't you have enough blood on your hands?'

'Not nearly enough, if you don't do as your told. It's time to clear out. I suppose you've worked out by now that you aren't in charge anymore. If you ever were. I'm going to need one of you to come with me.'

'What are you talking... Where?' Allison felt the blood drain from her face.

'Away. Of course. Except for those who are surplus to requirements. They'll provide some plausibility.'

'You've gone too far, Hemmings,' Rachel said. 'No one is going anywhere, especially after what you did.'

'As if you have a choice, you silly cow.' Hemmings looked at the women, sizing them up like a buyer at a farmer's market. 'All right. If there are no volunteers. Eeny, meeny, miny, moe, catch a—'

A distant explosion sent a shudder through the building. The lights flickered. Hemmings spun around.

'What the hell was that?'

'Vengeance,' Anne said, grinning fiercely.

Snapping orders, Hemmings grabbed Allison and began dragging her down the stairs. Rachel and Anne lurched forward, but the guards with Hemmings held their weapons on them. Another pair of guards hurried up the steps and, with minimal fuss, hefted the Child's throne off the ground and began to carry it down the steps.

More explosions, closer now, echoed in the control room. Despairing and impotent, Rachel and Anne watched as Hemmings disappeared at the door, with a struggling Allison in tow. The guards with the Child reached ground level, and then began pushing the chair, gathering speed before bursting through the door and into the corridor.

'Everyone, up here,' Rachel yelled.

The shell-shocked remnants of their team clambered up the stairs, some clutching each other for support. They gathered in the space afforded by the absence of the Child and waited the outcome of the battle now raging through the facility.

It took longer than they anticipated. It was a full half hour before men, not in uniform but bearing military weapons, pushed their way into the Control Room. They were led by a man in his late twenties, whose eyes blazed with intensity.

'Bill. Oh God, Bill!' Anne raced down the stairs, and the man came up to meet her. They roughly embraced, Anne cupping the side of his face and looking at him as if she couldn't believe he had come.

Bishop looked up at Rachel as she descended the steps.

'Professor Jensen, a pleasure to meet you at last. I've heard a lot about you.'

'And I you, Mr Bishop.'

'Major,' he said. 'Major William Bishop. You know, Professor, you should have agreed to speak with me. It might've avoided a lot of unpleasantness.'

Rachel frowned, and then it came to her. 'William. It was you who...?'

'The very same.'

Rachel looked at Bishop, appraising him. 'I take it you've mopped them all up. Where's Hemmings?'

'We've either killed or taken prisoner over thirty men. They were tenacious, I'll give them that. I don't know who Hemmings is, though.'

Rachel and Anne looked at each other. 'You've not seen Allison. Blonde woman, a bit shorter than me.'

Bishop shook his head. 'A friend of yours, Anne?'

'Allison Williams was the woman in charge,' Rachel said. 'Now she's gone. Along with certain important equipment. Destined for Moscow, I fear.'

'What makes you say that, Professor?'

'I've been looking through paperwork while we were cooped up here. I found a manifest. A container of equipment was shipped last week to a town in eastern Finland, close to the Soviet border.'

'You don't think they're going to send Allison and the Child to the Soviet Union?' Anne asked.

'Child? Is there a child with them?'

'It's complicated.' Anne touched her husband's shoulder with affection.

Rachel stood with hand on hip. 'Steal equipment, take key members of the team. It's likely they'll want to train a local contingent. But Hemmings has to get out of the country. Where?' She looked at Bishop. 'Bring one of those prisoners in, Major. Now.'

Bishop gave the order and, after a few minutes, two of his men brought in a man whose hands had been bound. They sat him in a chair and stepped back.

'We've no time for nonsense,' Rachel said, looking at the prisoner. His head hung low. She reached forward and lifted his chin up. 'Where were you taking those people?'

The man looked wildly about him. He was young, barely twenty. His face was flushed.

'Please, you've got to believe me. I had no idea things would turn out like this. We were told it was just a simple security job.'

'Well, it wasn't. People are dead. Their blood is on your hands.' Rachel jabbed him in the chest. 'You're probably going to spend a long, long time in jail. Unless...'

The guard looked at Rachel with hope. 'Jura. They're going to Jura.'

'And then?' Bishop leaned in, his face hard. The guard blanched.

'I don't know. They didn't tell us. Just that they're going to Jura. You've got to believe me.'

Bishop looked at Rachel, who nodded. 'All right, get him out of here. I've heard enough.'

Bishop's men dragged the guard away, who by now was sobbing.

'Jura,' Anne said. 'What's at Jura.'

'The Scapa Flow,' Bishop said. 'Deep enough for a boat or... a submarine?'

'So, the Soviets *are* involved,' Rachel said. 'Can we chase them?'

Bishop considered. 'I should think we can arrange something. We're not UNIT, but the Fifth has its own... methods.'

'Then...' Rachel's voice trailed off. She made a beeline to the terminal.

She tapped hurriedly at the keyboard. The monitor flickered into life and, as Anne and Bishop gathered around her, Rachel read the information tumbling down.

'Oh God,' she said, hand on her mouth. She looked at Anne and pointed to the screen. 'They've laid in two random targeting patterns.'

'Damn,' Bishop said, peering over Rachel's shoulder. 'Those co-ordinates are constantly shifting. Latitude and longitude all fall within a narrow band... It's been a while since I've had to... But I think that covers the whole of the British Isles. What am I looking at?'

'Death on a scale unimaginable,' Rachel said. 'The system will target two sites, to be chosen completely at random, somewhere in the United Kingdom, for attack. It's a tactic, to keep us off their backs while they make their escape and handover our technical knowledge. And judging by that countdown, we've got less than a day to find Hemmings and his crew, otherwise we'll be too late.'

CHAPTER NINETEEN

Thursday – East Berlin. 1.30am.

ON THE return trip, the Opel, with Gorkovich in, took the rear position in the convoy. Gorkovich, his collar turned up to do something to hide the stubble on his cheeks, sat in the rear, opposite Gilmore.

'You have cigarette?' the Russian said, hopefully.

When Gilmore shook his head, Gorkovich adopted a mournful look, then slumped back, eyes closed. Gorkovich had refused to hand over the satchel to Stanhope. Gilmore didn't blame him.

'Where's the safe house?' Gilmore asked as the convoy raced through the darkened streets. That information hadn't been discussed at the conference.

'We've an apartment in the British sector,' Stanhope said.

'Not London Block?'

'Too many curious eyes and loose tongues. We'll debrief our friend in relative quiet, then arrange for him to be shipped to another safe house in Britain for a more in-depth examination.'

'You make him sound like a side of beef,' Gilmore said, glancing at the Russian.

'Oh, our engineer friend here is more valuable than that.' Stanhope seemed relieved, as if a weight had been lifted from his shoulders. It was odd, Gilmore reflected, given they were still deep within enemy territory. 'He's worked in nuclear facilities. He'll have a very nice tale to tell our boys back home.'

'And those plans and photographs,' Gilmore said, feeling his stomach tighten. 'What about my wife?'

'If our friend's explanation how Woden funnelled the information behind the Iron Curtain stacks up, I'm sure your wife will be in the clear,' Stanhope said. 'Now be a good fellow and hush up. We're coming to the checkpoint.'

The brake lights of the leading cars flared, and Hannah brought the Opel to a stop. Spotlights positioned on the towers on both sides of the Wall moved constantly across the ground, illuminating the cars and trucks waiting on each side. Even at this time of night, there were lines of people waiting to cross the border from both sides. Through the thickening fog, Gilmore saw a structure rising above them into the night sky. With a jolt, he realised it was the Brandenburg Gate, still scorched and scarred by war. He just made out Victory riding a chariot drawn by four horses, before the swirling fog swallowed the structure.

Several guards spilled from the booth at the checkpoint, and the atmosphere in the car grew tense. Other guards walked up and down the line of waiting vehicles, many with Alsatians straining at their leashes. Gorkovich's eyes were open now.

'Put the bag on the floor, between your feet,' Gilmore ordered, as the guards began examining the paperwork of those waiting to cross. 'Hold tight and we'll make it through.'

The boot on the lead Opel stood open and guards clustered around it.

A German guard stopped beside their car and pointed a torch inside. Shielding her eyes, Hannah wound down the window. By good luck, a lamppost cast a long shadow over Gilmore and Gorkovich in the back seat.

'Everything all right?' Stanhope asked, leaning across and giving his most earnest smile. The guard glared at him. Up ahead, Gilmore saw the guards drifting away from the two lead Opels and towards them.

'Open the door,' the guard told Hannah, in a cold monotone. For a moment, Hannah froze, glancing in the rear vision mirror at Gilmore. His hand dropped to his Browning.

At that moment, a figure in black emerged from the shadow of the guard post. The tip of a cigarette glowed crimson in his hand. He wore a peaked cap, and there were tabs at his jacket cuffs and shoulders.

Gilmore froze. The uniform...

'That's a GRU officer,' Gilmore said, grip tightening on the

Browning. He leaned forward. 'Get the car started, Hannah. Do it now.'

Time turned to treacle. Hannah reached for the keys. The GRU officer flicked his cigarette into the street. He barked an order in heavily accented German. Guards materialised out of the shadows, converging on the lead car and began pulling the BRIXMIS team out. Shouting filled the air, swiftly followed by gunfire. The people waiting in the queues to pass either side of the border scattered. More gunfire, and several members of the BRIXMIS team went down.

Frenzied dogs barked, and the hysterical screaming of a woman wound up like an air raid siren. Gilmore saw one of the BRIXMIS team dragged from the second car. He struggled, fists and feet flailing. An Alsatian, pulled up on its hind legs by its leash, snapped its teeth inches from the soldier's face. Despite the numbers piling on him, the soldier managed to knock one of the German guards to the ground, before another guard shot him in the chest.

The guard who stood at Hannah's window swore in guttural German. He hesitated, looking down at Hannah, before his eyes fixed on Gilmore. He fumbled with the pistol at his hip as more screams filled the air.

'Go go go!' Gilmore shouted in Hannah's ear.

She started the Opel, gunned the engine and drove around the stranded lead cars.

A bullet punched through the rear window, thudding into the ceiling with a massive bang. Despite this, they shot through the barrier, shattering the wooden bar into kindling. Racing across the cobbles beneath the Brandenburg Gate, they crossed into West Berlin with gunfire raking the rear of the Opel.

Hannah turned a corner, wheels shrieking. Stanhope, his face white with fury, turned his rage on Gilmore.

'I'm the only person who can ensure your wife doesn't spend a long, long time in prison for selling secrets to the Soviets. Have a care how you speak to me.'

'Have a care? You blind, incompetent fool—'

'I'd leave out the chest thumping, fellas,' Hannah said. Her eyes flicked to the rear vision mirror, then back to the road ahead. 'We've got company.'

Gilmore and Stanhope turned and looked through the

damaged rear window. A pair of vehicles were closing with them fast.

'They've lost their minds,' Gilmore said. 'Crossing into West Berlin risks an international incident.'

'They want Gorkovich badly enough they'll do anything,' Stanhope said.

'That's all well and good,' Hannah said, wrestling with the steering wheel as the Opel skidded around a corner. The chasing car followed, the sounds of shrieking tyres echoing around them. 'But how do we get him to the safe house with this lot on our tail?'

'We can't,' Gilmore snarled, throwing a furious glance at Stanhope. 'We have to assume the location of the safe house has been blown as well.'

A foreboding silence filled the cabin.

Gilmore leaned forward, bracing himself with an outflung hand against the central pillar.

'Which hangar do you keep your Chipmunks?' He had to shout above the engine's roar.

Stanhope looked back at him. 'What did you say?'

'The hangar. BRIXMIS. He's right.' Hannah spun the wheel again, and the Opel described an arc across a near empty square, scattering pigeons who erupted into the air with a cacophonous thunder of wings. The Opel circled a fountain, four horses on each corner spouting water.

'Just get us there, Hannah!' Gilmore said, pounding the back of the seat and watching the lead car draw closer.

'Buckle up!' Hannah shouted.

She slammed the car through the gears, the engine screaming, the stink of burning rubber filling the cabin. Gorkovich sat pressed up against the corner of the seat, his eyes wide, flecks of spittle on his lips.

The Opel straightened its course as Hannah charged down a narrow street. Surprised pedestrians, those late leaving theatres or restaurants, watched the cars race along. Hannah dodged left and right, cutting off the chase car's attempts to flank them and force the Opel off the road. Distantly, police sirens began to vent their fury.

'That's torn it,' Hannah said, glancing at the rear vision

mirror.

Gilmore turned around. A pair of chasing police wagons joined the pursuit, swinging out of a side street and falling in behind the East German cars. Gilmore saw the upper body of a person in the chasing car emerge from a passenger window.

'I don't care who you have to call,' Gilmore shouted, as he watched incredulously as the East German aimed a weapon at one of the pursuing police vehicles. 'But get on the radio and call ahead. I want one of the Chipmunks fuelled and ready on the tarmac.'

Stanhope nodded curtly and reached for the Larkspur handset hanging under the dashboard. In short, staccato bursts of words, he barked instructions as Hannah kept the Opel racing down the road.

The boom of a weapon sounded above the engines. Gilmore saw the lead police vehicle weave from side to side, sending bins cartwheeling through the air. The driver jerked the wheel and the car crossed over the lines painted on the road. A wheel skidded on a patch of oil and the car swerved against a building. The sound of metal grinding on bricks was like a Banshee wail as the wall made short work of the car's paint job. The weapon boomed again, and the windscreen of the police car exploded inward, showering the occupants with glass and blinding the driver.

The police car suddenly veered to the right, clipping a shopfront. The front tyre exploded, and the vehicle tipped, the sound of tearing metal like the horrendous squalling of a monstrous baby. The car clipped the kerb and it tipped end over end, sending up chunks of bricks and torn metal into the air. It slid on its roof before slamming into a wall with an enormous crash. The last Gilmore saw of the wrecked police car were the wheels spinning lazily as steam from its sundered radiator spiralled into the night sky.

'Keep your head down,' Gilmore shouted at Gorkovich, who was more than happy to oblige. Winding down his window, Gilmore leaned out, Browning in hand. He pumped a couple of rounds into the chasing car. One sparked off the side mirror, sending glass flying. The other smashed a headlight, leaving the remaining one glaring at them like a pursuing cyclops. The man leaning out the passenger window slowly turned, and Gilmore saw his face twist into a grimace of rage.

'Aim for their bloody tyres,' Hannah shouted, spinning the wheel again.

They were now in an industrial sector. A long line of chain link fence appeared as they cleared a clot of buildings, and Gilmore saw the familiar lines of a low-slung hangar appear.

'There's the aerodrome,' Stanhope shouted.

'And there's the Chipmunk,' Gilmore said, ducking as a bullet ricocheted off the Opel's boot.

The guard station at the aerodrome entrance came upon them quickly. Hannah hit the horn, the winding sound shattering the night. Gilmore watched the police car shoot forward, closing the gap between it and their pursuers, only for the driver to suddenly peel away, dropping back as they neared the entrance.

'What the hell is he doing?'

'West German police have no jurisdiction over the Allied Powers, including coming onto areas under our direct military control,' Stanhope yelled.

He shouted orders into the handset. A guard emerged at the double from the guard house and raised the boom gate as Hannah cut the corner dangerously. Gilmore felt the Opel tilting onto two wheels before it thumped back down as Hannah straightened up. A wide-eyed guard watched them race past before he leapt for his life as the pursuing vehicle mounted the kerb and almost ran him over.

'They're not letting up,' Gilmore shouted, before he leaned out the window again and fired.

The other headlight blew out, leaving only the grey outline of the chasing car. Up ahead, a small aircraft sat on the tarmac. Several men stood around it. From the hangar, a jeep emerged and raced towards them.

'Can you fly that?' Stanhope called as Hannah turned onto the tarmac.

'Like a dream,' Gilmore answered, eyes staring raptly at the aeroplane.

The Land Rover zoomed past them, heading straight for the chasing car, which swerved to avoid a collision. It ran onto an expanse of grass, the wheels vainly striving for purchase. It fishtailed along, the jeep in hot pursuit.

'No time for relaxing, Group Captain,' Stanhope called. Hannah drew up to the Chipmunk and killed the engine. 'Let's get in the air. We're heading straight for home.'

A gunfight broke out on the grass as the men in the Land Rover engaged the East Germans. More gunfire shattered the night, and men from both sides sought shelter behind their vehicles. Gilmore turned and helped bundle Gorkovich out of the Opel then up the narrow steps into the Chipmunk.

'BRIXMIS has its own air force?' Hannah said, wide-eyed as she buckled herself in.

'Only a brace of planes,' Gilmore said, squeezing himself into the pilot's seat. 'Consider yourself lucky I'm not leaving you on the tarmac,' he said, flicking switches. The instrument panel lit up. 'These are usually two seaters, but they've been modified for the mission here.'

Stanhope helped Gorkovich buckle up, then he moved forward and sat beside Gilmore.

'Chocks away?' Stanhope said, looking at the instrumentation panel.

'This isn't bloody Biggles,' Gilmore said, signalling to the ground crew.

Thumbs up from the tarmac was enough for him. Slipping on his headphones, Gilmore engaged the starter motor. The engine rumbled into life. Flicking several switches, he felt a bump and the Chipmunk began rolling down the tarmac. Bullets sparked on the tarmac in front of them.

'Hold on everyone. This will be hairy,' Gilmore said into his headset microphone.

He heard a burst of static, then Stanhope's tinny voice.

'Just get us across the Channel in one piece, Group Captain, and then we can crack open the champagne.'

Checking his instruments again, Gilmore turned and glanced into the rear.

'Ready?' he called, grinning like a young boy with his favourite toy.

Hannah looked uneasy but nodded all the same. Gorkovich appeared to have fainted.

'Here we go.'

Hands on the yoke, Gilmore gunned the engines. The

Chipmunk shook as its propellers spun up, then it began racing down the runway. Lights buried in the tarmac flashed past, and the fence at the end of the runway drew closer with alarming speed. Depressing a switch, the clank of the ailerons fixing into place for take-off rang clear as a bell. A moment of weightlessness, then they were aloft. Rising rapidly, West Berlin rapidly dropped away from them. In a few minutes, they were heading along one of the main flight paths out of the city and across East Germany.

'Ladies and gentlemen,' Gilmore said into his microphone. He was almost giddy with relief, marked only by annoyance he had left behind the Lancaster model he had promised his son. 'There will be no drinks service this evening, but I can promise you a relatively smooth return trip. Sit back and relax and please obey all warning signs.'

Keying off the switch, Gilmore covered his microphone with a free hand and turned to Stanhope. 'I need the location of the safe house. And you better hope the East German air force doesn't scramble any jets. I'm good, but I'm not that good.'

CHAPTER TWENTY

Thursday – French Airspace. 3am.

DESPITE WORRIES about the East German air force, Gilmore piloted the Chipmunk across East German airspace without incident. He kept the aeroplane as low as he dared, to prevent radar installations getting a fix on them. His rusty German was enough to monitor the radio traffic while the others dozed. He only truly relaxed when the navigation beacon switched over to a West German station. In less than an hour, the Chipmunk crossed France and then flew over the open waters of the Channel. Gilmore nudged Stanhope awake.

'Tell your people we'll be over the landing site in thirty minutes. It's black as Hades out there – I want some flares laid down on the flattest paddock they can find.'

Stanhope grunted, and keyed his microphone. He dialled in the frequency on the radio and Gilmore heard a burst of static in his headphones. It cleared, and then a woman speaking in a monotone responded. Stanhope gave what sounded like a passcode, which was authenticated. Stanhope rattled off a series of instructions, then switched off his microphone. He settled back in the co-pilot's chair.

'They'll be waiting. Keep on following your heading. You'll see the landing site soon—'

A white light filled the Chipmunk's cabin. It was so brilliant, Gilmore lost his vision for a few moments. When it did come back, his eyes watered and all he saw were double images. There was no rumble of thunder.

'What in God's name was that?' he said, almost shouting.

'It came from the north,' Stanhope said, peering out of the window. The flash of light vanished as quickly as it appeared. The starry night spread out above them.

'Did you see that?' Hannah poked her head between the two chairs. 'A massive pillar of light, to the north.'

'Probably just lightning,' Stanhope said.

'Lightning? I've been flying for thirty years,' Gilmore pointed out, 'and I've never seen anything like that.'

'Well, there's a first time for everything, Mr Gilmore. Since its gone, let's just concentrate on getting this bird down on the ground safely, eh?'

Hannah returned to her seat, while Gilmore quietly seethed.

The White Cliffs of Dover vanished as they left the Channel behind, with the Chipmunk flying in a westerly direction. Gilmore heard Hannah's low cheer from the back, and he half turned in his seat and gave her a thumbs up. The young woman had proven resourceful, with her driving especially, but also the matter regarding Whateley. Which reminded him...

'What are you going to do about Whateley?' he said, keying his microphone so that only he and Stanhope shared the channel.

'He'll be handled appropriately,' Stanhope said, glancing at Gilmore.

'What does "handled appropriately" mean?'

'It means exactly that.' The buzz of static did nothing to hide the warning in Stanhope's voice.

'Don't tell me MI6 is going to sit on its hands and risk a proven traitor getting anywhere near Downing Street.'

'You worry too much, Group Captain.' Stanhope clapped him on the shoulder. 'Just get us home and it'll all be fine. You'll see.'

'There.' Stanhope pointed.

Gilmore saw lights flickering in the distance. He checked his position. They were over the landing zone. Pulling the yoke to starboard, Gilmore turned the Chipmunk in a great arc, before pointing the noise dead straight toward the distant, parallel smoking flares.

'Here we go,' he said, as turbulence struck the Chipmunk.

Reducing power to the engines, he corrected his approach, flicked a switch to raise the ailerons to slow their speed, then began his descent. The twin propellers thrummed, the sound filling the cabin. Turbulence struck them again, but Gilmore was more than a match for it. The ground rushed towards them, and the familiar sensation of terror and exhilaration filled him.

'Hang on,' he said over the microphone. 'This will be bumpy.'

As they descended towards the ground, Gilmore glimpsed a pair of Range Rovers standing to one side, several people clustered around them. The darker mass of a building to port shot by, then he had eyes only for the ground.

With the nose up, the Chipmunk landed on its rear wheels, before the slowing speed forced the nose wheel down. The Chipmunk bounced along the ground, as the propellers slowed. A rushing sound filled the cabin, and the lights flickered. There was a loud rattle and crash, and the bouncing smoothed out. Taxiing it in a circle, Gilmore directed the Chipmunk towards the waiting vehicles.

As the Chipmunk came to a halt, Stanhope removed the headset and unbuckled his seat belt.

'I've got to bring my team up to speed. We'll begin questioning Gorkovich as soon as we're set up. You should watch. It'll be educational.' Without waiting for a response, Stanhope squeezed between the two seats and entered the tiny cabin.

'How do you stand the man?' Gilmore asked when he joined Hannah in the cabin.

'I hold my nose and think of the bigger picture.'

'What does the bigger picture look like?' Gilmore reached over and shook Gorkovich's shoulder. He had slept through the landing. His eyes opened blearily, and he yawned, revealing gaps in his teeth.

'The security of the Realm,' Hannah said, turning to look at Gilmore. 'Isn't that what you signed up for when you joined the RAF?'

'I was running away from a broken heart,' Gilmore said. 'Comrade Gorkovich? Comrade? Come on, it's time to wake up. Don't forget your bag.'

'England?' Gorkovich said. His bloodshot eyes held something that looked like a plea.

'Definitely, England,' Gilmore said. Acting on an impulse,

he stuck out his hand. The Russian did the same and both men shook hands. 'Let's go, old chap,' Gilmore said, indicating the door. 'Hopefully Stanhope has laid on some vodka. Truth to tell,' he said, smiling at Hannah, 'I could do with a nip or three myself.'

Gorkovich lumbered down the stairs, where a pair of hulking men, wearing identical black trousers and skivvies, greeted him. They guided him towards one of the Range Rovers and bundled him inside. Stanhope finished talking, then came over.

'Gordon, you're in charge while I'm interviewing Gorkovich,' he said. 'Watch everything, record everything. I'll need a report typed up and ready to telex to HQ by 6.ooam. Are you up to it?'

Hannah nodded. 'I am. Thank you, sir.'

'Don't thank me yet,' Stanhope said. He lifted his hand and jangled a set of keys. 'Come on if you're coming.'

The building Gilmore glimpsed while landing proved to be a low-slung farmhouse. Around it were several outbuildings; a whitewashed cottage, a cold store, empty stables and a shed containing a tractor that appeared to date back to the Great War. Stanhope parked the Range Rover next to its twin, and they all exited in a clatter of doors.

'The place was a gift given to MI6 by a former agent when he died. It has all the attributes – remote, with visibility from all sides.' Stanhope led them through a shadow haunted garden to the front door. 'One road in and out. Nearest transportation link is a train station a mile from here.'

Blacked out windows confronted them. The door stood open, with a blank faced guard standing beside it, a submachine gun cradled in his arms. He nodded at Stanhope but gave Gilmore a blank faced glare.

'I'll have to protest to management,' Gilmore murmured to Hannah as they passed the guard. 'The staff are decidedly unfriendly.'

Most of the furniture in the farmhouse had been removed. Empty room after empty room confronted them as Stanhope led them deeper into the dwelling. Only in the centre of the building, off a main corridor lit by a string of bare bulbs hung along one wall, did Gilmore glimpse furnishings. They stopped in front of a room filled with camp beds.

'How many in your squad?' Gilmore asked, looking around.

'Excluding Stanhope and me, there's another nine on the grounds. We're pretty remote, but you can never be too careful.' Hannah yawned hugely, then looked embarrassed. 'Sorry,' she said. 'Long day.'

'Going to be a longer night. Are we here for an extended stay?' Gilmore nodded to the beds.

'Depends,' Hannah said. 'If Gorkovich spills his guts without any fuss and bother, we shouldn't be more than a day or two.'

'And if he decides to parse out his information to gain better terms on his new life in the West...?'

'Best get used to a thin mattress then.'

'Let's have a look at this observation room.'

Hannah led Gilmore to it. Two television sets stood against a wall, the cabling for each going through a duct into the interview room. A static image of the interview room could be seen on each screen, from opposite corners. Sitting on a low shelf beside one of the televisions was a square device, with a reel-to-reel tape inside the plastic housing.

'One-way mirror?' Gilmore wondered, standing in front of the glass dividing both rooms.

Nodding, Hannah pointed to the televisions. 'We'll record the feed from the video camera and send the tapes to London.'

Gilmore nodded. The interview room contained a narrow table, with a chair at either end. A temporary lighting rig stood in one corner, illuminating the space. In opposite corners, each trained on an empty chair, stood a tripod holding a video camera, each wide lens staring blindly at the other. From the speakers in the television sets, he heard the door open and watched Stanhope and Gorkovich enter. Stanhope held a folder in one hand. Hannah nudged Gilmore.

'See how his hands are shaking? Smokes like a chimney.'

Stanhope closed the door. The rattle of chairs came through the feed as both men sat down.

'Here we go,' Hannah said. She moved to the video recorder and depressed one of the keys. The reels turned.

'For the record, Comrade Gorkovich,' Stanhope said, his voice tinny in the television speakers. 'Could you please give us your name and occupation?'

'Yuri Gorkovich. Nuclear scientist.' Gorkovich looked edgy.

His eyes flicked to the corners of the room, then back to Stanhope.

'Nuclear scientist? Which facility did you work at?'

'Beloyarsk nuclear power station. In Sverdlovsk Oblast.'

'That's east of Moscow, yes?'

Gorkovich nodded.

'Sverdlovsk is the nearest city?'

'Yes, but I live in Zarechny, which is closer to the facility.'

'What did you do there? Your research, I mean?'

'Nuclear medicine. For treatment of cancer.'

'How interesting,' Stanhope said, in a voice that sounded as uninterested in nuclear medicine as it could be. 'We have a copy of your file; did you know that? In fact,' he said, opening the folder he had carried in, 'I have it right here. It says something about my social life that this is the most entertaining bedtime reading.'

Gorkovich shot Stanhope a look that Gilmore found unreadable.

Stanhope smiled. From his jacket pocket, he pulled out a packet of cigarettes and shook one loose. He offered it to Gorkovich, who took it like a man reaching for a lifejacket in a storm. From his other pocket, Stanhope retrieved a matchbook and slid it across the table towards Gorkovich. Gorkovich, his fingers trembling, took two tries before he was able to strike a light. The flame danced as he lit the cigarette. The spent match he tossed into the ashtray.

'You say you're involved in nuclear medicine. But that's not what your file says. Your secret file, I mean. Don't look so surprised, my dear fellow. We have our methods. Did you think we would simply accept you with open arms without really checking out who you were and what your research really was?' Stanhope looked down at the file open in front of him. 'For instance, you never worked at Beloyarsk, did you?

'No answer? That's a pity. No, you were based in City Forty. A closed city, site of one of the Soviet Union's most secret nuclear facilities.' Stanhope paused, and gave Gorkovich a look of pity. 'You are a long way from home, aren't you?'

'What's he talking about?' Gilmore asked.

Keen to hear about the plans Gorkovich had with him, he was impatient for Stanhope to get to the point.

'He's talking about Ozersk,' Hannah said, her eyes shining

with excitement. 'The birthplace of the Soviet nuclear weapons programme. Gorkovich was lying about working in nuclear medicine. He's directly involved in the Soviet nuclear programme.'

'Nuclear weapons... What does any of this have to do with my wife?' Gilmore felt a creeping sense of dread.

'Nuclear medicine,' Gorkovich said stubbornly, stabbing the hand holding the cigarette at Stanhope. The tip of the cigarette flared, then Gorkovich took a nervous drag on it.

'Sure, nuclear medicine.' Stanhope glanced at the window, then looked back at Gorkovich. He tapped the report sitting in front of him again. 'But it wasn't though, was it? Let's cut to the chase, comrade. You've been working on... well, let's keep that quiet for the moment. But it is to do with research developed here. A little of your own work, but a lot of it from... a third party, close to home. For one of us.' He glanced again at the window, perhaps sensing Gilmore glaring at him through the glass. 'A pity about the accident, of course.'

Gorkovich started. The trembling in his hands grew stronger.

'It was an accident, wasn't it, Comrade Gorkovich?'

Narrowing his eyes, Gorkovich nodded slowly. 'Yes, yes. An accident.'

'If you say so. You defected before the Commission of Inquiry could meet.' Stanhope turned a page of the report and pretended to examine it, before looking across the table at Gorkovich. 'It must've been bad. Twelve of your colleague's dead.'

Gorkovich face went white.

Watching with Gilmore, Hannah shook her head. 'Stanhope has his hooks in him now.'

'So, he lied about what he does,' Gilmore said. 'Why is it so important?'

'It goes to why he decided to defect. A man in a desperate need to be anywhere but at the centre of responsibility might do or say anything to tempt the other side to accept him.'

'You think he forged those Woden documents? I saw those plans, Hannah. You haven't. I recognised them. They're what Woden has been working on for years, using my wife's research.'

Stanhope stood, then leaned on his balled fists, staring straight into Gorkovich's eyes.

'Let me put it to you straight, Comrade Gorkovich. We have a report that squarely puts the blame at your incompetence causing an explosion in a laboratory that left twelve men and women dead. That contaminated the surrounding five square miles with enough radiation to ensure they had to plough it all up and ban anyone from the area for the next fifty years. Strange how you made it out alive. Or did you know it would all go pear-shaped, but went along because you were too gutless to tell your masters the tests were doomed to fail?'

'It was an accident,' Gorkovich said, almost pleading.

'An accident that painted a target right on your back,' Stanhope said, emphasising his point by stabbing a finger at the hapless defector. 'There was a gulag in your future, wasn't there, Gorkovich? If you were lucky. Or a bullet to the head if you proved too difficult an issue to make disappear. Enough reason for you to forge those documents you hold to your chest so tenderly, so they could be used to tempt us into accepting you.'

'These papers are real,' Gorkovich said. 'I risked my life to steal them, to bring them to you. The work we did with them, we showed that man, Vatley, he visited our lab—'

'Enough.'

A tense silence filled the room.

'Did he say Vatley?' Hannah said, turning to Gilmore.

'Vatley?' Gilmore's eyes widened. 'Oh God,' he said, hand almost clawing at the glass. 'Whateley. Whateley's been to the USSR. That's the proof my wife is innocent.'

He banged on the glass. Gorkovich flinched. Stanhope ignored it.

'You're mistaken, Comrade Gorkovich,' Stanhope said. He checked his watch. 'But it doesn't matter now. None of it does.' He glanced at the window, at Gilmore and Hannah standing impotently on the other side of the glass. He smiled.

A dawning horror swept over Gilmore. 'Why is Stanhope armed?'

'He shouldn't be armed. Perhaps he forgo—'

An explosion rocked the farmhouse. Dust and plaster rained down from the ceiling in the observation room, filling it with a choking white cloud. Before it filled the interview room, Gilmore saw Stanhope unhurriedly draw his revolver and put two bullets in Gorkovich's chest. The Russian's face creased with incredulity as blood soaked his shirt black. He struggled to stand, a hand reaching out imploringly, then Stanhope shot him in the face. Gorkovich was dead before he hit the floor.

'Stanhope,' Gilmore shouted. 'You murdering bastard. He's the one who blew the mission.'

Gunfire filled the farmhouse as Gilmore drew his Browning. He put his foot to a chair and shoved it across the floor, where it jammed under the door handle.

'Get your damned gun out, girl!' he yelled at Hannah who stood, dumbfounded. He heard screaming from elsewhere in the farmhouse. The chatter of submachine guns was awful.

Casting around, Gilmore saw the only exterior window was boarded up. The door rattled from the pounding on the other side. It began to splinter, and the chair jamming it in place skidded an inch.

Adrenaline poured through Gilmore's veins. Jamming the Browning into his belt, he lifted one of the televisions and heaved it at the two-way window. The vacuum tube inside the set exploded as the window shattered. Drawing the Browning, Gilmore fired at movement inside the interrogation room. Stanhope swore, then the door flew open and he escaped outside.

The dust began clearing, and Gilmore saw the satchel holding Gorkovich's documents lying on the floor. Careless of the shards of glass still in the frame, Gilmore leaped through, rolling to a standing position. Someone ran past the half open door and was then cut down by the chatter of a submachine gun. Gilmore picked up the satchel and slung the leather strap over his shoulder. He spared Gorkovich a glance, the dead man's face a mask of white dust and blood, then crossed to the door.

Smoke poured down the corridor. He saw a figure wearing a gas mask loom out of the roiling cloud. Gilmore fired and shot the figure in the head, wincing as blood fountained from it. He jumped over the body sprawled headlong on the floor.

A man armed with a submachine appeared from within the gas cloud. Gilmore clubbed him to the ground with a savage punch.

More gunfire. Where was Hannah?

He almost shot her when she appeared out of the gloom. He tossed the gas mask to her.

'Put that on,' he shouted, as another figure appeared.

He lunged at Gilmore and, for a moment, the two men grappled. Gilmore slapped away the gun hand, then punched his attacker in the throat with the butt of the Browning. He felt something crunch under it, and the man went down, choking.

Turning, Gilmore grabbed Hannah by the hand. 'We have to get out of here. Is there another—?'

Hannah raised her pistol and fired over Gilmore's shoulder. The pressure wave made his head feel like it was bulging like a balloon. His ear rang like a bell. He turned and saw a figure dead at his feet.

'Upstairs,' Hannah shouted, her voice muffled by the gas mask.

The gas was thick now, and with his eyes streaming and convulsed by a coughing fit, Gilmore staggered after Hannah. He followed her up a short flight of stairs. The gunfire slowed. It was dark on the stairs, and it was only by luck that they made it to the landing without tripping.

A coughing fit brought Gilmore to a stop. His throat burned and tears dripped down his cheeks. Hannah hovered over him, looking anxiously towards the stairs.

'Why?' Hannah asked. 'Why has Stanhope betrayed us?'

Whateley. The name rang in Gilmore's head like a bell. Gorkovich had seen him, seen him in Russia. At his secret facility? And Stanhope...

'He's protecting Whateley,' Gilmore said. 'Stanhope used the BRIXMIS process to get to Gorkovich, get him here, so he could kill all three of us. With us dead, no one is any the wiser about Whateley and Woden. Bambera has been played. I've been played.'

More gunfire erupted. They heard boots on the stairs. They backed down the corridor, towards a boarded-up window.

'We have to get out of here,' Hannah said. 'We have to tell...'

'Who?' Who can we trust? If Woden has suborned an MI6 officer, their tentacles reach deep.'

A shot rang out, and plaster exploded from a wall. Gilmore fired twice, and whoever had been coming up the stairs retreated.

'A good thing Stanhope was too cocky to take our weapons from us. We can't stay here, though.' He indicated the boarded-up window with the Browning.

Gas began to creep down the corridor. Reaching the window,

Gilmore began prising away the planks.

'Woden has its damned fingers in everything,' he said, tossing aside a board. Silvered light from the moon shone across an empty paddock. 'Politicians like Whateley, police, bought and paid for out of Woden's profits.' Another board came free.

He heard slow clapping. He turned. A masked Stanhope materialised out of the gloom, torches behind him piercing the rolling gas.

'Not quite the dim military mind, eh, Group Captain?' Stanhope said. Even with the mask on, his derision was as clear as a bell. Stanhope held his pistol by his side. 'Why don't you be a good chap and hand over that satchel?'

'Why?' Hannah shouted. 'Just so you can hide your treason. Bloody Alex Stanhope. All that talk about Queen and Country. You're just a damned whore, willing to sell out to the highest bid—'

A shot rang out. Hannah coughed and staggered. Gilmore grabbed her shoulders, and she sagged into his arms. He felt her press something hard into his hands. A hot wetness scalded him. He looked down and saw that Stanhope had shot her in the throat. Blood pulsed from the terrible wound. Her hands scrabbled weakly at him. Behind the mask, Hannah's eyes were wide, frantic. Then the light fled from them, and she was dead.

Too heavy for Gilmore to hold, Hannah slid from his grasp, landing with an awful thud on the bare floorboards.

'Now see what she made me do,' Stanhope said. He looked at Hannah's body in much the same way he might if his dog had made a mess on the floor. He dragged off his mask and smiled at Gilmore. 'The Service soiled itself when it hired the likes of her. England deserves better, don't you think?'

'You murdering thug,' Gilmore raged. He used the cover of his crouching body to slip the tape Hannah had handed him into a pocket.

'Sticks and stones, Mr Gilmore,' Stanhope said, ironically echoing an earlier comment. 'I won't ask again. Be a good fellow and give me the satchel.'

Surging to his feet, Gilmore fired blindly. Stanhope clapped a hand to the side of his face as he spun away. Turning, Gilmore charged towards the window, leaping at it with his arms crossed over his face.

He burst through it in a flurry of shattered timber. Cold air rushed over him as he fell.

His short-lived flight ended with a thud. Instinctively, Gilmore let his body go loose and he rolled several times. Pain flared in his ribs and his breath exploded from him. He heard shouting.

He scrambled to his feet and stumbled away...

CHAPTER TWENTY-ONE

Thursday – Home Counties. 4.10am.

THE DREAM had followed Gilmore in the years since the Second World War. Falling, always falling, rushing through the night as artillery barrages exploded around him, as bombers fell shrieking through the darkness, blossoming red and black on impact. The ripple of the airframe, metal shivering like water as the Lancaster thundered through the night. The terrible sense of vulnerability, a frail bundle of bones and skin, waiting to be burst by a shell lobbed into the air to keep the bomber fleets at bay.

Gilmore woke in a cold sweat.

Groggy, he looked around, grunting at the pain in his shoulder. He glanced at it, saw the deeper black of his blood-stained jacket, and realised where he was.

The face of the man who had climbed into the train carriage loomed briefly in Gilmore's memory, the deafened cry when shot mercifully brief. The train clattered on, leaving behind all sounds of pursuit. An hour or two later, slumped against the open door watching the silhouetted countryside passing-by, Gilmore started to recognise the landscape.

A wild hope blossomed. As the train slowed approaching the next station, satchel in hand, Gilmore jumped from the carriage onto a grassy slope.

The station was unmanned, a single lightbulb flickering over the station's covered entrance. Gilmore glanced at the station's name, which read Paddock Wood. He offered up a silent prayer of gratitude.

Wincing at the sharp pain in his shoulder, Gilmore climbed onto the platform and stole along it, exiting into the car park. Several vehicles stood alone, their owners travelling up to London.

Feeling guilty, but desperate, Gilmore tried the door handles of each and found one unlocked. The little Morris Minor groaned under his weight as he half fell inside. He quickly went through the glovebox and found a key. Giving silent thanks to the trust rural dwellers had in their neighbours, Gilmore started the car and drove off.

Driving north, he left the slumbering town behind him, and switched on the radio. That brilliant pillar of light remained seared in his memory; he desperately wanted to know what it was. He felt in his bones it had to do with the satellites. But static laced with music filled the tiny cabin, so Gilmore turned down the volume.

The moon emerged occasionally from behind the clouds, but he didn't need its light to navigate. Gilmore knew where he was going.

Emerging from the tunnel, Gilmore drove for another fifteen minutes. The headlights swooped as he navigated the bends in the road. A familiar low stone fence came into view, then a massive oak. He drove on for another mile and saw a gravel road stretching to the right, its stones glimmering in the wan moonlight.

'Rachel will hate this,' he muttered to himself. 'As if I have a choice.'

He steered the Morris Minor onto the gravel and drove on. Within seconds, a cottage emerged from the darkness, its white-washed walls and thatched roof evoking memories laced with conflicting emotions.

Abruptly, the pips sounded, and Gilmore turned up the radio volume as the car coasted towards the cottage.

'The news that the Prime Minister visited Her Majesty late last night, out of all known precedent, to request that Parliament be dissolved, has been greeted by the opposition parties. Mr Harry Whateley, leader of the Freedom Party, which many commentators believe may hold the balance of power in the next Parliament, was forced to cut short a controversial business

engagement. Mr Whateley, attending in his capacity as director of Woden Armaments at an arms' trade fair in West Berlin, flew out on the last flight shortly before midnight, and arrived in London in the last hour. Speaking to reporters at Heathrow, Mr Whateley said he welcomed the announcement.'

Whateley's voice came on the radio.

'It is well past time this rotten government was tossed out for a new, energetic leadership based on the great British values the Freedom Party promotes...'

Exhaustion rolled over Gilmore. He sagged forward, only righting himself in time to avoid crashing into a fence. With suddenly clumsy hands, he parked the car and switched off the engine. Numbness crept through him. Dimly aware that shock was catching up with him, Gilmore watched the light over the cottage's front door flare into life.

He pawed at the driver's door and opened it on the third attempt. The interior light came on, almost blinding him. The next seconds were staccato images.

A figure, lit from behind, stood framed in the doorway, cradling a shotgun. He staggered forward, one arm stretched out.

'Ian?' A familiar voice called out. 'Ian, is that you? What the hell are you doing here?'

'Running for my life,' he mumbled, feeling utterly spent. Then he fell into the woman's arms with a groan. 'Edith,' he said, then the night swept him away.

Gilmore woke to familiar surroundings. The kitchen stood empty, but he heard banging in a room somewhere in the cottage. His jacket and Browning were gone. The satchel was still in his grasp. He touched his forehead and felt a sticking plaster over the cut. His shirt was gone, and he felt blood seeping down his exposed arm. Sweat ran down his face and the pain in his shoulder stung with the fierceness of a stab wound.

'Still with us?' Gilmore's ex-wife came into the kitchen.

A broken shotgun sat on the counter, gleaming in the light from the bulb overhead. She was tall, angular, and had a shock of shoulder length grey hair. It had been auburn, once. She dressed practically, in trousers, shirt and a cream-coloured jumper.

'Only just.'

'Don't be a girl,' Edith Gilmore said. She knelt by his side and critically examined the wound. 'The way you're talking, your arm has been shot off. Nicked, maybe, but definitely still attached.' Opening the first aid kit, she glanced at Gilmore. 'You're lucky I'm still a light sleeper. When I heard your car coming up the drive at this God forsaken hour, I knew trouble was on its way.'

'I'm glad to see your bedside manner has improved,' Gilmore said. Wincing, he sat straighter.

'Everything does, with time,' Edith said. Again, softly now, she asked, 'You wouldn't let go of that satchel. It must be important.'

'Very,' Gilmore said, his voice barely above a whisper. 'People have died because of it.'

'Died? What the hell have you got yourself into?'

'Trouble.'

'Trouble? That's it? You've been shot, while wearing your old uniform and driven through the dead of night like the Devil is at your heels, *and* all you've got to say is *trouble*?'

'Big trouble,' Gilmore said, with a flicker of a smile.

'My bedside manner has improved, but your sense of humour hasn't.' She pressed a hand to his forehead. 'You're freezing. Shock. Wait here.'

Gilmore watched as Edith went to a cupboard in the kitchen, opened it and pulled out a bottle of Scotch and a glass.

'Here, pour yourself one while I start stitching that wound.'

Balancing the glass on his thigh, Gilmore undid the cap with one hand and poured himself a healthy slug of Scotch. The liquid burned a trail down his throat, shocking him with its strength. The shaking in his hands lessened.

'Please don't tell me you drink this regularly.'

'Its purposes are medicinal only,' Edith said, drily. She took a bottle from the first aid kit, undid the top and poured a healthy measure over a square of folded cloth. 'This will sting.' Without pausing, Edith dabbed disinfectant on the wound.

'Damn it, Edith,' Gilmore said, hissing at the flaring pain.

'You're being a girl again, Ian.' Edith examined the wound with a critical eye. 'You're lucky, though.' She sealed the bottle and replaced it in the kit. 'Whoever shot you took a chunk out, but it will heal nicely.' She glanced up at him. 'You really should stay the night. You're dead on your feet.'

'I have to keep going,' Gilmore said. The pillar of light haunted him.

'How you ever recovered in that hospital at the end of the war I'll never understand,' Edith said, as she cleaned away the blood around the wound.

'Your less than tender ministrations couldn't have been the reason,' Gilmore said, hiding a pained smile with another mouthful of the Scotch.

'I might very well stitch this and your mouth shut if you keep up with that sort of talk. I was a damned good nurse back then. Still am. Fair warning,' she said, glancing at Gilmore. 'This will hurt as well.'

Fortified by the Scotch, which was now a comfortable warmth in his stomach, Gilmore watched while Edith stitched the wound. When she finished, she bandaged his shoulder, then wrapped a length around his chest to anchor it, before tying off the knot.

'Well, then,' Edith said, looking critically at her handiwork. 'I've done you a favour. Now you owe me. What the hell is going on?'

Looking at the bottle of Scotch again, Gilmore frowned then replaced the cap with some regret. 'I need some clothes,' he said, looking down at his tattered and bloody uniform. 'Please.'

Edith narrowed her eyes for a moment, before disappearing into the depths of the cottage.

When she returned, carrying a shirt, jumper and trousers, Gilmore was standing beside a window, looking out into the front yard.

'Expecting visitors?' Edith asked, handing him the clothes.

'I hope to God not. Though I'd be happier if you fetched your shotgun. Just in case.'

'Just in case?' Edith put her hands on her hips, which Gilmore knew from experience presaged an argument.

'Don't argue with me, woman. Just get the damned thing.'

'Woman? I bet you don't refer to your... professor like that, do you? I'll give you a couple of minutes to get changed in privacy. Though I'll only be seeing what I've already seen.'

Without waiting for a reply, Edith left.

Discarding what remained of his uniform, Gilmore dressed. When Edith returned, she was holding the shotgun.

'You should burn those,' Gilmore said, pointing to his uniform lying in a heap. 'And by should, I mean you must. Hide I was ever here.'

'You arrive here all torn up, asking for help. I think I'm owed an explanation.'

'It's... not safe.'

Edith arched an eyebrow. 'You don't say. Is your... Is Rachel all right?'

There was an old hurt there so obvious Gilmore couldn't miss it. 'She's fine,' he said, and then thought of Stanhope. Sudden panic flared in him.

Edith must've seen it in his face. 'What is going on, Ian?'

Gilmore glanced at his ex-wife. There was still something of the beauty that had drawn his eye after the war while he recovered from the injuries sustained on the Lancaster's return flight home. It should've worked, indeed, if he had been someone else, someone who had never had that night on the beach...

'It's all too much,' he said, shaking his head. 'The country faces a terrible danger and I have no earthly idea what to do about it.'

'You fight,' Edith said. 'You fight and you fight and you fight. That's all we can do, Ian. That's all we've ever been able to do.'

'You don't even know what I'm talking about.'

'There's the old Ian,' Edith said with real bitterness. 'The man who thought I was too stupid to stay married to. I don't have to understand what you're talking about. You arrive in the dead of night, covered in your own blood, wearing that bloody Browning. I see a man fleeing danger when he should be looking it square in the face. You let me down many, many times, Ian. I won't lie. But you were always someone who knew what was what, and what to do about it.'

'I'm sorry I disappointed you,' Gilmore said, voice barely above a whisper. An old shame haunted him. 'That failure is on me, not you.'

'I'm sure Rachel would disagree.' Edith looked aside, breathed in deeply. 'Are you happy?'

Glancing at her, Gilmore hesitated. He recognised the bittersweet look in her eyes.

'I... we, are.'

'And that lad of yours... Dillon, isn't it?'

'How do you know?'

'We still have mutual friends, Ian.'

Gilmore shook his head, smiling. 'He's a bright one. Smarter than his father, that's for sure.'

'Wouldn't be hard,' Edith said, glancing away again. When she looked back, she blinked rapidly. 'So, what will you do now? It sounds like the safety of the country depends upon you.'

'Avoid the people hunting me, get back to London, somehow bring a politician down before he betrays us all.' A sudden panicked thought gripped him. 'I had some things with me. A tape. And my wallet.'

Edith nodded. She went into the kitchen and returned with Gilmore's uniform jacket. Wrapped inside were the car keys, the black plastic tape Hannah had pressed into his hands as she lay dying, and his wallet.

'The blood on the tape is dry,' Edith said. 'It's not yours, is it?'

Gilmore shook his head. 'Someone... brave died tonight. I have to honour her sacrifice by getting that tape to the people who can use it.'

'Then you must succeed, Ian. For her sake. And yours.'

After adding the jacket to the pile of discarded clothing, Gilmore buckled the holster in place. Gingerly, he lifted the satchel's strap over his head and settled it against his hip. Picking up his wallet, he thumbed through the contents and found the card Bannerton had given him. After a moment's thought, he returned the tape and wallet to a pocket, then patted his trousers.

From the rear of her jeans, tucked into the belt, Edith took out Gilmore's Browning.

'Looking for this?' She handed it to him.

Gilmore nodded gratefully and holstered it. For a moment, they stood looking at each other, the clock on the wall ticking loudly. Gilmore coughed.

'I have to go.' He half turned, then looked back. 'Thank you, Edith. I... thank you.'

'Where will you go?'

'London. There's a man who needs to hear that tape. Afterwards... afterwards will take care of itself.'

Edith nodded. Gilmore went to the front door and opened it.

'Ian, wait.'

Gilmore turned and Edith was suddenly inside the circle of his arms. She kissed him on the lips, warmly, then stepped back. A flush bloomed on her cheeks.

'For old time's sake,' she said. 'We had some good times, didn't we?'

Gilmore nodded. A knot squeezed his throat. 'We did. You... you take care, Edith.'

Before Edith could respond, Gilmore stepped outside and walked to the car. Grunting, he slid behind the wheel and closed the door. Starting the engine, he glanced at the cottage and saw Edith framed in the doorway again.

He was about to drive off, when her words about fighting hit hard. He thought about the card in his wallet.

Raising a hand in salute, he drove off into the night.

CHAPTER TWENTY-TWO

Thursday – London. 5am.

'**ARE WE** doing the right thing?'

Rachel glanced at Anne, who looked nervously out of the window at a house looming over them. The engine cooled, the ticking filling the cabin. On their right stood a large rectangle of garden, hidden by the darkness. Distantly, they could hear traffic; delivery vans and trucks, the lifeblood of London.

'Walsingham has betrayed his country,' Rachel said.

Bishop nodded. His face was in shadow, and when he moved forward into the dim light afforded by a streetlamp farther along, it was set and determined.

'We brace this coward in his home, ask him a few questions. He'll tell us where his men are taking Allison and those technicians.'

'How?' Anne asked.

Bishop twisted in his seat. 'Not politely, that's for sure. This is the side of my work you've never really... liked. So, come on if you're coming, but only on the understanding that I have a job to do here.'

Anne swallowed. Looked at Rachel.

'Saving the world can have a cost,' Rachel said.

'Don't I know,' Anne muttered, and took a deep breath. 'Very well. Lead on, Bill.'

Houses lined the footpath in a deep 'U' that came in from Brompton Road, before turning on itself and exiting back into it. Cars lined the street; fancy cars, expensive cars. The buildings themselves were a mixture of exposed brick and stuccoed walls.

Wrought iron railings fronted many, and the doors gleamed in the faint light.

'This is how the other half live,' Bishop said. 'Built on the blood and bones of the rest of us. Of course, someone like Walsingham lives here.'

Clearly uncomfortable with her husband's attitude, Anne looked around. 'Do you know which one he lives in?'

'I do,' Rachel said. 'When he hired Ian, he invited us to dinner to celebrate. The food was awful muck.' She nodded to a house several doors up. 'It's that one.'

'Is Walsingham married?'

Rachel shook her head. 'Married to the job, he would say.'

'Staff?' Bishop asked.

'He served us himself when we had dinner, which probably explains why it was awful. Staff during the day, none at night. There certainly aren't any servant's quarters.'

'Any thoughts on getting inside?'

'He took the time to show us around. Top to bottom. All three floors and the garage. There's a small gate down a narrow lane. Come on, I'll show you.'

Rachel led the way, with Bishop and Anne behind him. They were soon confronted by high walls forming a constriction forcing them to walk single file. Rachel stood beside a gate, a shadow in the darkness. Bishop grabbed the bars and pulled. A chain and padlock rattled.

'No such luck,' Rachel said. 'Any ideas?'

Bishop looked the gate up and down. Gaps in the wrought iron bars offered a view into an expansive back garden, filled with trees. Branches moved in a slight breeze, and there was rain in the air. 'Wait here.'

Bishop returned in a few minutes, holding a tyre iron. He slotted it into the shackle, then, carefully, leaned into it. They all heard a muffled crack before the shackle few off. Bishop caught the padlock and pocketed it. He unwrapped the chain and left it piled on the ground.

'Cheap trash. You can be as wealthy as King Midas, but that doesn't stop people from cutting corners to save a few pennies.' Bishop turned the handle and the gate opened silently.

Inside, a patio led to a set of French doors. The lights were off. They could see shadowy furniture inside.

'No sign of a security system,' Bishop said. He cast around and took a stone from a garden bed. 'What do you reckon?' he said, hefting the stone.

'Try not to bring the whole neighbourhood down on our ears,' Anne said.

Bishop grinned, and Rachel shook her head. Clearly, Anne had lived a very different life to the one Rachel had previously imagined. She may have been a little more cautious than her husband, but Anne Bishop was no shrinking violet. She'd lived more than enough dangerous times, and, perhaps, had become a little bit blithe about them.

Rachel considered her few years in the Counter-Measures Group over a decade ago. Had she been so much different before the halls of learning tempered her once more?

Bishop smartly rapped a glass pane next to the handle. There was a pop, and a piece of glass fell out. It skittered across the parquetry flooring. They all froze, then, after a minute of silence, Bishop reached in and unlocked the French door.

The interior of the house was silent. There wasn't even the ticking of a clock to disturb the quiet. Gesturing, Rachel led them through the kitchen area, to a set of heavily carpeted stairs leading upwards.

'We got the grand tour,' Rachel whispered, leaning towards her companions.

Slowly, they ascended, the stairs turning at the landing then taking them to the first floor. Several dark doors lined a corridor.

Rachel led them to Walsingham's bedroom door. Gently, she turned the handle and pushed the door open. Darkness confronted them. Their eyes adjusted, and they could see a wide bed beneath the outlines of what was no doubt a gaudy looking chandelier. Rachel stayed with Anne by the door, while Bishop crept up to a huddled figure sleeping beneath satin sheets.

Bishop paused, then waved at Rachel. She flicked a switch.

A glare bright enough to put to shame the unveiling of the Blackpool Illuminations bloomed in the room. The figure in bed groaned and rolled onto his back, waving a hand feebly over his eyes as if that would keep the blinding light at bay.

'What the hell...?' was all he could mumble before Walsingham focused bleary eyes on Bishop, who stood over him, grinning.

'Be a good fella and keep your trap shut, eh?' Bishop grabbed Walsingham by the shoulders and dragged him from the bed and across the carpet to an overstuffed leather chair sitting in the corner.

Walsingham tried to put up a struggle but gave it up when Bishop shoved him into the chair.

With his silk pyjamas and bald head, Walsingham looked like a slightly eccentric professor trying to work out why the undergraduates were playing a prank on him. But as his eyes adjusted, and the sleepiness sloughed off him, his features became more alert. Anger bubbled beneath him.

'Who the bloody hell do you...? Rachel? What in God's name is going on?'

'I think you know, Peter,' Rachel said, softly. She walked over to him. He tried to stand, but Bishop shoved him back into the chair.

'I don't know anything of the sort. Tell your trained ape if he puts his hands on me again, I'll see that he...'

Rachel lifted a hand, and Walsingham's words jerked to a halt. Bishop could tell he didn't like being hushed.

'All we want is information,' she said. 'That's all.'

'Again, I have no idea why you're here. This is... this is criminal!'

'So is betraying your country,' Bishop said, leaning forward, his teeth bared.

'Bill,' Anne warned. He shot her a look, which she matched.

'Let me lay it out for you, Mr Walsingham, very clearly,' Bishop said, 'very succinctly. Your company has been dealing with the Soviets to gain access to Eastern Europe to sell arms. You are prepared to hand over secret technology and people to the Soviets relating to the Cerberus satellites, as a down payment for that access. Tell me if I'm getting warm.'

Walsingham looked at Bishop, then Anne and finally Rachel. He shook his head, and chuckled.

'You idiots are going to spend a very long time in jail over a fantasy. Not one syllable of what this fool has just said is—' Walsingham's voice grew strangled. He looked down and saw Bishop had buried the barrel of his pistol in his stomach. Bishop leaned forward.

'Your goons held my wife hostage. They shot one of her colleagues dead, in front of her. That's something a man can't forget or forgive. Anne's more forgiving. She doesn't want me to beat you within an inch of your dirty little life. I have far, far less scruples. Am I making myself understood?'

For the first time, Walsingham looked uncertain. He glanced pleadingly at Rachel.

'Rachel, I don't know what you've been told, but surely you trust me. Ian and I... We've done great things together with the firm. It's madness to think otherwise.'

'And yet here I am,' Rachel said quietly. She glanced around the room, taking in the rich furnishings and decor. 'You've done well, Peter. You started on the bottom rung. Had to fight tooth and claw to get to where you are today. But you've lost your moral compass, I very much fear. When was it I wonder that money replaced ambition? You should be remembered for reviving British industry in the arms sector, much as it sickens me. But we have incontrovertible proof that you've sold your soul to the Soviets.' She walked forward, stopping short of him. 'Where is Hemmings taking my colleagues? Tell us, and I'm sure our friend here won't shoot you. Dead men tell no tales, but I'm reliably informed that gut wounds are excruciating.'

Again, Walsingham looked at each of them in turn. This time, though, his face was slick with sweat and he had gone pale. He licked his lips, then, slowly, unwillingly at first, then in a babble of words that spoke of a man having held his guilt too closely for too long, he talked.

Later, as they drove away down Brompton Road, Anne spoke from the darkness in the back seat.

'Well, I feel thoroughly dirty after that.'

'So do I,' Bishop said. 'But we do what we must.'

'Speaking of must,' Rachel said, 'we must speak with Bambera. The government needs to be informed and the military is our best shot. After all, it's their fault we've got Armageddon floating over our heads. And the clock is ticking.'

Bishop nodded. He glanced in the rear vision mirror, and saw Anne staring out the window. 'He'll be at his London accommodation.'

The darkness was beginning to lighten a little, as a rosy glow painted the clouds.

'You wouldn't by chance have another weapon, would you, Major?'

'Rachel...' Anne sounded tired.

'It's fine, Anne. Major? Do you?'

Bishop shot Rachel a surprised look.

'Don't worry, I've had training,' Rachel explained.

'I've got several in a locked box in the back.'

'Very good. How long till we get there?'

'Fifteen minutes.'

CHAPTER TWENTY-THREE

Thursday – London. 6am.

GILMORE GRABBED a half hour of sleep after parking the car behind a copse of trees at the side of the road. After rousing himself, he pushed on to London, by way of a quick stopover in a county village. There, he surprised the postmaster. Once he had accomplished what he needed to do, Gilmore headed straight for London, venturing into the metropolis just before six. His shoulder was sore, but manageable. He flicked on the radio as the pips completed sounding, dreading what the news might bring.

'Police and the security services are currently looking for the whereabouts of Ian Gilmore, Woden Armaments consultant and a former air vice-marshal in the RAF. Gilmore was in attendance at the annual West Berlin arms fair but disappeared after an incident involving the West Berlin police, and elements of the East Berlin security forces. Authorities believe Mr Gilmore returned to England, though his current whereabouts is unknown. A spokesman for Woden Armaments refused to comment. It is understood Mr Gilmore is sought in connection with the death of a woman. Gilmore is considered armed and dangerous and should not be approached.

'Turning to other news now, reports of an oil rig on fire in the North Sea have been disputed by the government, which is preparing to enter caretaker mode with the calling of the General Election. The Department of Energy has released a statement which says that unusually fierce storm activity has resulted in a loss of communication with Brisingamen Platform in the North

Sea...'

Gilmore switched the radio off and shook his head in frustration.

Lies and more lies.

He stared out the car window, deep in thought.

'Bambera.'

Could he trust Bambera? After all, he had brought Stanhope and Gilmore together. But the way Bambera had spoken about his suspicions of Woden and Whateley...

'If Bambera doesn't help me, the whole show goes under, taking him as well.' Aware he was talking to himself and not liking it, Gilmore came to a quick decision.

Crossing the Thames, Gilmore drove north, away from Westminster. A few delivery trucks rumbled about, leaving the streets eerily empty. Gilmore turned off a main road and entered the leafy London suburb of Kensington.

Fingers of light stretched across the sky, pushing back the darkness. Driving slowly down a familiar street, Gilmore counted off the large townhouses lining both sides of the road.

'There you are.'

He drove past the building he had been looking for. He parked further along the road. Angling the rear-view mirror to give him the best view, Gilmore waited for a few minutes. The only foot traffic was an elderly man trailing behind his dog, which sniffed its way passed where Gilmore had parked.

Exiting the car, satchel in hand, he glanced up at the lightening sky. As the stars slowly disappeared, he sensed the orbiting Cerberus satellites, waiting to strike.

A cold wind blew, sending fallen leaves dancing along the footpath. Distant traffic hummed like a swarm of bees in summer. Gilmore caught glimpses of movement behind the windows of some of the homes, as families began their morning rituals. His heart suddenly ached for Rachel and Dillon. A deep weariness came over him and, with it, a burning anger.

'Now or never,' he muttered.

Looking around, Gilmore ducked into an alley that ran beside the townhouse he had marked earlier. A red brick wall formed the boundary of the townhouse. There was a gate set in the wall, but it was padlocked from the inside. Most of the people living in the street knew exactly who resided there but made it their business not to share that knowledge with the outside world. It was a peculiarity that Gilmore often remarked upon that the Minister of Defence, with the entire British Armed Forces at his disposal, had almost nothing in the way of personal security. The British belief that no one in their right mind would attack a Minister was about to prove extremely useful to Gilmore.

'Bloody hubris.'

Using the cracks in the wall, Gilmore clambered up and over it, dropping into the garden on the other side. He did his best to ignore his aching shoulder. He knelt for a moment, senses ranging out. The shadowy garden was empty. Bushes screened the rear wall. A silent fountain sat at the centre of a neatly clipped lawn, itself bordered by a garden bed. Steps led up to the back door.

Gilmore tested it and found it locked. Patting his pockets, he noticed that Edith had left a handkerchief in one. Silently thanking her, he wrapped it around the butt of the Browning, and rapped hard on a small window beside the door. There was a muffled crack. Gilmore picked out a few pieces, which allowed to reach in and undo the lock.

The door opened silently. Closing it, he walked through the laundry and out into a corridor. Somewhere deep within the house, a clock ticked quietly to itself. The television and radio were silent. Gilmore did a quick recce. It was, as he suspected, empty, brooding while it waited for its master's return.

Whether Bambera was staying in the city after a night of Cabinet meetings, or seeing a secret lover, Gilmore didn't care a whit. Bambera would return. Gilmore could wait.

At the kitchen sink, Gilmore washed his hands and his face, glad to feel clean after the events of the past day. He glanced at his reflection in the window, not liking the new lines cutting deep into either side of his mouth, nor the pools of darkness within which his red-rimmed eyes glimmered.

Filling a glass of water from the kitchen tap, he drank it, then went to the refrigerator and opened the door. Some leftover casserole presented itself, and without bothering to heat it, Gilmore wolfed it down while standing over the sink. He left the remains sitting on the sideboard, then went to find Bambera's study.

Fifteen minutes later, he heard a car stop in the street. Indistinct words with the driver, then the sound of the car driving away. Footsteps on the pavement, then up to the door. It opened silently. Gilmore heard the clatter of autumnal leaves across the front path. The door closed. A heavy tread approached the study, then it veered away towards the kitchen. He didn't hear anything for a few minutes.

In the darkness of the study, seated with his back to the window and facing the doorway, Gilmore's patience eventually bore fruit.

'So, you're alive.' A bulky shadow filled the doorway. 'I hope you liked my dinner.'

In the gloom, Gilmore could see Bambera's glittering eyes. He reached across and turned on the desk lamp. On his knee, Gilmore rested the Browning, the barrel not pointed at Bambera. Yet.

'It was passably good,' Gilmore said. 'My compliments to your housekeeper.' He indicated the other chair with the pistol. 'Sit down.'

Bambera did as instructed, the chair creaking beneath his bulk. The man looked exhausted.

'Busy night? You're missing out on your London residence. The taxpayers will shake their heads.'

'PM got it in his head he wanted to have a crisis meeting about the satellites. Couldn't make his mind up what was more important – the impact on the election campaign if the news gets out, or the prospect of British cities burning.'

'What was decided?'

Bambera flicked his hand dismissively. 'Nothing. Lots of talk. I think they hope to sweep it under the carpet long enough to worry about later.' He leaned forward. 'How did you survive? According to the reports I've seen, the safe house is a burned-out ruin, and the area is littered with corpses.'

'Luck,' Gilmore said, bitterly. 'Have you heard from Stanhope?'

Bambera shook his head. He looked uncomfortable. 'Should I?'

'Pray you don't.' Gilmore waved his hand at Bambera's quirked eyebrow. 'I'll get to that in a moment. Do you trust me?'

'You've got a gun in your hand and I'm still alive. On balance, I'd have to say yes, but only just.'

Gilmore watched Bambera for a few moments, while the Minister did the same to him.

'I take it you've heard the news?' Bambera said, breaking the silence.

'On the radio. No doubt the printing presses in Fleet Street are running hot. You've done a good job stitching me up for what happened in West Berlin and that safe house.'

'You're wrong,' Bambera said, nostrils flaring. 'What has happened over the last day has nothing to do with me or the government.'

'Don't you dare sit there after what's happened and lie to me.' Gilmore tapped the barrel of the pistol on his knee in agitation. 'Stanhope's a traitor, did you know that? Stanhope and that bloody Whateley.'

Eyes narrowing, Bambera opened his mouth, then closed it. After a few seconds, he spoke.

'Tell me everything. Tell me what happened in West Berlin.'

Gilmore wasn't a Catholic, but the next few minutes were what he suspected confessing to a priest felt like. The words spilled from him in a torrent, chapter and verse of the betrayal that had cost lives and threatened the nation.

'So, Stanhope killed his own agent and Whateley has a GRU handler?' Bambera said, incredulous.

'Succinctly put.' Gilmore dismissed the idea of telling Bambera about the recording. He wanted his own revenge, safe from the hands of a meddling politician. He shook his head, then stopped as a memory surfaced. 'I saw something on the flight back; a massive shaft of light, in the North Sea. Don't tell me there's storm activity out there.'

Bambera pinched the bridge of his nose, as if trying to contain a headache. Gilmore saw how exhausted the Minister looked.

'That shaft of light was one of the Cerberus satellites. It was tested again.'

'Could the Soviets have control of the satellites?'

'I think it is too soon. We've been working our sources inside the Kremlin. No one is saying anything, and someone always says something if it is happening. The Foreign Secretary called

182

in the Soviet ambassador overnight, gave him a roasting about flight incursions over Scotland as a cover to see if there was anything he would give away about the destruction of the rig. Nothing. If the Soviets had control of the Cerberus satellites, we'd know by now.'

'You'd be better off leaking the news to the press,' Gilmore said. 'That would get a response from everyone, the Soviets included. You'd know about leaking, after what you did to me.'

'I did not leak to the press what happened at the safe house,' Bambera snapped. 'What would I have to gain?'

'A damned scapegoat, that's what. A convenient one, on the eve of an election.'

'You think I leaked this to the press? Cabinet dithered over the satellites, but they're right to wait and hope that things turn out all right. You're many things, Air Vice Marshal, but you're no politician.'

'Thank God for that,' Gilmore said, bitterly. 'I've served my country my entire adult life. I've supplied more information on Woden's misdeeds than you've been able to get your hands on in years and now I'm being called a traitor the length and breadth of the country. You'll forgive me if I don't believe everything that comes out of your mouth.'

'Why would I turn the guns on my own side?'

'When was I ever on your side?' Gilmore asked, almost shouting. With a visible effort, he calmed himself. 'From the very beginning, I've been pushed and pulled into doing something I wanted no part.'

'No part? I've never seen someone so thankful to be given such a thankless task as spying on their own employer. You were rotting away in the shadows, Gilmore. I pulled you back into the light.'

'And the thanks I get is to be effectively blackmailed into clearing my wife's name, and now we're both in the frame for treason.'

'Ian,' Bambera said, leaning forward in his chair to emphasise his words. 'I did not set you up. I have had suspicions about Woden's activities stretching back almost a decade.'

Gilmore's eyes grew wide. 'Almost a decade? And you didn't tell me that when you asked me to spy on them?' He paused, calculating. 'Woden have been selling secrets to the Soviets for that long?'

Bambera nodded. 'Even when I was serving, there was muttering that whatever Woden supplied under contract, we would be facing the same on the battlefield if it ever came to the big show in Europe.'

'And no one did anything?'

'No one could do anything. The bloody Establishment... A bunch of parasites who look after their own. The same people in the same families for generations... They dine together, drink together, go shooting together, bed each other's wives. And they tolerate treason, you mark my words.' Bambera leaned forward. 'Ask yourself, why didn't Oswald Mosley dance from the end of a rope when the war finished, eh? One hand washes the other while the nation is sold down the river to its enemies.'

By the time Bambera had finished, sweat stood out on his brow. 'I entered politics to try and clean the whole mess up. But it's worse than I ever imagined.'

'All right then,' Gilmore said. 'If you didn't tell the press, who did? It can't just have been Stanhope.'

'Stanhope? He's the last link at the end of a very long chain. I trusted the man, and he's betrayed us all.' Bambera shook his head. 'It's the same people. Woden. Their mates in the security services. There's talk of groups, or an association of them, far in the background, who have used Woden for their own ends. But other than a whisper, there's never been any evidence.'

'Until now,' Gilmore said. Wincing, he reached into the satchel and pulled out the paperwork Gorkovich had given his life to bring to the West. He handed it to Bambera.

'This is it,' the Minister said, after spending several minutes silently paging through the documents. 'This is the whole show.'

'That's definitive proof that Woden's documentation was leaked to the Soviets. Their seal is all over that paperwork. What about Whateley?'

'You're certain it was Whateley who met with a GRU officer?'

Gilmore nodded. 'I was as close to him then as I am to you now. And the woman Stanhope killed, Hannah Gordon. She confirmed Whateley was talking to a high-ranking member of the GRU.'

'And the attack on the safe house. Was it the Soviets? Were they with Stanhope?'

'No. The attackers only spoke English. They were our own.'

Bambera abruptly stood and began pacing his study. He didn't seem to care that Gilmore still held a weapon on him.

'Worse and worse,' Bambera said. 'Whateley in the pocket of the Soviets. If he gets anywhere near Downing Street after the election... And if those forces I mentioned earlier have allied themselves with the Soviets, it's worse than I—'

Glass exploded from the study window. Bambera spun around and collapsed at Gilmore's feet. Instinctively, Gilmore smashed the desk light with the Browning and dropped to the carpeted floor. Bambera was breathing heavily.

'Sniper,' he managed through gritted teeth.

'Where are you hit?' Gilmore moved to a position behind Bambera.

'Chest,' Bambera said. He was still lucid, though his voice whistled.

Gilmore grabbed Bambera by the shoulder as more slugs blew out the window. One ruffled Gilmore's hair, and he cringed away, but dragged Bambera into the corridor and out of the direct line of fire.

The firing stopped, leaving an echoing silence disturbed by Bambera's ragged breathing. Gilmore worked by touch in the gloom. He felt a hot damp patch underneath Bambera's right collar bone, and further examination elicited a grunt of pain from the minister. Shuffling around, Gilmore examined the opposite side of Bambera's shoulder by touch. He couldn't feel an exit wound.

'Bullet's still in you. Probably stopped you bleeding out on your own floor.'

'I'll buy a ticket for the pools then,' Bambera said. His breathing had settled.

'We have to get you out of here.'

A sudden noise from the rear of the house had Gilmore on his feet in one swift movement, the Browning held out before him. After a moment's hesitation, he moved past the entrance to the study, and crept down the corridor towards the kitchen.

An awful tension gripped the townhouse. Darkness claimed it. A door creaked, and a shadow climbed a wall. Gilmore was about to shoot, when more gunfire poured through the shattered remains of the window in the study, shredding the wall opposite.

'I will shoot to kill!' Gilmore shouted, moving forward, bent at the waist.

He stopped by the door into the kitchen, holding his breath, feeling the thud of his heart. He counted to three, reached into the kitchen, slapped on the light and rushed forward.

A man aimed a gun at Gilmore's head. For a moment, the two men glared at each other over their gun sights. Gilmore felt his finger tighten on the trigger, then, impossibly, a familiar voice rang out.

'Ian. For God's sake, don't shoot him.'

Gilmore saw Rachel standing by the sink. She pointed the weapon she held at the floor. A woman he vaguely recalled stood beside her, face white. The man confronting him glanced at Rachel.

'You know him?'

'He's my husband, Major Bishop. Ian, what are you doing here?'

'I might ask the same thing, my dear,' Gilmore said, warily watching Major Bishop. Cautiously, he lowered his weapon. Bishop did the same. 'Major Bishop... That name rings a bell.' He nodded at the other woman. 'Which makes you... Anne Travers. Lethbridge-Stewart's old team.' Gilmore jerked a thumb over his shoulder. 'I'd love to chat, but I've got the Minister of Defence lying on the floor in the corridor with a bullet in his shoulder. Someone just tried to assassinate him.'

Bishop started, swore, then ducked through the kitchen door. Gilmore and Rachel looked at each other for a moment, then he went over and folded her in his arms. He winced as she hugged him.

'Are you hurt?' Rachel stepped back, seeing the sticky plaster on his forehead for the first time.

'Just a flesh wound.' Gilmore tapped his shoulder with the Browning and hissed.

'A flesh wound, really?'

'It's fine. Far better than what I've unearthed.'

'How bad is it?'

'Apart from treason and subversion, and the sniper peppering the townhouse with slugs, and the fact your technology has been stolen and used to make satellites armed with laser arrays, it's pretty bad. What are you doing here,

Rachel?'

'Devesham is... We had to escape.'

'Escape? What the hell happened?'

'Woden's what happened. They've sold the secret of my research to the Soviets for access to the East European market.'

'I know,' Gilmore said. 'I'd love to compare notes, but time is short.'

'If you three could stop chatting for a moment,' Bishop called out, 'I'd love some help with Bambera.'

'The both of you keep an eye on the back door,' Gilmore said, before joining Bishop in the corridor.

Together, the two men carried Bambera into the kitchen and settled him on the floor.

'How bad is he?' Rachel said.

'Tell your wife I won't bleed to death on her account,' Bambera said.

Under the kitchen light, the blood on his shirt was startlingly red. Bishop began pulling open drawers, quickly returning with several dishcloths.

'We have to get him out of here,' he said, kneeling beside Bambera.

'I agree,' Gilmore said. 'Any idea how you propose to do that without being ventilated by our sniper friend?'

Bishop folded a dishcloth and pressed it to Bambera's wound. The Minister groaned.

The front door rang out under a series of blows. They all heard the crack of splintering wood. Moving to the kitchen entrance, Gilmore ducked into the corridor for a moment, and saw the dim outline of a figure through the shattered front door.

Gilmore fired at the door, the Browning's bark loud in the confines of the corridor. The figure in the door spun away, shrieking.

Glass shattered in the kitchen. Turning back, Gilmore saw Anne retreat as a figure climbed through the window. Both Gilmore and Rachel fired simultaneously, and the figure fell forward onto the floor. Gilmore went to the body and rolled it onto its back. He pulled off the balaclava, revealing a pale face. The eyes opened.

'You think you're so clever,' Gilmore said, leaning forward. 'Follow me at a distance, knowing I'd have to meet Bambera with the information I have. Then kill him and pin the blame on me. Disgruntled ex-RAF officer goes mad in a murder-suicide pact. Who are you?'

'We're the coming storm,' the figure said, choking on blood.

Gilmore heard the floorboards in the main corridor creak. Signalling to Bishop, they aimed and fired through the wall several times. A cloud of plaster bloomed in the air. They all heard a grunt, then the sound of a body hitting the floor.

Cautiously, Gilmore stepped into the corridor and saw the man slumped against the wall. A rifle with a telescope attached fell from nerveless fingers. Gilmore kicked it aside and checked the man for a pulse. Nothing.

Gilmore returned to the man he and his wife had shot. Rachel knelt beside him. She looked at Gilmore. 'He's still alive. Barely.'

'Your sniper friend is dead. You're the only one left alive. Who are you?' Gilmore repeated, kneeling beside the man.

Eyelids fluttered; the eyes glacial blue. A shock of white hair gleamed in the low light.

'Race traitors like you will find out soon enough,' he said, revealing blood-stained teeth. His back suddenly arched and he coughed, spraying blood into the air. His eyes fixed on Bambera, and his teeth pulled back in a snarl. Then his head lolled to one side.

Silence descended over the townhouse. Bambera's laboured breathing replaced the echoes of gunfire. A dog barked somewhere down the street. Gilmore felt the urge to run.

'I'll call for help,' Rachel said, reaching the phone.

Once the call had been placed, she turned back to her husband.

'You can't be here. Not with half the police force looking for you.'

'Someone has to stay with Bambera,' Gilmore said.

'We have to go north,' Rachel insisted. She looked at Anne, then Bishop. 'We spoke with Walsingham and—'

'When?' Gilmore looked incredulous.

'In the last hour,' Bishop said. 'He didn't want to speak but...'

'We didn't give him much choice,' Anne said.

'He's not in a good place,' Rachel said, with some satisfaction. 'And he talked. Remarkable how quickly a bully folds when pressure is applied.'

Glancing at Bishop, Gilmore decided he didn't want to know what sort of tactics had been used to make Walsingham talk.

'What's up north?' he asked instead.

'The Devesham Mission Control team, or part of it,' Anne said. She glanced at Rachel.

'They've kidnapped an old colleague of ours,' Rachel said. 'Allison Williams.'

'Allison?' Gilmore shook his head. He hadn't seen her in years. It was like the Counter-Measures Group was being drawn back together. 'What the devil do they want with Allison?'

'She'll be handed over to the Soviets,' Anne said.

'The government doesn't control the satellites,' Rachel said. 'Woden does, or at least they will, if we let them get away with the Devesham team.'

'How long do we have?' Gilmore asked.

'Woden has already sunk a naval vessel in the Indian Ocean. And destroyed an oil rig in the North Sea. We heard about that on the radio. There's a countdown happening now to another attack, possibly somewhere in London. We've only got a few hours to retrieve the Devesham team from Jura. If the attack succeeds, you can bet Whateley will raise hell about it. It'll be enough to swing the election his way.'

'Don't worry about Whateley,' Gilmore said, thinking of the note he had left with the tape recording. He looked at Bambera. 'Make sure no one touches Whateley. He'll condemn himself out of his own mouth, and soon enough.'

Bambera nodded, though he looked unsure.

'You'll just have to trust me, Minister,' Gilmore said. He turned to the others. 'Let's focus on right now, shall we? Jura? It sounds like the kidnappers have got too much of a head start. We'll never make it in time by road.'

'Then we fly, dear,' Rachel said.

Gilmore looked nonplussed at her. He was running on fumes. 'Fly?' he asked, aware he was missing something obvious.

'The flying school near home. The Piper?'

Gilmore could've kicked himself. He looked at Bishop. 'This is for me and Rachel to sort out.'

Bishop nodded. 'We'll stay with Bambera,' he said, looking at his wife. 'I've got men scattered here, there and everywhere, who need to be in barracks. My operation is... not quite sanctioned, certainly not by Fugglestone.'

'You can't spare any men?' Gilmore asked.

Bishop started to shake his head, then stopped. 'I have a few friends up Jura way. Ex-Fifth. I'll make some calls. Expect some friendly faces when you land on the island.'

'Minister?' Rachel said. 'Can you spare some men?'

'There's no time,' Bambera said. 'If you're going, you have to go now.'

Gilmore nodded. There was something of the general he had once been still within Bambera. He looked at Bishop.

'Thanks for looking after Rachel.'

'I daresay she'd say the opposite,' Bishop said, smiling ruefully.

'I daresay,' Rachel said, drily.

Bishop looked around the ruined kitchen. 'Good luck, Professor. It's been quite an experience.'

'It certainly has,' Rachel said. She stepped forward and embraced Anne. 'We'll get Allison back. Don't you worry.'

'Give them hell, Rachel,' Anne said. She looked at Gilmore. 'Both of you.'

'Whatever transport you have, ours is better,' Bishop said. 'Plus, it has the virtue of being loaded with enough military ordinance to invade a small nation. Our friends in the north will appreciate the help. Here.' Bishop tossed Gilmore the keys to his Land Rover.

Rachel stepped forward and caught them deftly. 'You look like Hell, Ian. I'll drive, you get some sleep.' She tucked her pistol into a pocket. 'Ready to save the country, Mr Gilmore?'

He could only smile. 'Always,' he said, with a grin. 'And it's group captain now.'

'Really?' Rachel seemed less than impressed. 'You men and your titles. Come along, then.'

CHAPTER TWENTY-FOUR

Thursday – London. 6.50am.

RACHEL DROVE only a few streets before she began peppering Gilmore with questions. She was, Gilmore reflected, less than satisfied with some of his revelations. *So much for having a rest,* he ruefully thought.

'I understand why you were spying for Bambera,' she said, after they left London via the A10. 'Woden is an awful organisation, and they've clearly betrayed the country, and stolen my research. But why didn't you tell me?'

Gilmore chewed on the thought for a minute. 'I suppose if I did, it would be an admission I was bored and frustrated with my life.'

'You're bored and frustrated with Dillon and I?'

'Of course not. It was just hard to admit that after a lifetime of service, I was surplus to requirements. I had done things, important things, and now I was forced out. It stung.' He looked at his wife, then reached out and touched her shoulder. 'But I was never bored and frustrated with you or Dillon. You are the only things keeping me... The only bright light in a life suddenly dimmed.'

For a long stretch of time, an uncomfortable silence descended over them.

'And... Edith. You saw Edith.'

'I did,' Gilmore said. He had debated leaving that part of his story out, but there had been too many secrets in their marriage in recent months.

'I suppose I should thank her for patching you up. How is

your shoulder?'

Gilmore moved his arm. It still hurt, but the bandage felt secure. 'Better than it was before I saw her. She did ask after Dillon, if that's any interest.'

'She has at least one redeeming feature, then,' Rachel said. 'But don't make a habit of visiting her. The warmth I'm feeling towards her is a fragile thing, let me tell you.'

Gilmore chuckled at that, which immeasurably improved the atmosphere of the drive.

'All done,' Gilmore said, closing the Land Rover's tailgate.

It had been somewhat unnerving transferring several long rifles and ammunition onto the Piper, but he had seen the necessity of it. He had completed his pre-flight checks on arrival, so it was only a matter of a few minutes before they were taxiing towards the runway. Gilmore had a flash of memory from fleeing West Berlin, and marvelled at how much had happened in such a short period of time.

'Buckle up,' he said to his wife as he slipped on a pair of headphones.

Settled into his seat, Gilmore's eyes ran over the instrument board one final time, then, satisfied, he opened the throttle. Their speed picked up, and soon they were racing down the runway. There was a bump, and then they were climbing into the air, Cambridge falling away as Gilmore turned the Piper in a wide arc and pointed the nose north.

'Next stop Jura,' he said, flashing a smile at his wife.

'Very good, dear,' Rachel said, looking out her window at the lightening landscape below. 'By the way, do you know if Jura has a landing strip?'

As it turned out, Jura did have a landing strip, a long stretch of grass that ended at a cliff overlooking the sea. It was Rachel's turn to rest, and she dozed for much of the flight. The hum of the engines proved a comfort to Gilmore, who relished being in the air without the thought of East German fighter planes being dispatched to shoot him out of the sky.

When the navigational beacon chimed, Gilmore started his descent routine. The Piper's rudimentary navigational system locked onto the beacon on the island. Rachel woke at the sound of the beacon. Rubbing her eyes, she sat up.

'Have we arrived?'

'In a few minutes,' Gilmore said, looking out the window on his side and spotting the landing strip.

The grassy runway provided a bumpy landing, but not dangerously so. Gilmore saw sheep standing in tight huddles on either side of the runway, testimony to the rural nature of the island. The airstrip was deserted apart from a pair of Range Rovers that sat waiting beside what looked like a shed.

'Is that Bishop's welcoming party?' Gilmore said.

'It has to be.'

And so it proved when Rachel and Gilmore disembarked. Four men, all burly looking farm types, emerged from the Range Rovers. Gilmore decided, as he approached them, they had the look of wolves leashed for too long.

'Gentlemen,' Gilmore said, stopping short of them.

'Group Captain Gilmore, is it?' the man closest to Gilmore asked. He had a luxuriant moustache, and a suspicious look in his eyes.

'The very same,' Gilmore replied.

'The last captain I met, I knocked out,' the man said. He turned his head and spit. 'Will it be the same this time?'

'Depends.'

'On what?'

'Whether I knock you out first.'

The man glared at him for a moment, before the men behind him broke into laughter.

'Go easy, Jock,' one of the men said, a relatively youthful looking man compared to his companions.

'I take it you're all ex-Fifth Operational Corps?' Rachel said.

'Well, according to a piece of paper I signed, my answer is I don't know what you're talking about.' More laughter from the other men. Jock looked Rachel up and down. 'Who might you be?'

'Judging by this conversation, the brains.' That provoked more laughter.

'The brains it is,' Jock said. 'All right,' he said, as rain began slanting down. 'What's this mission that the major had me pulled away from my breakfast for?'

With the weather worsening, they all piled into the shed

that proved to be part weather station, part office. Maps were pinned to several cork boards, and a desk was jammed into one corner. There was a small sink, a hotplate, and to everyone's satisfaction, a kettle and a tin of coffee. As Rachel rustled up some brews, she laid out the situation.

'You've seen things that you could never tell your wives or your girlfriends. This is the same,' Rachel said, bringing over a tray full of steaming cups. The men gathered around and took a cup each. 'A group of traitors have kidnapped British scientists and are travelling here to sell them to the Soviets. If we don't stop them, the Soviets will have their hands on technology which will allow them to dominate the world.'

Rachel's words dropped like a stone in a well. The men looked at each other and nodded.

'Saved the world a few times with the Fifth, Miss,' Jock said. 'I can stand to do it again, if you've a mind to.'

'Oh, we do,' Gilmore said. He pulled a relief map of Jura off the wall and spread it out over the desk. 'You men are locals. You tell me where on this coast a submarine can safely surface.'

The day dragged on. The rain came and went, before settling. Soon enough, the afternoon was shading into darkness when the telephone rang in the shed. Gilmore, who had been dozing, jumped. Oscar answered it. The other men, Jock, Angus and Simon, watched coolly.

'It has, has it? Make sure the ferry turns back. There will be no one leaving Jura tonight without our say so, all right?' He hung up. 'Last ferry from the mainland. My uncle tells me they dropped off a small bus, with blacked out windows. It's heading to the northern cove right now.'

'That's our cue,' Gilmore said. He looked at Rachel. 'I take it you won't stay behind?'

'Not for all the tea in India.'

'I assume she knows how to handle herself,' Jock said, cocking an eyebrow at Rachel.

Rachel pulled the pistol from her belt, removed, racked the slide and caught the ejected bullet. She glanced at Jock, smirked, thumbed the bullet back into the magazine, and slapped the magazine into the Browning. Then she cocked the hammer and pointed it at Jock's head.

'The safety is on, Miss,' he said in a soft voice. Then he smiled, his moustache bristling. 'If this pale Sassenach proves too soft for you, would you take up with a red-blooded Scotsman?'

'You men,' Rachel said, uncocking the hammer and shoving the Browning into her belt again. 'And the answer is no,' she said to general laughter. 'Ian is man enough for me. Now, are we going to stand around all night talking, or get the job done?'

Rachel squeezed into one Range Rover, and Gilmore into the other. While the men had brought their shotguns, they eagerly accepted the semi-automatics that Gilmore took out of the Piper.

With Gilmore's vehicle in the lead, the little convoy began making their way towards the northern coast.

'High tide's in half an hour?' Gilmore asked, checking his watch.

'Aye,' Jock said, turning the wheel as they exited the airfield. 'Don't worry, laddie. We'll be there in time to give those dirty Russkies a fine old welcome, don't you worry.'

The bus bounced and swayed over the rough road. The trip north had been a nightmare. After being hustled into a bus with blacked out windows, Allison had watched as the guards had lifted the Child into the rear of the vehicle, through the emergency exit. Seats had been removed beforehand to provide space. Allison and the few technicians with her were then forced aboard. A half dozen guards, who had escaped the attack, rode with them, with Hemmings seated at the front. At speed, they had left Mission Control, driving through the sleeping village, before emerging into the open and driving off into the night.

They stopped after a few hours. From the rear, Allison heard Hemmings arguing with someone. The bus turned off the main road north, and ventured down country lanes for half an hour before stopping in an ill-tended layby. There, with the atmosphere in the bus rank with the closed in atmosphere and tension, they waited.

Close to sunset, the bus started again, and they drove off. It seemed that Hemmings had been spooked about being on the open road during the day. Now, with darkness claiming the land, they sped north again.

Most of the technicians were dozing when they came to the ferry. Not even the swaying and jolting as the bus drove onto, then shortly afterwards, off the ferry disturbed them. Allison hadn't slept at all. She sat at the rear of the bus, tending to the Child.

'How are you doing?' Allison whispered. She didn't expect an answer. She was still experiencing some shock at the events of the last day. It comforted her to speak to someone who wasn't pointing a gun at her head.

Hemmings stood at the head of the bus, gripping a metal pole while giving instructions to the driver. There was a wild look in his eyes, as if he didn't quiet expect to be where he was. The pistol strapped to his waist was clearly visible.

'I'm not doing well,' Allison whispered, as if confiding to a girlfriend. 'Everything I've worked for the last five years... We were meant to be doing something good, to benefit not only Britain, but the world. Faster communication, the spreading of ideas more easily than ever before. And all for nothing. I've been tricked. Used. We've delivered a weapons platform capable of reducing a city to cinders.'

Allison looked into the Child's eyes. They were dreamy, occluded, hiding secrets only the girl who had grown into a broken adult knew. Hesitant at first, Allison reached up and pulled aside a strand of hair from her face.

'What we did to you, Judith. That was unforgiveable.'

The bus lurched, throwing Allison against the casing within which the Child sat. She looked ahead again and saw that they had breasted a rise. Moonlight shimmered like quicksilver on the waves in the bay ahead of them.

She heard Hemmings' voice begin to rise, then the front window of the bus blew in.

Simon Hemmings felt his pulse thudding in his ears. He was furious; not at himself, because Simon Hemmings had spent a lifetime ensuring someone else was always to blame. Walsingham, Woden, those bloody women at Devesham. He blamed them.

The mission had gone to schedule, until those three shrews had concocted a plan to bring it all crashing down around him. He and some of his men had got away, but not in the manner, or with all the people, that the plan demanded.

Now he was here, trapped on this bus, without all his men, getting ready for the hand off. He glanced to the back of the bus.

The technicians were all asleep. Weak and soft, they dozed in their seats. Only that woman, one of the Gorgons, Allison Williams, remained awake, tending to that *thing* encased inside that tin can.

For months, he had tolerated Rachel Gilmore's high-handed manner to the breaking point, listened to the inane chit chat of Allison and Anne about their personal lives, but he could not cope with the creature they so relied on to ensure the satellites worked as intended. If it were up to him, he'd have put a bullet in the thing's head and be done with it.

He didn't like to admit it, but he had panicked on the drive north. No one had responded to his calls on the walkie-talkie. He was flying blind. The decision to get off the main road had been his to make, despite the objections of some of his men. Whatever the cause of the communications problems, he was getting these people to Jura, come Hell or high water. And indeed, it proved fortuitous, as their arrival was now timed to the approach of high tide.

High tide, and transport to the East.

The ferry operator gave them an odd look; a bus with blacked out windows. But some cash and a quick word purchased agreement and silence, and soon enough, they were rolling off onto Jura.

The road wound around and around, through wild pastures and sheep farmer's crofts that seemed to merge with the countryside. Rain whipped the bus and the temperature plunged as the night drew in. Hemmings was looking forward to dumping his cargo with their new masters, and then hightailing it for sunnier climes.

Dreams of the Caribbean were interrupted when the bus lurched as it breasted a rise. His grip on the metal pole tightened, and Hemmings leaned forward, looking towards the open harbour and the waves, dark as metal, glinting in the moonlight.

'That's the place. Get us down there n—'

The front window blew in.

CHAPTER TWENTY-FIVE

Thursday – Jura, Scotland. 9pm.

THE RAIN turned to sleet and the temperature hovered just above zero. Behind them, waves crashed on a narrow shingle beach, which was bounded by twin spits of land.

'Out there are the remains of the German navy,' Jock said after they had parked the Range Rovers behind a fold of land off the main track. 'Scuttled after the war.' He pointed to the Scapa Flow, the body of water that separated several islands in this part of the North Sea. 'You English then decided it would be better to salvage most of it for your foundries. Fella who did it lost his shirt, but now it's basically open water out there. Perfect for a submarine.'

Gilmore listened stoically to the history lesson while feeding ammunition into his submachine gun. 'How's the tide? Must be running high now.'

'Aye, it's just about hit its peak,' Jock said.

The other men, and Rachel, were spread out on either side of the track, which was wide enough to accommodate a large vehicle. Or a bus, as Rachel had pointed out earlier. There was a turning circle at the bottom of the track and the beach itself.

'I want to minimise casualties as much as possible,' Rachel told them after they arrived. 'I've got people on that bus I care about. I don't want to be attending their funerals because someone got too excited.'

'She's a firecracker, this one, Group Captain,' Jock said. 'No, Ma'am, we're more interested in keeping those dirty Russkies jumping and dodging than killing our own.' He turned to the other men. 'All right, you lads know how to stage an ambush. Only this time, it should work – we're fighting Brezhnev's boys, not grubby little green fellas who want to eat your faces. Get lively,' he said, his voice descending into the sergeant's growl he used when in the service. The men scattered.

'Promise me you'll stay out of the line of fire,' Gilmore said to his wife, who stood gazing at the water.

'I'll do no such thing,' she said, turning to him. Her face was white and her eyes wide and shining. 'I fought in the war, just like you. I survived Shoreditch, just like you, and survived more than my fair share of dangerous situations with the Counter-Measures Group, just like you. I'm not afraid of some thugs who have betrayed our country.'

Smiling, Gilmore enveloped his wife in a hug, ignoring the whistles of the nearby men.

'That's my girl,' he said. Letting her go, Gilmore saluted her. 'Give them hell, Rachel.'

The growl of an engine rolled over them. Gilmore saw a bus crest the rise at the top of the track, and begin a slow, careful descent. At that moment, Jock called out, pointing to the water. An uprush of bubbles from several hundred yards out was clearly visible in the moonlight. Amid that turmoil emerged a coning tower, blacker than night.

'That's it,' Gilmore said. 'Here we go.'

Seeking cover, Rachel rushed over to the other side of the track. Gilmore remained in place.

With half the team keeping an eye on the water, and the other half on the bus' approach, Gilmore had time to review the plan. It was basic; a hammer where he preferred a scalpel's blade. But time and circumstances dictated otherwise. Taking careful aim, he fired.

The bus's front window blew in, revealing the driver with an arm up to protect his face. A shadowy figure standing next to the driver glittered with shards of broken glass. Sporadic gunfire began, pinging off the bus, designed to keep anyone armed inside down. The bus lurched to one side, ran off the track and buried its nose into an earthen wall formed by a fold of land.

Scattered firing began from behind them. A rubber dinghy, filled with half a dozen marines, rapidly approached them, its outboard motor buzzing.

'Here come the Russkies!' Jock shouted, his voice full of excited delight.

He and his men began peppering the dinghy, which took evasive action, dodging left and right as it rode the waves racing to shore. One of the men cried out and toppled into the water. The others hunkered down as best they could. The dinghy ran aground several hundred yards away, the metal hull grinding along the single beach before coming to a stop. The survivors clambered out and scattered across the beach and vainly sought shelter. Firing began in earnest.

With the Soviets pinned down, Gilmore took the opportunity to approach the bus. Desultory fire came from one of the broken windows, sending up plumes of dirt around his feet. Seeking refuge against the side of the bus, Gilmore saw his wife coming up closely behind him.

'Are you sure you'd rather not be back with the Piper, dear?'

'I'd sooner be here, by your side, making sure you don't make a hash of things.' Clearly enjoying herself despite the danger, Rachel smiled broadly.

'They are trying to kill us.' Gilmore slung the submachine gun over his shoulder then took out his Browning.

'I won't hold it against them as long as they keep missing. What are you planning?'

'Frontal assault. Have to hope the crash took most of them out.'

At that moment, one of the blacked-out windows shattered, revealing a familiar face.

'Ian Gilmore? Rachel? What the hell are you doing here?' It was Allison Williams, more careworn than when he had last seen her at his wedding.

'Rescue mission,' he shouted. 'How many armed men are inside?'

'One,' Allison said. 'The accident took care of almost all of them.' She suddenly looked up.

Her eyes widened, then she was brutally shoved away. A hand holding a gun emerged from the window and began firing wildly. Gilmore and Rachel threw themselves aside. They scrambled along the ground to the rear of the bus.

'That's Hemmings,' Rachel said, breathing heavily. 'He organised the kidnapping at the facility.'

'Right,' Gilmore said. The firing from the beach had lessened sharply. They seemed to have the upper hand. 'Let's get this one sorted, then we can tend to the wounded.'

Gilmore grabbed the handle to the emergency exit. With a groan, he overcame the resistance and pulled it open, revealing a strange throne-like chair. Gilmore had a moment to glimpse a pale figure slumped inside it, then pandemonium broke out inside the bus, as figures rushed the narrow aisle, forcing back a figure waving a weapon.

Taking his chance, Gilmore climbed inside. A smell came off the figure in the chair, of refrigerant and decay. His nose wrinkled, and he stepped around it as quickly as he could. There were several men, lying unconscious. Either the accident had done for them, or their hostages had overwhelmed them. Browning raised, he picked his way forward, seeking out Hemmings.

A man who he presumed was Hemmings stood outside the bus, holding Allison around the throat with one arm, a gun barrel pressed to her temple. Allison's face was white with fright, her eyes wide.

'Let her go,' Gilmore said, stepping off the bus.

The technicians had scattered back up the trail. He glanced back, and saw Rachel crouching in the doorway, watching events keenly. Down on the beach, bodies were slumped on the shingle and floating in the water.

'You're in no position to start giving orders,' Hemmings snarled. His lips were flecked with spittle, and his eyes bulged, rolling from side to side like a cornered dog. Allison struggled in his grip, and he tightened his hold until she started choking.

'I think I am,' Gilmore said. He stood with the Browning aimed at Hemmings. 'Let her go and you live. If you don't...'

'Shut up!' Hemmings snarled. He backed down the trail, dragging Allison with him.

Gilmore kept pace.

'Do you really think the Soviets will give a fig about you, once they have Allison? You'll be lucky they don't shoot you and dump your body in the North Sea. Maybe they'll do something exotic and push you out a torpedo tube, but either way, they have no earthly use for you.'

'You say what you like, but Mr Walsingham will make sure

I'm looked after.'

'Looked after?' Gilmore saw Rachel from the corner of his eye. She held her weapon by her side. 'From what I hear, Mr Walsingham was cowering in his bedroom after my wife had a stern word with him. I imagine the authorities are asking him some very sharp questions right about now.'

Hemmings' eyes wavered. He glanced over his shoulder, down at the beach. What he saw he clearly didn't like.

Gilmore saw Hemmings' finger tighten on the trigger. Time seemed to stretch. Then he saw Allison lift her foot and slam it down on Hemming's foot. Hemming's howled and his grip on her loosened. It was enough for Allison to wriggle free. She shoved him, then ran up the slope, where Rachel grabbed her.

Hemmings regained his footing and aimed his weapon at Gilmore.

'It doesn't matter, anyway,' the man said, laughing, the sound unhinged. 'That thing in the bus is already doing what needs to be done. A city in Britain will burn toni—'

Gilmore fired, and Hemmings spun around, his gun flying away. He fell to the ground in a crumpled heap, blood pumping from a wound in his chest. Walking over, Gilmore prodded him with his booted foot. There was no response. He pocketed the discarded pistol, then stood and assessed the situation.

The empty dinghy floated some distance from shore. All the Soviet marines were dead. None had made it above the beach. A figure appeared on the conning tower. Light sparked off binoculars. Gilmore feared more marines would be dispatched. After another minute, the conning tower slipped beneath the water. The slap of waves on the beach filled the air.

'What a waste.' Rachel shook her head at the carnage all around them.

Jock and his men were on the beach, checking that the marines were indeed all dead. Unbidden, Gilmore wrapped an arm around Rachel's shoulder and held her tight.

'Have you forgotten something?' It was Allison, her voice hoarse from Hemmings' hold on her throat.

'What do you mean?' Gilmore asked, unease creeping through him. Then he remembered Hemming's final words.

'Everything has been such a rush,' Rachel said, wiping a tired hand over her forehead. Her face hardened. 'Hemmings forced us to enter a firing sequence for a Cerberus satellite stationed over Britain. It's on an automatic countdown with a random target programmed in.'

'We've got no equipment, Rachel,' Allison said. Despair was etched into her face.

'But we have the Child,' Rachel said. 'We can get her to countermand the order.'

Allison and Rachel exchanged an unreadable look, then they turned and hurried back to the bus. Confused, Gilmore followed them into the interior.

Glass crunched under their boots as they hurried down the aisle.

'Help me with this,' Allison called out to Rachel, who joined her.

Together, they undid a series of locks holding the cowl in place, then lifted it back.

'What in God's name has been done to her?' Gilmore felt queasy just looking at the cables which ran from the back of the skull and disappeared into a recess in the unit.

'Gave her a life she had lost.' Allison turned to Rachel, ignoring Gilmore. 'You remember what happened to her after Shoreditch, Rachel. Or do you? You quit, wrote your book, started a family, then decided to ascend back to your throne in Cambridge. The rest of us had to put the pieces back together after all we experienced.' Allison turned to the Child. Drool hung in a thin line from her slack lips. 'I saved her. She'd be dead without me.'

'She'd be better off dead, given what you've done to her.' Gilmore shook his head in amazement. 'She's that little girl we encountered.' He glanced at his wife. 'Did you know about this?'

'She was in this state when I first arrived at Devesham. It was too late to reverse what had been done, and her parents agreed to it in any event. Better this than the alternative, they said.'

'This... what's been done... it's an abomination.'

'It's progress,' Allison said, her eyes glittering. Gilmore looked at her in shock, as if seeing her for the first time.

'Enough, Ian.' Rachel laid a hand on her husband's arm. 'The time for scruples is later.'

Gritting his teeth, Gilmore nodded. 'You said the firing

sequence is still counting down. Can you stop it?'

'Us, directly?' Rachel shook her head. 'No. Her mind lies at the heart of the Cerberus satellite's control mechanism. We thought we were designing a mechanism for controlling the satellites; instead, Woden overrode our work and turned her into targeting mechanism. There are sub-routines wired into her that make direct contact impossible.'

'So, we can't even ask her to stop the sequence?' Gilmore was incredulous. 'You've put a monstrous engine of destruction in the hands of a thing you can't control?'

'Unless...'

Gilmore and Allison looked at Rachel.

'We can't communicate verbally with her, correct? What if we were able to create a link with her. Mind to mind? We could tap into that latent telepathic field she exhibits.'

'We have no equipment, even if it could be done,' Allison said. She rubbed her hands anxiously.

'Not here,' Rachel said. 'But there's communications equipment at the airfield.'

'Do you think you can cobble something together?' Hope kindled in Allison's eyes.

'My skills at lashing disparate pieces of equipment together wouldn't go near what the Doctor managed,' Rachel said. 'But they will have to do.'

'Right then,' Gilmore said. 'Let's go.'

They managed to get the bus back onto the road. With Jock at the wheel, and Gilmore driving a Range Rover, they returned to the airfield in smart time.

Given the lack of space inside the airfield office, Gilmore stationed Jock and his men outside. The Child's throne took up fully a third of the space, and that was after they had dragged the desk out.

Gilmore stood to one side, watching as the women broke down the communications equipment to its components, then brought them together into a new configuration. Someone had found a soldering iron, and the smell of burning metal and plastic filled the tiny space. For her part, the Child remained as she had been all along, despite the fire and fury; comatose, her eyes endlessly flicking from side to side.

'So, who is it going to be?' Allison said. In one hand, she held up a crude looking metal circlet, covered in cabling which ended in a plug she held in her other hand.

'I will,' Rachel said.

'This looks dangerous,' Gilmore said, looking uneasily at the circlet. There was exposed wiring on either side of it. 'How does it work?'

Allison answered. 'It's a known fact, amongst certain fields of science at least, that everyone generates a low-level telepathic field. No one has ever been able to tap it, so all we experience are dreams we think tell the future, or flashes of déjà vu.' She nodded to the circlet. 'What this does is amplify that field—'

'Albeit very crudely,' Rachel said.

'But it does the job,' Allison said. Her arms were folded. 'It should be me.'

'I taught you,' Rachel said. 'Whatever road you've gone down, for whatever reason you've gone down it, I'm responsible.' She took the circlet and considered it for a moment. 'All right then. Plug the cable into that unit.'

Allison did as instructed. The unit throbbed with power. The smell of ozone filled the room

Rachel looked at them. 'There may be a moment of pain, but whatever you do, don't break the connection until I tell you.'

Before Gilmore could ask how she would be able to tell them, Rachel placed the circlet on her head. There was a spark, and the smell of ozone intensified, then she collapsed writhing to the floor.

A young schoolgirl skipped in a circle within a white expanse of nothing. A little earlier, she had heard distant shouting, but had ignored it, as she ignored everything she thought she saw or heard. The only thing that mattered to her was the white light pulsing through her head. It gave her comfort, eased the pain that had blighted her life before the woman had found her and taken her in.

Then she heard a voice. She continued skipping while reciting numbers, hoping the voice would go away. The voice became insistent, urgent. Then a shape seeped out of the air. Reluctantly, the schoolgirl stopped, though she kept reciting numbers. She crossed her arms and glared at the shape.

'Go away,' she said. In between each word she recited a number. Each was less than the one before. This was her place. Her safe place.

'Do you remember me?' the woman said. Her face swam into view. The girl recognised it, from a long, long time ago. She didn't like thinking about that long-ago time. It hurt to be reminded.

'I do,' the girl said, between numbers. Smoothing her school dress, she held her head high, watching the woman.

'Can you do something for me?'

'Maybe,' the girl replied. More numbers.

'Maybe?' The woman smiled. 'You do know you are in control here, don't you? This...' The woman waved her hand around. '...all this is yours to command.'

The girl nodded and smiled. It sounded good to hear someone acknowledge it. Numbers filled her head and her mouth.

'So, you're aware you can stop it?'

'Of course,' the schoolgirl said, reciting numbers again and again between the words. She waved her hand.

The whiteness dropped away, and the two of them floated next to a satellite. The girl looked down and saw the earth. She could make out the outline of Britain, smudged with clouds. A terrible energy throbbed from the very metal of the satellite and, as she watched, several of the huge panels began to align themselves.

'That satellite is readying itself to fire on a city, down there, in Britain,' the woman said. 'People, many people, will die tonight, unless you halt the firing sequence.'

'Please.' Numbersnumbersnumbers.

'Sorry?'

'You didn't say *please*.'

'Would it help if I did?'

The girl shrugged.

The woman cocked her head and looked at the girl.

'Are you happy?'

'Happy. Sad. Angry. Lost. Angry. Sad. Angry angry angry angry angry...' The numbers came in a blizzard now, a blurring of sound that threatened to overwhelm her. The need to get to zero became acute, a desperate lunge to the finish line...

The simulation around them stuttered. Great blasts of static replaced sections of the imagery. The woman looked wildly about.

'You have to stop the firing sequence,' she shouted, her voice fading. 'Please. Otherwise tens of thousands will die. Men, women. Children. Children like you will di—'

The woman disappeared.

Amid that howling maelstrom of static, the little girl named Judith, who never really had a childhood, whose life had been one of pain and loss, looked down curiously at the small blue green world and the tiny island. And then she decided.

Rachel stopped convulsing after a few seconds. Gilmore knelt by her side and pulled the circlet off, despite Allison's protestations. He could see Rachel's eyes moving beneath their lids.

'Rachel? Rachel? Can you hear me.'

Rachel groaned, and her eyelids fluttered open. 'Did it work?' She clutched her head and moaned.

'Did what work?' Gilmore looked at Allison. 'You've only been gone for a few seconds.'

A shout from outside drew their attention. The door to the shed opened. It was Jock, his face shining with excitement.

'Come out and see this.'

Helping his wife to her feet, Gilmore guided her outside. Jock pointed to the sky, where the wind had blown a ragged hole in the cloud cover.

Gazing upwards, Gilmore saw a fitful, pulsing light grow brighter and brighter. He held his breath, expecting to see a vast shaft of white light flash down, as he had on the flight back from West Berlin.

Instead, there was an expanding ball of light. Tendrils of it streaked out in all directions. For an instant, daylight laid claim to Britain, before it faded and darkness returned.

'Well, did we win?' Jock said, looking at them expectantly.

'Yes,' Gilmore said, looking at his wife before embracing her. 'We did.'

CHAPTER TWENTY-SIX

Monday – Cambridge. 8pm.

IT WAS, Gilmore decided, good to be home.

The local constabulary on Jura hadn't taken kindly to the bodies lying on the northern beach overlooking the Scapa Flow. They took it even less kindly when men from the Ministry of Defence and MI6 appeared and claimed possession of the corpses of the Soviet marines.

While the issues of jurisdiction were being argued over, Gilmore and Rachel took their leave. Allison stayed behind to supervise the return of the Child back to Devesham.

'I shall come up in a few days,' Rachel had said, after embracing Allison. The younger woman nodded tiredly. There were new lines on her face, and her eyes were haunted.

'When you're ready, Rachel. We'll have to put the satellites in a holding pattern until we find out exactly what Woden did.' She had looked at Gilmore. 'What will happen with Woden?'

'If I had my way, I'd burn the whole organisation to the ground and salt the earth. We'll see. Take care, Allison.'

They were quiet on the flight back. The clouds had gone away, leaving the moon to command the skies.

'What shall we tell Dillon?'

'Once the MoD has publicly cleared my name, the truth.' Gilmore glanced at his wife. 'What are you thinking?'

She turned to him and smiled tiredly. 'That I'll be glad to have both my men home and safe.'

Her words did much to hearten Gilmore. He knew they would have to talk about him lying about working for Bambera, but it now felt less like something to dread.

A couple of hours later they were home. There had been no one at the airport to greet them, which Gilmore had expected. In the car, the attempted assassination of Bambera led the news, overshadowing the calling of the General Election. It was expected, the newsreader said, that after a short stay in hospital, Bambera would return to his London residence to recuperate. In light of recent events, he would be assigned a protection detail.

'I bet they will,' Gilmore had said, shaking his head.

While it was good to be home, to shut the door on a strange and chaotic world, it felt different, all the same. Dillon was still away; he wouldn't return until tomorrow evening. It felt, Gilmore decided, like it had the day after he had buried his father. There had been a subtle but profound shift in his life, and everything felt a little off kilter.

During the afternoon, the telephone rang. Rachel took the call, her eyebrows knotted together as she listened. Finally, she nodded then handed the receiver to Gilmore, who had been lurking in the kitchen.

'There's a fellow, name of Bannerton. Says he wants to speak with you.'

A jolt ran through Gilmore. He took the receiver and pressed it to his ear.

'Jack? Ian, here.'

'Gilmore? My God. The grapevine is absolutely humming, and it's speaking your name. What the hell did you get up to in West Berlin? And something about Jura. You've been a busy lad.'

'Maybe I'll tell you all about it one day. What did you want?'

'I'll hold you to that and don't forget it.' There was a long pause.

Gilmore imagined the Bannerton was checking to make sure the door to his office was firmly closed. Eventually, he spoke.

'I got the tape. My God, man. It's real, isn't it?'

'As real as you or I.'

'I read your note. This GRU officer... He's a monster, from what my contacts have told me.'

'Perfect company for a traitor, then.' Gilmore's voice was flat.

'You do know Whateley is booked for tonight's show?'

'Is he?' Gilmore said. 'What a coincidence something like

this has fallen into your lap.'

'I'm going to use it, tonight. He won't know what's hit him.'

Gilmore let the silence stretch before he responded.

'Good.'

He hung up the call.

'What was that about?' Rachel asked.

'We're watching BBC1 at eight tonight, dear. I think you'll find it... inspiring.'

They enjoyed a quiet dinner, then settled in front of the television. The television announcer advised the rest of the evening's schedule, before introducing the next show.

'And coming up is *Politics with Jack Bannerton*. Tonight's guest is Harry Whateley, leader of the Freedom Party, and the man many say will hold the balance of power in the House of Commons after the General Election.'

Gilmore sensed Rachel's glance and he nodded.

After the titles, Bannerton appeared on screen. He smiled, then introduced his guest.

'Tonight, I'm speaking with the leader of the Freedom Party, Mr Harry Whateley.'

After the formalities, Bannerton got down to business.

'Welcome back from West Berlin, Mr Whateley. As a director of Woden, do you have anything to say about one of your employees, Mr Ian Gilmore?'

'No. On the advice of our lawyers, I can't say anything at the moment. I'm happy to let the authorities deal with him as they see fit.'

'And yet you were part of the delegation with Mr Gilmore that attended an arms trade conference.'

'Well, yes. But I had nothing to do with him. Fellow vanished as soon as we booked into the hotel. I'd prefer to concentrate on politics, if it's all the same to you.'

'I'm sure you would,' Bannerton said smoothly. 'I think it is safe to say, Mr Whateley, that your party stands for several things. A strong Britain, a Britain that looks to its own concerns, and a Britain that hues closer to its traditions. Would that be right?'

'Spot on,' Whateley said, clasping his hands and leaning forward. 'For too long, the elites in this country have sold out the average man in the street. For too long, we've sent money overseas to support corrupt governments, and accepting the worst of them in return. My party, the Freedom Party, will ensure that Britain will be for the British.'

'He's about as subtle as a brick to the face,' Rachel said, appalled.

'I see,' Bannerton said. He smiled. 'You would argue then that the government's response to repeated Soviet incursions into British airspace are a sign of weakness?'

'Oh, absolutely. This government is far too cowardly when it comes to the communist threat this country faces.'

'The sheer gall of the man,' Gilmore muttered. Whateley was trying to brazen it out.

'And yet we've just heard this evening that there's been a call between Downing Street and Moscow,' Bannerton said. 'The Soviets have announced that issues with navigation beacons have been behind the crossings into British airspace and that further accidental incursions won't take place. What do you have to say to that?'

'Why are we talking with them? Talk is another way of doing nothing. We consistently do nothing, despite their constant provocations. Instead, we cosy up to the Communists in China and ignore the menace closer to home. I mean, they're all the same, the Reds, aren't they?'

'I'm sure the Soviets in Moscow would say something different about their comrades in Peking. So, you are stridently anti-communist, would you say?'

'Oh, absolutely. An absolute menace. Made worse by the fact the government did nothing about these incursions from the North Sea. Now they wave this announcement around as if that is proof of their ability to deal with Moscow. We must be tough on Communism, everywhere.'

'I see,' Bannerton said. He leaned forward. 'We have some audio we'd like to play, Mr Whateley. I'd be interested in your response once it is finished.'

Looking nonplussed, Whateley nodded. Bannerton sat back, smiling the sort of smile a shark would blush at, Gilmore decided.

There was a hiss then voices could be heard. In the background, Gilmore could just hear the Australian poker player speaking.

'We have to wait.'

'The timing is not up to you anymore, Vatley.'

'So that's it. For all my work—'

'Comrade Vatley, your allegiance to the Motherland is not unappreciated. But events are moving at their own pace. When the election is called, you will do as I have instruct—'

As the recording played, Whateley's face grew darker and darker. Gilmore could see his hands tremble, and his eyes darted from side to side, like a rat trapped in a pipe.

'We're did you get that?' Whateley asked, nearly shouting.

'I'm not at liberty to reveal my sources,' Bannerton said smoothly. 'But what I am interested in is why you would be conversing with a known GRU officer in West Berlin. It seems very much like you're taking orders from him. Would you care to explain?'

Whateley very much didn't want to explain. By the time the interview finished, several chaotic minutes later, it seemed to Gilmore that Whateley's political career was over.

'You engineered that,' Rachel said.

'I did. It's the least I could do to honour the death of a brave woman who recorded it.'

And Gilmore told Rachel about meeting Hannah, and her bravery, and how she died.

Shortly afterwards, Gilmore took a phone call.

EPILOGUE

LATER THAT night, while most sensible people, like Gilmore and his wife, were asleep, in another home in central London, another man took a very different phone call.

Suitcases sat beside the front door. The Mercedes was parked in the street. His hand was on the door handle, ready to open it, when the telephone rang. The noise made Walsingham's blood run cold.

He hesitated, glancing at the suitcases. Since the attack on him, his home had become an alien place. The shadows in rooms seemed deeper. Sounds lingered longer than they had a right. He had rattled around the house, unsure what to do, transfixed by the news on the radio, worried that his front door would be smashed down and police officers would boil through. He had watched on in horror as Whateley crucified himself on television, saw a political career burn in front of his eyes.

He had packed in a hurry afterwards, intent on catching a ferry to the Continent and then driving somewhere, anywhere into the interior. It seemed, he thought, as he picked up the receiver, that events were catching up with him.

'Hello?'

There was a pause, then a series of clicks, then another pause. Walsingham had the sensation the call was being transferred through several switchboards. His heart raced. He knew what was coming.

'Mr Walsingham.' It wasn't a question.

That sibilant voice was all too familiar to Walsingham. He felt a chill again. He looked longingly at the door, knowing it would do him little good to hang up.

'Mr Ratcliffe.' Walsingham closed his eyes.

'You disappoint me, Mr Walsingham. It seems you want to cut and run. I wonder where you think you can go, hmm?'

The voice was that of a younger man, but it frightened Walsingham. Very little did, but this voice...

'I... I am just taking a holiday,' he said, knowing how pathetic it sounded. 'Work's been quite busy recently, and now that the launch of the Cerberus rockets is behind us—'

'I'm not sure which I hate more. Being lied to or being let down. Perhaps both, which you have managed to do with some aplomb, Mr Walsingham.'

Walsingham felt his resolve begin to crumble. 'I appreciate everything you contributed to making Woden a success. Money. Connections. But I did everything that was asked of me in return, Ratcliffe. Everything!'

'I don't think you did, do you? After all, I asked that you succeed at the tasks I set. The Cerberus rockets are no longer in your hands. Whateley is very much a busted flush. And Gilmore and his wife are still alive.' There was a pause, and Walsingham glimpsed all sorts of horrors in that yawning gap. 'I see now I was wrong to place my faith in you.' Ratcliffe's voice became clipped. 'My father always said that if a tool is broken, don't repair it. The best thing to do is dispose of it, as cleanly and as quickly as possible. Would you please do me a favour and look out your front window, Mr Walsingham? And come back and tell me what you see.'

Walsingham placed the receiver on the table and walked over to the front door. The suitcases beckoned to him. Instead, he flicked aside the curtain and glanced outside.

Brampton Court was quiet. Cars, very expensive cars, lined the street. It was, however, one car, not very expensive, that caught his eye. It sat under a streetlight, quite deliberately, and he saw two men sitting in the front seats. Ice gripped his heart.

With a slow step, he returned to the telephone.

'Mr Walsingham? You're still with us? Good. Very good. What did you see?'

'Two men...' Walsingham swallowed and started again. 'Two men, sitting in a car, in front of my house.'

'Excellent. Those men are very, very reliable. I ask them to do something and they will do it.' That horrible silence again. 'I can't afford to have you going off on holiday, Mr Walsingham. Men on holiday relax too much, talk too much, feel the need to fill the silence with blathering. They end up talking with people from the security services, sent on their trail to stop them from escaping. That sort of blathering I won't tolerate. So, regrettably, I must sever my relationship with you.'

'Sever, how?'

'Really, Mr Walsingham. Need you ask? I'm sure a man like you sees the reality of what is heading your way.' Again that pause, and when the voice returned, there was steel in it. 'Either my men deal with you, painfully, or you do the right thing, the honourable thing, and sort it out yourself. Trust me when I say, you really do want to take ownership of this matter.'

The receiver clicked.

The room around Walsingham pitched and tossed like a ship in a storm. His mouth was dry, and his face gleamed with sweat. Again, like a condemned man walking to the gallows, he went to the front door and peered through the curtain. The car was there. But it was now empty. A strange fright filled him.

He turned and hurried to his study. Once inside, he closed and locked the door. He should have known better than to get in bed with Mr Ratcliffe and the Association...

Walsingham unlocked the desk drawer and pulled out the pistol. He swallowed.

What other choice did he have...?

To be continued in...
Birds of Prey

GANGSTERS BY PHILIP MARTIN

Novelisation of the classic gritty 1970s British drama. John Kline is an ex-SAS officer recently released from prison who finds himself hired by the secretive DI6 police organisation to go undercover in the Birmingham underworld. Infiltrating a violent gangster organisation, Kline soon finds himself making some dangerous enemies, with his loyalties trapped between two opposing forces.

Gangsters is a novel of money, power and violence, the story of racketeers who grow fat on the profits of illegal immigration, drug trafficking – and death.

Also available from Candy Jar Books

GANGSTERS: DEATHTOUCH BY PHILIP MARTIN

Death comes to Birmingham disguised as W.C. Fields...

John Kline's gone straight. Or he's trying to. The restaurant business isn't all he'd hoped for – not with his old nemesis Inspector Khan pulling the strings of the liquor licencing board.

Khan's willing to cut a deal – but he isn't the only one. Shadowy forces of conspiracy and counter-conspiracy converge, and Kline has a choice: play the respectable citizen... or play his own game.

By his side, Anne Darracott, off the needle but on guard. She and Kline share a history – but not all of it.

Meanwhile, a new danger rises in the east. The White Devil, a legend out of the arcane, death himself – if death had a prehensile penis, anyway.

One thing's for sure, Birmingham's changing...

Philip Martin's Gangsters: Deathtouch is the final installment in a saga that began in 1976, with the cult classic BBC series. Uncompromising and anarchic, Gangsters combined realism with pulp fiction, social commentary with the absurd, winning the opprobrium of Mary Whitehouse, a legion of admirers, and to this day standing out as one of the most singular shows ever to be broadcast.

KKLAK! THE DOCTOR WHO ART OF CHRIS ACHILLÉOS

Kklak!: The Doctor Who Art of Chris Achilléos covers for the official Target novelisations, which began in the early '70s, defined a generation's image of the Doctor and his adventures – particularly after the show disappeared from British screens in the late '80s.

Lavishly detailed, with psychedelic overtones and an unapologetically pulpy sensibility, these covers perfectly captured the eccentric appeal of the classic series.

Kklak!: The Doctor Who Art of Chris Achilléos collects the entirety of Achilléos' *Doctor Who* artwork in chronological order, along with commentary from Achilléos himself (as well as some fans) – presenting the definitive guide to his seminal work. The book also includes a small contribution from twelfth Doctor Peter Capaldi and a foreword from Achilléos' long-time friend and collaborator, the late Terrance Dicks.

100 OBJECTS OF DR WHO BY PHILIP BATES

"So, all of time and space, everything that ever happened or ever will: where do you want to start...?"

100 Objects of Dr Who is a celebration of everyone's favourite sci-fi show. Perfect for fans, no matter your mileage – whether you've just started your journey through all of time and space, or have lived through the highs, the lows, the Wildernesses, the Androzanis, and the Twin Dilemmas.

Inside, you'll find: A terrifying army of three Daleks! Death's Head's head! A really quite astonishingly heavy door! Dinosaur fossils! A framed piece of wall!

And much, much more!

This is a book about *Doctor Who*. But probably not the one you're expecting.

DOWNTIME: CHILD OF THE NEW WORLD BY ANDY FRANKHAM-ALLEN

Kate Lethbridge-Stewart joins her father, Brigadier Lethbridge-Stewart, in a mission to save her son's life!

For the last nine years Kate's life has been one full of contentment. Other than a minor blip in 2003, she hasn't had to worry about aliens bothering her or her son. Indeed, her biggest concern is Gordy's first girlfriend. But it all changes when a face from her past appears, bringing with him a warning.

The Brigadier and Kate set off on a mission to the ruins of Det-Sen Monastery in Tibet where an ancient power is about to rise. It's a mission that will tear the Brigadier's family apart, bringing them face to face with their worst fears and inner demons!